PRAISE FOR THE NOVELS OF TIM GREEN

ABOVE THE LAW

"Heroic Casey is a delight . . . The story line is fast-paced and, like Casey's previous appearance, filled with terrific spins."
—*Midwest Book Review*

"Green builds the momentum into an explosive climax . . . As always, Green delivers an engrossing thriller—based on horrors that are all too credible."
—**BookLoons.com**

"Nothing can stop the book's velocity . . . one of those fast-paced novels written with the urgency of a Twitter post. Like James M. Canin or Robert B. Parker, Green writes as if he's being charged by the word. He sets a fast pace, then picks up the tempo . . . and he's a heck of a mystery writer."
—**CreativeLoafing.com**

more . . .

AMERICAN OUTRAGE

ABOVE
THE
LAW

TIM
GREEN

GRAND CENTRAL
PUBLISHING

NEW YORK   BOSTON

This book is a work of fiction. Names, characters, places, and incidents are the product of the author's imagination or are used fictitiously. Any resemblance to actual events, locales, or persons, living or dead, is coincidental.

Grand Central Publishing
Hachette Book Group
237 Park Avenue
New York, NY 10017
Visit our website at www.HachetteBookGroup.com

Grand Central Publishing is a division of Hachette Book Group, Inc.
The Grand Central Publishing name and logo is a trademark of Hachette Book Group, Inc.

Printed in the United States of America

Originally published in hardcover by Hachette Book Group
First mass market edition, February 2010

10 9 8 7 6 5 4 3 2 1

For my love, Illyssa

ACKNOWLEDGMENTS

With each book I write, there are many people who help with essential steps along the way, and I would like to thank them.

Esther Newberg, the world's greatest agent and my dear friend, for her wisdom. Ace Atkins, my dependable, brilliant, and talented friend, for his careful reading and fantastic ideas. Jamie Raab, my publisher, and Jaime Levine, my editor, who polished this story with unmatched insight and creativity. As well as all my friends at Grand Central Publishing, beginning with our leader, David Young, Chris Barba and the best sales team in the world, Emi Battaglia, Karen Torres, Flamur Tonuzi, Martha Otis, Jim Spivey, and Mari Okuda.

My parents, Dick and Judy Green, who taught me to read and to love books and who spent many hours scouring this manuscript so that it shines.

A special thanks to Dr. Kathleen Corrado and Katherine Unger at the Onondaga County Medical Examiner's Office for their insight into crime scene DNA; Deputy

Chief Michael Kerwin, the good cop who's been with me from the beginning; fellow officer Kevin Murphy for his assistance with gangs; Marc Harrold, Tommy Rosser, and Rehien Babaoglu for their insights into immigration law; Onondaga County District Attorney William Fitzpatrick for his friendship and guidance; Tim DeMore for his expertise in civil procedure; and Mike O'Connor of the US Border Patrol, who helps keep us all safe.

CHAPTER
1

Headlights crept up the wall before jetting across the ceiling and blinking out. Elijandro stiffened at the familiar purr of the engine and clatter of rocks off the undercarriage as the white Range Rover descended the hillside lane. He left the sagging bed and the warmth of his young wife's body, skirted past the crib, and eased open the front door, letting himself out into the dark of predawn.

Elijandro clutched himself and stepped gingerly across the dirt yard until he stood shivering beside the Range Rover. The hills and the thick clouds above glowed in the orange flare from some distant lightning. Damp ozone floated on the small breeze. The new leaves on the lone willow tree shifted restlessly and the window hummed down, muffled now by the rumble of the approaching front. White teeth shone out at Elijandro, but the spade-cut smile and the familiar face of not the wife, but her husband and his boss, staggered him.

"You come good to the call," his boss said, grinning like a mask.

"The call?" Elijandro said.

"Like a tom turkey," the boss said, grinning, then clucking like a hen with a puck, puck, puck. "The sound of this Range Rover. The sound of my wife."

Elijandro stuttered until the boss interrupted.

"Screw her. Get your camo on, Ellie," he said. "Kurt said you put a flock to bed in the oaks out on Jessup's Knob and there was a big bird in with them. That right?"

Elijandro nodded eagerly and could see now that the boss wore camouflage from the neck down.

"Then let's go get his ass," the boss said. From the passenger seat he raised a bottle of Jack Daniel's and took a good slug before smacking the cork home with the palm of his hand.

Elijandro peered at the western sky. "Rain coming."

"So we'll get wet," the boss said. "Bird'll come to the call rain or shine. Lightning gets 'em excited. Go on."

Elijandro turned for the tenant house, scratching the stubble on his head, hopping barefoot through the stones, picking his way until he reached the porch.

The house had been built along with two dozen other shacks for migrant workers some sixty years ago. Like them, it sagged wearily under its rumpled tin roof, propped up off the dirt and more or less leveled on four cinder-block stacks. Being drenched in weather and heat for all those years had rendered each of the houses gray and had shrunken the slat-board siding like an old man's bones. Unlike the others, theirs squatted in the lowland by the Trinity River, where cattle inevitably got bogged down in the muck and had from time to time to be roped and dragged free with a mule. The boss's father was the one who had this shack sledged away from the company of its brethren by a team back in '67. By tradition, the place went to the top Mexican, a worker trusted enough to quickly shepherd the livestock free from the muck as soon as they began to bray and before they could do harm to themselves.

With a trembling hand, Ellie scrawled a note to his wife saying he'd be back from the hunt by breakfast. Quickly, he removed his camo gear from its nail, slipping it on before he scooped up his shotgun and grabbed the turkey vest, which clattered to the floor, lumpy and awkward from pockets filled by turkey calls and shotgun shells. He bent for it, and when he rose up he saw comets of light in the corners of his vision. His heart hadn't stopped pounding since he saw the boss's face.

Ellie jogged out to the Range Rover, climbing into the passenger seat and smelling the familiar scent of its fine leather and somewhere the hint of her favorite perfume. His boss reversed the SUV out to the main track and headed up the hill, then ran the ridge before dipping down into the river's wash, across a steel bridge, and up the other bank, talking all the while about his wife being a dirty slut who didn't deserve a Range Rover and slurring his words until the SUV came to rest at the bottom of a field plowed for corn.

His boss killed the engine and the two of them sat listening to it tick down to nothing while the boss turned a shotgun shell end over end with his manicured fingers.

———

Ellie watched and waited until he could stand it no more. He pointed up the field toward the wooded ridge and said, "Them birds are up on top."

His boss smiled funny at him and got out. They eased the Range Rover's doors closed. Elijandro let the silence of predawn settle on them for a moment before he cleared his throat, cupped a hand to his mouth, and let fly the low sonorous call of a barred owl. Nothing came back at them but the echo of his call as it bounced away between the low hills.

Elijandro eyed the eastern sky. A line, pale yellow and flush with the horizon, had begun to melt away the ink of night to a navy blue promising day. The storm would come from the other side of the knob, where the flicker of lightning continued to illuminate the oncoming clouds.

Elijandro cleared his throat, then tried again.

Halfway through the call, the big tom erupted from the top of the knob with a gobble that sent a surge of blood through Elijandro's heart. He grinned at his boss and in the dark saw his boss's teeth. His boss raised his shotgun in one hand as though victory were already theirs, and together they pulled camo masks down over their faces.

"Let's go kill him," his boss said.

Elijandro set off into the woods, keeping just inside the trees and following the edge of the field up toward the top. By the time they were fifty yards from the far end of the field Elijandro could hear his boss's labored breathing. He directed his boss to the base of a big oak close enough to the edge of the woods for a good clean shot and slipped out into the field, the newly turned dirt damp and sucking at his boots. He set the decoys, crouched, spun, and darted across the soft ridges of dirt toward the spot where he'd left his boss. He found an old stump in a clump of bracken not twenty feet from where his boss sat, but closer to the decoys so that his call would better match their location. He settled in, resting the lower part of his back against the trunk, and glanced over his shoulder at his boss, who gave him a thumbs-up.

Elijandro popped the diaphragm call into his mouth and began turning it over with his tongue to soften it, then settled into the silence, absorbing it and the grand expanse of the brightening sky. He took deep breaths of the crisp air, his mind clearing itself of the people he worked for, his responsibilities on the ranch and to his own little family. He loved to guide turkey hunts, not for the kill but in order to participate in the birth of a new day.

The horizon below glowed golden now and the smaller stars began to blink out. A breeze stirred and overhead the dark roiling clouds at the edge of the storm front crept toward the coming dawn as if racing the sun to its rise. Thunder rumbled. A song sparrow peeped nearby and fluttered past Elijandro's head, finding a high spot on the stalk of bramble to clear its throat and offer up the first song of the morning. After that, the other birds woke, too. First slowly, like an orchestra tuning its instruments, but growing in number and volume until they produced a crescendo of chirping and trilling and whistling that ignored the coming storm entirely.

The time had come. Elijandro cupped his hand to his mouth and uttered a sharp hen cluck, then a staccato of high-pitched clucks as he twisted his hip and slapped his hand in a flutter against his rump: the sound of the first hen flying down from the roost. He heard the answering cluck from a real hen awakening on the ridge, then he called to the tom, a raspy, longing sound that rose and fell. The gobble of the big bird was so immediate and so close that Elijandro started and grinned and couldn't help but glance back to see if his boss was ready. The birds weren't on the top of the ridge, but much closer, immediately inside the woods at the end of the field.

His boss had been on enough hunts to know what it all meant and he fumbled with his shotgun, raising it and resting it across his knees, ready to shoot. Elijandro called again, and again the dawn exploded with the vibrant gobble of the trophy bird. The clouds began to spit fat drops of rain and the current of air became a steady breeze. Thunder clapped and the turkey gobbled angrily back at that. Two real hens flapped, clucked, fluttered, and then floated down from the high oaks toward the decoys, gliding in and milling among them, calling now themselves. The tom went crazy, gobbling at his hens and warning the storm clouds to stay away.

Elijandro brimmed with glee and excitement. He bit his tongue to keep himself from bursting into laughter as the big bird barked and pounded his wings against the air and drifted from the sky like a dirigible coming to land among his flock. Puffing out his feathers in full strut, clicking and drumming and fanning his tail, he appeared to be five times the size of his mates. More hens poured down from the trees like a pack of hussies.

The tom, an enormous ball of feathers no more than twenty yards from the edge of the field, slowly turned away and Elijandro knew his boss had the perfect chance to raise his gun and aim, then wait for the naked head and neck to reappear since the thick feathers of a turkey were better than a Kevlar vest. Thunder rumbled again and lightning flashed. As the tom rotated back and his head came into view Elijandro held his breath, anticipating the gunshot.

It came, but in an odd way. Elijandro felt the roar of the gun. Something flew out and away from above him, a dark chunk of bark, but then he realized there was no tree trunk above him and he reached for the top of his head as he felt himself tilting sideways and spilling toward the ground. The spit of rain became a faucet, water spilling down his face as if he were directly under the spigot. It didn't hurt, but as his fingers came to rest on the spot above his brow, he realized the firm fruit he felt protruding from a jagged capsule was his own broken skull and brains.

The liquid streaming down his face was a torrent of blood.

His body rested against the ground and it annoyed him that he couldn't remove his hand from the mess that had been the top of his head. His eyes focused in and out, like a quick zoom, then fixed on the flock of birds struggling up into the air, away from the danger, frantic for the safety of the woods. Elijandro saw the big Tom among them, dragging his long beard as he disappeared into the trees all in an instant. It was the same instant that the day was born.

The sun appeared bright in Elijandro's eyes, blinding him and washing over him until all was lost.

CHAPTER
2

Up Maple Avenue halfway to Love Field was a Sunoco filling station. One day, one of two partners disappeared with all the money he could carry. The weather-worn building sat empty long enough to lose half its windows to vandals and the cinder-block south wall facing the street caught a new shellacking of graffiti every other week. The pumps stood like upright corpses, dead to the world beneath a metal roof built to entice patrons in out of the sun or a thunderstorm to fill up.

When Casey rounded the corner she wasn't surprised to see every bit of the shadow under the roof occupied. From the rectangular crowd, a single line of people connected the pump area to the filling station like a human umbilical cord. It was 8:57 in the morning and people knew Casey's clinic opened at nine. Monday was the day they interviewed people for new cases. Like a school of fish, they turned in a single motion when her Mercedes rocked up over the lip of broken asphalt from the street, groaning and yipping on shocks gone bad twenty thousand miles ago.

She pulled around to the back of the building, thankful she'd laid down the ground rules over a year ago, when she first moved into the neighborhood. Unlike the shoppers at Neiman Marcus, these people had a quiet dignity and respect for others that superseded even their own tragic lives. They would wait for her to open the front door for business.

As she unlocked the back door, she heard a muffled flush from the exterior bathroom she shared with her clientele. The doorknob rattled and an overweight woman with long dark hair hanging from the fringes of a dirty white cowboy hat let herself out with a red-faced frown, hurrying around the corner to regain her place in the line.

Casey gave her Mercedes a fleeting look. Hubcaps and hood ornament had been stolen in her first week on Maple Avenue, and without the protection of a garage, the Texas sun had overcome German engineering, blistering the midnight-blue paint in several places, giving the car a leprous quality. Inside the filling station she bolted the door behind her and flicked on the AC unit in the boarded window. The burst of rank air that ran until the unit got going made her seek refuge in the outer room. There she breathed deep the smell of fresh-made coffee, then poured a cup.

Casey had known from the little red Fiesta out back that her two associates, Sharon Birnbaum and Donna Juarez, had beaten her to the clinic, but the coffee was proof positive. Casey sighed and surveyed the little storefront room where people had once purchased unhealthy snacks and paid for their fuel. It now served as the reception area for the Marcia Sales Legal Clinic for Women. The old single-bay garage, partitioned into three offices and a conference room by a friend from Habitat for Humanity, was where the women sat, as would a third associate if they could ever find another lawyer willing to work so hard for so little.

Casey's lawyers sat waiting at the plastic picnic table in what they called the conference room, poring over some documents, each with a laptop in front of her and each clutching her steaming coffee with two hands.

"Full slate this morning," Casey said, nodding toward the garage door and the crowd she couldn't see through a sheet of plywood put up over the broken glass. "Sharon, you've got court at two, right? Let's skip the meeting. Just remember, don't get into it with traffic violations. Tell them to check the guilty box and pay the fine. We'll get going as soon as Tina gets here."

Tina served as the clinic's interpreter.

"*We* can start," Sharon said.

"Right," Casey said. "*I* can start when Tina gets here."

"You gotta learn the language."

All three of them turned. In the doorway stood José O'Brien in faded jeans, wearing a denim shirt over his white tank top to cover the Glock he carried under his arm and the little nickel-plated snub-nosed .38 he kept tucked into the back of his pants.

"When I went to school," Casey said, pushing a wayward lock of long red hair behind her ear, "everyone took French."

"*Je suis désolé*," he said, telling her he was sorry.

"How do you know French?" she asked.

"School," he said. "No need to relearn Spanish. My mother said English didn't make any sense. I got all the Spanish I needed from the cradle on."

"Yeah, but think about the number of people I could help in the time it would take me to learn," Casey said.

José smiled at her in his easy way, white teeth flashing like small blades, and shrugged. His long dark eyelashes fluttered with their bashful tic. It was hard for Casey to imagine how he'd gotten the reputation he had when she saw that handsome, winning face with big liquid brown eyes that misted over at times when other men might stare blankly or look away. An ex-cop who'd become the youngest homicide detective in Dallas PD history, José had given up the force after just eight years to become a private investigator and satisfy his young wife's demands for more time and money.

With the same determined zeal, he built a ten-person investigation firm that catered to wealthy divorce candidates looking for angles. Three years into it, his own wife played an angle, taking him for nearly a million dollars and half his income until their daughter reached eighteen. José sold the business and became a one-man show, working for just enough money to pay the rent and his greedy ex-wife, and, recently, giving the rest of his services away to Casey's legal clinic, which desperately needed an investigator.

José was just over six feet with arms that tested the limits of his shirtsleeves and the wide V-shaped torso of a linebacker. The cops Casey knew still talked about his time as a patrolman on the street and the way the sight of José in blues would send gangbangers scrambling for cover. One story had him snatching a chrome-plated .45 right out of the hand of a drug dealer and beating him senseless after he'd threatened to kill José and his partner.

"And," José said, "this place wouldn't be the same without Tina."

On cue, Tina, a small dark girl with waves of kinky black hair, appeared blushing beside José and apologized for being late.

"No worry," Casey said. "We're going to skip the meeting and open the floodgates. Is Stacy here yet?"

"Waiting for all of you!" Stacy Berg shouted from the other side of the wall. "And the line's not getting any shorter."

"So, here we go," Casey said.

José gave Casey an unusual look and angled his head toward her office, disappearing that way himself. Casey got up from the plastic table and walked past Stacy, who sat behind the filling station counter, ready to direct the human traffic that came in the door.

"Before you send me anyone," Casey said, "I need five minutes with José."

"You and every red-blooded woman on the planet," Stacy said, eyeing the investigator as he disappeared into Casey's office.

Casey followed him in and closed the door.

CHAPTER
3

ISODORA HEARD THE CAR. SHE'D OPENED THE WIN-
dows after the short storm gave way to glaring sun in
hopes of capturing the small breeze. She wondered why
Elijandro hadn't returned in the Range Rover. The hands
of the clock showed ten before noon and she smacked her
dish towel against the metal sink, twisting her frown into
a snarl. She hated when he did this, leave her a note that
said he'd be back at one time and then arrive four hours
later. She took the carton of juice from the refrigerator for
the second time and set it down amid the stagnant breakfast things, then went to the door.

Shading her eyes, she studied the car as it materialized
from its cloud of dust. When she saw the rack of lights
and the police emblem, her stomach turned. Behind her
the baby stirred in the crib, giving off a little groan and a
small sigh that faded into sleep.

Isodora knew the tall police chief from before the baby
was born, when she worked in the big house. Whether it
was the ambassador from Brazil or the singer Toby Keith,

whenever Elijandro's boss had important guests, Chief Gage would be there with his bolo tie and icy blue eyes, drinking whiskey with just a single cube of ice. Isodora remembered the senator's wife, too, a skinny blonde who laughed like a hyena. The police chief fixed the hat on his head and knit his thick brows so they showed over the rims of his mirrored sunglasses. He scuffed the heels of his cowboy boots in the grit, leaving a small trail that Elijandro would call a man track.

"I got some bad news for you, missy," the police chief said.

Isodora tucked a strand of hair behind her ear. She shook her head and turned her face as if bracing for a slap.

"There's been an accident," he said. "I'm sorry, but Ellie's dead."

"No," she heard herself say, "I have breakfast for him. I know he's late."

The porch creaked under her feet and somewhere out back a calf bawled for its mother. A hiccup escaped her and she pressed her fingertips to her lips, her face flushing with embarrassment, and still she shook her head.

"I'm sorry," the police chief said.

"I'll put the eggs on," she said, opening the screen door and slipping away from him.

She moved through the tiny space, removing the box of eggs from the fridge and cracking them into the pan and lighting the stove, still hiccupping.

"Missy," the police chief said, his voice following her through the screen door, "I need you to come with me. There's some papers you need to sign."

Isodora kept right on cooking. She ignored the police

chief, and after a time she stopped hearing his words over the crackling eggs. She didn't hear him enter, and when he touched her shoulder, she shrieked and cringed.

"You got to at least sign this," he said, looking at his watch. "Sign it, and I'll leave you be for now, but when I come back later, you and the baby will have to come."

She put the spatula in her left hand and signed the paper with her trembling right hand, anything to have him go. He looked at the paper and nodded and she turned back to her work.

When the sound of his car disappeared over the hill, she put out her breakfast the way she knew Elijandro liked it and sat down to wait, staring blankly out the window, hiccupping all the while and listening for the sound of his voice, which she knew she'd hear at any moment.

———

Isodora had no idea how much time passed before the next knock came at the door. The room had grown hot, not summertime hot, but warm enough for the sweat to bead on her upper lip. The baby had been up crying in her crib, then playing quietly before crying again and falling back to sleep. Isodora knew this because the knock at the door woke up the baby and set her to crying again.

From where she sat at the table, Isodora could see that it wasn't Elijandro and it wasn't Gage, either. The man and woman wearing green jackets in the heat didn't knock twice. They came in, the woman bending over the baby's crib and the man approaching her and talking gently.

Like the boogeyman from an adult fairy tale, he wore a jacket bearing the letters ICE. The Icemen, that's who

they were, the Immigration and Customs Enforcement
agents who came in the middle of the night and stole husbands from their wives, tore babies from the arms of their
mothers. A scream bubbled up out of her throat, breaking her trance. She jumped up and pounced at the woman
who had her baby. The man grabbed her arms, restraining
her and deftly snapping metal cuffs on her wrists.

The woman laid Isodora's baby on the changing table,
wincing at the smell as she undid the dirty diaper. The
man kept his voice low, but it didn't keep him from escorting her out through the front door against her vio-
lent thrashing. The baby's screams pierced even her own
and Isodora boiled with rage and indignation, her vision
blurred with steamy tears.

A white county van waited outside next to the agents'
car. The Range Rover belonging to the senator's wife was
there, too, and she got out and approached Isodora.

"It's better this way," the senator's wife said, with a
face twisted in pain. "Please, believe me."

Isodora thrashed and struggled and spit at the wife's
face.

Through her rage, Isodora was aware that two women
with short hair climbed out of the van and spoke to the
Iceman about the baby. The two took Paquita from the
woman agent and put her into the van, snapping her into a
car seat in the back and driving off while Isodora howled
from the cage in the back of the ICE agents' car. As the
van disappeared over the hilltop, Isodora felt her throat
constrict and she choked and gagged and banged her head
against the glass until everything went black.

CHAPTER
4

CASEY SAT DOWN BEHIND HER DESK AND REMOVED a file from her briefcase. José dug into a beaten leather valise, pulling out several files of his own, then holding up one like a card for her to see and placing it on the desk before he sat down.

"Statements," he said.

"Statements?"

"Telling what kind of guy our dead coyote really was. And pictures."

"Of ?"

"Rosalita wasn't the first woman this asshole tried to leave in the middle of nowhere," he said.

Casey opened the file, looked at the pictures, and quickly closed it.

"Can we connect him to this?" she asked.

"Had an old friend run some DNA," José said. "He was a randy little son of a bitch."

"That's not even funny," she said.

"I didn't mean it to be," he said, nodding toward the file.

"There's six. Just the ones they found. I got persuasive with one of his mules. Word is that he'd peel off one lucky girl for every trip he made."

"Which is?"

José shrugged. "Twenty, thirty a year. He's been in business five. He picked them up at the bus stop in Nuevo Laredo and took them downriver where he kept a shitty boat, shuttled them over, and took them on a fifty-mile hike through the hills."

Casey flipped open the file again and stared for a moment, the blackened skin clinging to the bones like mold. She gritted her teeth. "Too bad he died so quick."

"A .357 hollow point tends to end things pretty abruptly," he said. "But even if it was quick, you gotta admit getting your balls shot off is no way to go. Can you get the DA to drop the charges against Rosalita with this?"

"If she were a sorority girl from Tech?" Casey said, closing the file for a second time and shoving it away from her. "No problem."

"I didn't see her wearing no pin when I spoke to her."

"Exactly," Casey said, shaking her head. "He'll offer us a manslaughter plea."

José whistled low. "Five to seven."

"Instead of the steak dinner we owe her for cleaning up that garbage. If I have to, I'll go to trial."

"Like in the movie?" he asked.

Casey blushed. In her past life she'd represented a law professor who turned out to be a homicidal maniac. The whole thing made national news. She got him off at trial, then helped to nail him when she learned the truth of his guilt. Hollywood got ahold of it, and the story ended up as a Lifetime Movie of the Week with Susan Lucci playing Casey.

"About the only thing real in that thing was me being a damn good trial lawyer," she said, unable to meet his big brown eyes.

"Hey, I like how you take all this stuff personally."

Casey studied his face, looking for the joke.

"I mean it," he said. "You live this stuff."

"I wish you could've seen our old offices," Casey said, looking around, her eyes resting briefly on the plywood slab and the diesel-smudged window above.

"In that glass tower on Commerce?" he said, shaking his head. "I met you there, remember?"

"You never saw the office, though," Casey said.

She'd met José getting off the elevator. Instead of getting in, he followed her into the lobby, asking if he could buy her coffee. When she asked him his business there, he told her he was an investigator for one of the attorneys on the tenth floor. She replied that she'd have coffee if he'd track down a witness for her in a case where a young woman was being prosecuted for possession of drugs, just for being in the backseat of a car driven by her older brother. When José called with the witness's new number and address by the end of the day, he asked to take her to dinner instead. She agreed, but only if he'd make it a working dinner.

"That place was for divorce lawyers and ambulance chasers," José said.

"I'm just thinking about the dignity of these people," Casey said, angling her head toward the door.

"These people—my people, I guess—don't need leather and brass for dignity," José said. "Give them a job and a paycheck and they'll hold their heads high."

"I didn't mean it that way," she said. "The place was nice, that's all."

"And hard to get to," José said. "Bet they never stacked up outside the door on Commerce Street. I'm sorry about the grease and gasoline smell, but this is the right place for your work. I'd have to charge if you were still in that glass tower."

"And we'd get about half as much done without you," she said. "So, it's all good."

"One thing is not so good," he said, reaching into his briefcase, leaning forward, and laying a second file down on the desk. "That guy you got the restraining order against?"

"For Soledad Mondo?"

"Yeah, her husband, that guy, Domingo Mondo," José said. "Just keep your eye out."

"For what?"

"I'm sure it's fine," José said, "but I leaned on him a little and there was something about him. I don't know. He didn't make a threat or anything like that, but he had a look. I'm sure it's just me being overcautious."

"Like he's going to come after me?"

"No. Just keep your eyes open. If you see him, or notice something funny, you call me. Don't worry about it. Just be smart. You still got that little .38 I gave you?"

Casey patted the desk drawer beside her knee.

José grinned and slapped his knees, rising as he said, "Speaking of smart, I got a little redheaded wife who's taking personal training to a whole new level, but they keep changing where they go so I can't ever get set up on them."

"Redhead?"

"Not red like yours," José said, scooping up his files and stuffing them into the valise. "The orange kind."

Casey touched her own hair and felt her cheeks warm.

"Thank you for the photos," she said.

"You'll make it up to me one day," he said, winking and drawing the bolt and letting himself out the back.

Casey went to the door to watch him go. As he climbed up into his F-350, she felt a reply bubbling up from the knot in her stomach. She even opened her mouth to speak and he paused with his hand on the truck door, but the words tangled themselves into a snag and hung up in her throat.

So she waved goodbye.

The throng pressed in on her. A tide of human misery and injustice seeking asylum. Casey wished she were God and could make all their problems disappear. Women bound to men like slaves so they could get green cards. Women working for poverty wages with infants who needed lifesaving operations. Women hiding from abusive husbands, desperate for the protection of a law whose effectiveness worked on a sliding scale dependent on wealth. Women robbed of their virginity, their dignity, and their savings by a race of criminal opportunists without conscience or fear of judicial retribution.

At eleven-fifty she ushered a pregnant teenage girl— hoping for child support from the married executive of a large software company—out the door with promises of help. She thanked Tina and told her to take lunch. As Tina passed through, Casey saw Stacy marching toward her with a file. Before she could get her office door closed, Stacy jammed her foot between the door and the frame and barged in, closing it behind her.

"Wait," Stacy said. "One more."

"Give it to Sharon."

"She says she'll only see you."

"I've got a lunch and I've got the DA," Casey said, looking at her watch.

"Just one more."

"There's always one more," Casey said, rounding her desk and stuffing some files into her briefcase.

"Maria Delgado," Stacy said, slapping a hand on the desk. "You helped her older sister get away from some creep. She has another sister, younger. Her husband's dead. She's got a two-year-old baby, and they've got her in custody and the baby in some foster home."

"Drug dealer?" Casey asked, glancing up.

Stacy shook her head. "A hunting accident."

"It's really important?" Casey asked, snapping the case shut.

"Absolutely."

"Then tell her to wait," Casey said, slinging the briefcase over her shoulder and making for the back door. "Paige Ludden and her friends provide about half our operating budget and I'm already going to be late for lunch, and then I've got a meeting with the DA about Rosalita Suarez, who's looking at manslaughter one.

"If it's really that important, then she'll be here when I get back. You can tell her that."

"Go if you have to," Stacy said, hands on her hips, wagging her head toward the waiting room. "But if you could see this woman's face? You wouldn't be worrying about lunch."

CHAPTER
5

"WE GOT AN OPEN CONTAINER LAW IN THESE PARTS."

Teuch squinted through the tail of cigarette smoke leaching from his nostrils. Frowning, he told the old white man behind the counter to kiss his ass, then opened the forty-ounce bottle of King Cobra, popping the twist top with his teeth and taking a long hard pull. He wiped the foam from his mouth on a bare, tattooed arm and belched. The old whitey had already given him the address he needed so there was no longer any reason to pretend to be polite.

He scooped up his groceries and stepped outside, the cuffs of his baggy jeans dragging in the grit, the noon sun smacking him in the face, and the heat waffling up from the parking lot. He hawked up something from the long drive and spat, expecting it to sizzle like hot grease on the blacktop, disappointed when it didn't. The midnight-blue Chevy pickup rode low with twenty-inch Neeper Titans buried in the wheel wells. He dumped his bag on the passenger floor, then slid in and eased back into the reclined seat, pulling out onto Highway 45 and into the little four-corner town of Wilmer. On the seat next to him, a MAC-10 rested under an army blanket. He reached in to fondle it, then took a bottle from the bag on the floor and drank as he drove.

He turned left and after half a block the dusty trees opened up onto a small stone church built on a gravel lot. A wooden cross marked the high point on the arch above the doors and two small stone belfries stood out front like midgets hawking tickets at the big top entrance. The priest looked up from his broom on the flagstone stoop and squinted at Teuch.

Teuch stopped and leaned across the seat.

"Father Diego," he said.

The priest nodded, leaned the broom against the stone wall, and crossed the gravel yard in his heavy brown robe until he stood at eye level with Teuch.

"Teuch?" the priest said, his eyes small but languid beneath the blunt border of his dark bangs.

"You're good with names, Father," Teuch said, speaking English for the priest.

"Paquita's godfather," the priest said, speaking in Spanish, his eyes going sad. "How could I forget? We were able to repair the nave window with your donation. I'm sorry about your brother."

"Sorry doesn't do anybody any good, Father," Teuch said, still in English. "An eye for an eye, a tooth for a tooth. Doesn't it say that?"

"And turn the other cheek," the priest said.

"Not me."

"I should show you something," the priest said. "It was something I showed your brother, a tragedy for our people."

"We both know what really happened to my brother, don't we?" Teuch said. "He couldn't keep his snake in his pants."

"Your brother was a good family man," the priest said, shaking his head. "You should know what he tried to do for others."

"That doesn't matter to me, Father," Teuch said. "Only the people who did this matter."

The priest shook his head. "Maybe you could help. The Lord brings His blessings to those who help the weak."

"I gave that money to your church because of my god-daughter," Teuch said. "Sorry, Father. I help my own. I have an appointment."

Teuch pulled away, kicking up a cloud of dust that made the priest cover his nose. Teuch carried on until he hit Belt Line Road. He turned right and kept on the main thorough-fare until he came to an auto-body shop on a parched and stony half-acre behind a rusted chain-link fence.

He pulled in and drove around to the back. Each of the three bays held a car in some stage of repair. A handful of Mexicans milled about in gray jumpsuits. They reminded Teuch of his brother. Sorry-ass beaners working for grin-gos who were no better than the *chilango* politicians in his own country, whores and thieves who hid behind the law. They didn't fool Teuch with their laws. He had a dif-ferent law. He knew how to get even and he knew how to protect his own, as a Latin King should. He had his eyes on the third crown of his chapter, the warlord, and a ter-mination this big would guarantee it for him.

The one who'd murdered his brother was a big *gaba-cho*, as big as they got. That's why he'd taken the trip up from San Antonio. That's why he'd play the Mojo slave,

just to get close. Respect, that's what it was about. Teuch
got out and ambled into the first bay, scanning the area for
whites and seeing none.

He adjusted his wraparound Oakley sunglasses and
ran his hand through the ragged thatch on his head, then
walked through the bays as if he belonged there, assessing
the men who worked there, looking for a sign that might
tell him who would talk. The two old-timers rebuilding
the front end of a Ford Explorer didn't even look up. In the
next bay, though, a skinny kid with a pock-scarred face
and wearing a red bandana on his head glanced Teuch's
way, showing off a bit of gold with a half-smile.

In Spanish, Teuch asked the kid how he was doing.
The kid wiped his hands and stood up from the hubcap
he'd been lining up. Teuch told him he was from out of
town and looking for work. He told the kid he'd heard
about a big ranch outside town where they'd hire men
without papers.

One of the old-timers wandered over with a paint gun
in his hand. Through his mask he told Teuch that he didn't
look much like a ranch hand. Teuch told the old *naco* to
kiss his ass and that got a giggle out of the kid. Teuch
observed that this job must be a pain in the balls for a
kid who didn't like to take shit from ignorant old *nacos*.
The kid showed his teeth and agreed out loud that they
were a sorry bunch, and then Teuch asked again about
the ranch.

Sure, the kid said with jittery eyes, Lucky Star Ranch,
east of town out on Malloy Bridge Road. There was a big
stone fence with an iron gateway that read LUCKY STAR,
but that was to the main house. He'd want to take the next
gravel road after that. If he crossed the river, he'd gone too

far. Or he could wait like the rest of them outside the rail yard about six in the morning. That's when those who didn't get work at the yard got picked up for day labor. The ranch always had someone there to pick up some cheap hands.

Despite the scowls the kid drew from his coworkers for talking too much, he kept going and told Teuch the name of the man who did the hiring, an Indian half-breed by the name of Bill Ells. The kid said he ought to try the rail yard first, though, because they paid only two dollars an hour out at the ranch and even if you caught on for any length of time, the water in the bunkhouses sometimes went bad.

When Teuch asked about the Mexican who got killed out on the ranch the previous week, the kid shut right down. Teuch didn't push it. He had what he needed and he took his time shuffling out of the shade of the building and back into his truck. When he got there, he reached in and drained off the rest of his King Cobra forty-ounce. It had begun to warm, reminding Teuch of piss. He tossed the bottle up by the neck so that it hung in a high arc before smashing outside the bay where the two old-timers worked. That got their attention, but neither of them moved toward him or the glass.

Teuch figured it was weak-ass old-timers like them who gave being Mexican a bad name.

The kid wandered out, though, grinning. Teuch gave him a wink, lit a fresh cigarette, and climbed in. It wasn't far out to the ranch and Teuch gritted his teeth as he pulled past the gravel drive meant for Mexicans. The gringos, they all wanted workers, but they didn't want to treat them like people. That's why the Latin Kings thrived. If you were a King or a Queen, you got respect.

Teuch doubled back and got a thirty-dollar room at the Texas Road Inn on Route 45. He rolled a couple of joints and put his feet up on the bed. He planned on being at the rail yard by six. That would be the safest way into Lucky Star, the least conspicuous, even if it took a couple of days to get picked up. He certainly didn't want to pull up to the ranch looking for menial work with a thirty-thousand-dollar pimped-out lowrider. Even the old-timers at the garage had pegged him for more than a wetback fresh in.

He blew a cloud of smoke toward the water-stained ceiling, confident that by week's end he'd be able to line himself up for a shot at the boss who did Elijandro. Teuch patted the MAC-10 nestled into the covers beside him and smiled, because with a gun like that, how could he miss?

CHAPTER
6

W HO'S WHO SOLD BIG PREMIUM BURGERS TO THE women who could afford to shop in the adjacent stores, some of Highland Park's finest. Casey parked her old Mercedes next to a gleaming new white one and marched up the steps. Paige Ludden flagged her from the wooden deck amid the buzzing throng of women taking a break from their shopping sprees and the lucky few who sat with husbands in crisp tailored suits.

Casey sat down, happy for the umbrella that offered some shade.

"Thanks for ordering," she said. "I've got a meeting with the DA at one. Sorry."

"Well," Paige said, arching her back, "what do you think?"

Casey caught her breath and assessed her friend, the only holdover from her past life. There was a lot to look at. Paige wore her brass-blonde hair swept back and held in place with plenty of spray. Her nails, like her lipstick, were fire-engine red. The white sleeveless dress she wore was punctuated by black polka dots and the red belt around her narrow waist matched her nails.

"My boobs," Paige said in her syrupy Southern drawl. "Don't tell me you can't see *them*."

"Oh," Casey said, "of course. Fantastic."

"C to a D," Paige said, leaning forward to issue a hushed secret. "In and out in two hours."

"C is pretty big to begin with," Casey said, glancing down at her own modest chest.

Paige reached over and slapped Casey's hand. "How do you think I got Luddy in the first place? That's what they like, you know that. We ought to get you some. And where's your makeup? Good Lord, you've got to put it out there for them a little bit. You wouldn't fish without a worm, would you?"

Casey lifted her burger off its plate and sank her teeth in, shaking her head and relishing the taste of blood.

"One rich husband is enough for one lifetime," she said with her mouth half full.

"Doesn't have to be a Ludden or a Jordan," Paige said, chattering like a wren, nibbling at her burger, and dabbing the corner of her lip with a paper napkin. "No one needs *that* much money. But something for between the sheets, anyway. What about that Mexican you got working for you?"

Casey gulped some diet soda and choked.

"His name is O'Brien," she said. "He's half Irish and he doesn't work for me."

"Mexican, Irish, whatever. God, that's a man," Paige said, sipping through a straw. "Has he asked you out?"

"He can't be much more than thirty. What? Seven, eight years younger than me?"

"Age," Paige said, flicking her fingers. "I'm almost twenty years younger than Luddy. Fix up that face and wear something a little less, I don't know, frumpy."

"Paige."

"I'm sorry, but I'm your friend," she said. "Pleated pants? That mustard blouse? So last year, honey. I remember when you and Taylor came up from Austin for the Margarita Ball that one time. My God, that strapless thing? Shoulders like a goddamn statue. You were the talk of the town."

Casey chewed and took another bite, but couldn't help glancing down at herself. She straightened her back and swallowed.

"I'm going to start running again," she said. "I don't know, it got cold over the winter and one day I just said the hell with it."

"Don't worry about that," Paige said. "You don't have to be as skinny as a model. It's not natural for a girl to run six miles every morning anyway. I'm talking about some style, perfume, heels, a little lace for God's sake. I can see the industrial-grade bra from here. Send out some signals. Date the Mexican if you need to. God, my mother must be rolling over in her grave. I'm serious about the boobs. You only live once, honey."

Casey looked at her for a minute, unable to keep from smiling. She'd known Paige since college, the debutante who took her under her wing like a sister even though Casey came from a poor family in a West Texas cow town.

"Even if I wanted them," Casey said, "they cost too much."

Paige rolled her eyes. "Don't even bring up money with me. Who told you to let Taylor off like that? You could have been rich, no strings attached."

"Well," Casey said, finishing her last bite and removing a twenty from her purse, "I never wanted what wasn't mine."

"Your money's no good with me," Paige said, snatching up the bill and stuffing it back into Casey's purse. "Luddy said it was yours, by law. Not that he ever would, but he said if we were quits he'd be obligated to keep my allowance coming *and* give me half the house as well as either Aspen or Grand Cayman."

"It's not about that anymore," Casey said. "I'm not saying I'm right and you're not. I wouldn't even be able to do half of what I do without your money, and your friends."

"It'd be more if my trust wasn't set up that way," Paige said, her face dropping into a worried look. "You know that, honey. One million a year for charity sounds damn good, but when you have to split it ten different ways? I asked Luddy if I could funnel it to the clinic another way, but he told me that'd be some kind of fraud and I don't like the sound of that."

"No, you're extremely generous," Casey said. "And you're happy."

"Yes. I suppose."

"And you're helping," Casey said. "Believe me, what you're doing is just as important as what I am. These people need help and my staff can't afford to work for nothing."

"You shouldn't, either," Paige said with a pout. "I tell you that. You're a lawyer. You should get paid. A hundred thousand? Luddy's driver makes that. Pay yourself, and buy yourself some clothes and some boobs. You were one of the best. Susan Lucci, for God's sake, no matter how old she is. How many women lawyers can say that? How many women?"

Casey wiped her hands and kissed Paige's cheek.

"I'll see you at the tea," Casey said. "You've got some good prospects lined up?"

"Only Mrs. Cavanaugh and Sissy James, two of the richest women in Dallas. We'll get you out of that god-awful gas station yet."

Casey smiled and said, "You're great. I'm sorry I have to run, but the DA isn't easy to get time with."

"You know Luddy's caddy's son got a DUI and that man wouldn't let him off? Luddy called him himself. I don't know how a man like that gets elected and calls himself a good Republican. Oh, Luddy gave him an earful. Don't mention my name when you see him. It won't help at all."

Casey blinked and searched her friend's face to see if she was serious. She was.

"I won't," Casey said with a smile. "Thanks for the burger, and the tip."

CHAPTER
7

THE TWELVE-STORY COURTHOUSE BUILDINGS STOOD like twin rectangular guardians between downtown Dallas and the scrubby greenbelt feeding off the murk of the Trinity River. By now, the sun's work assured heat from below as well as above, leaving the blacktop pliant and pulsing with thermal waves. Casey parked in the deck out back, took a side entrance, passed through the screeners, and rode the elevator up to the top where Dustin Cruz could survey his kingdom from a corner office full of leather and mahogany.

Casey drank in the vista through the floor-to-ceiling smoked glass and felt a pang of envy. Dustin Cruz swiveled around in his high-backed chair with the phone to his ear, the salt-and-pepper hair on his head so thick it looked like a rug. His bristly mustache, shoe-polish black, seemed to jump off his face and tended to distract people from the red blotches that worried his olive skin. The big DA nodded at Casey and signaled for her to hold on while he finished his business. She shifted from foot to foot until he hung up.

"Would you like to sit?" he asked, his low voice rumbling.

Casey did. She took out the file José had given her, slid it across the desktop, and said, "Dustin, I want to ask you a favor."

"Do I owe you a favor?" the DA asked, snorting and pointing to himself. "I must have missed that."

"I'll owe you one," Casey said. "And it won't cost you anything, no political capital. You won't take a shot in the papers. In fact, I'm betting that they'll love it."

"Love what?" Cruz asked.

"Your compassion."

"I don't have compassion," he said, the bags under his eyes giving him a weary cast. "I'm the DA. The judges—some of them—have compassion. Not my job."

"But you could have."

"Ms. Jordan," Cruz said, "I don't know you. I didn't see the movie, though I heard about it from my wife, and I read about you in the papers at the time, so I admire you. Also, I'm glad you've kept yourself busy with green cards and restraining orders, and left the real dirtbags in this city to me. That's why I'm sitting here talking to you when I've got five murder trials on the docket in the next three weeks. But right now, you're close to abusing the courtesy I've given you as a kind of celebrity."

Cruz forced a smile and looked at his watch.

"I'd like you to drop the charges against Rosalita Suarez."

Cruz narrowed his eyes. "The girl who killed the coyote?"

"Before you say anything," Casey said, "look at this."

She removed the file from her briefcase and slid the photos across the desk.

"This man smuggled illegals across the border from the bus stop in Nuevo Laredo for five years and these are some of his other victims," she said. "Women he peeled away from his group, the same way he tried with Rosalita, women he raped and then killed. The only difference is that when he got Rosalita off by herself, she had a .357 in her skirt, thanks to a cautious older brother. I've got the DNA reports on the other victims in here."

She flopped the rest of the file down on the edge of the desk.

"How did you get this?" Cruz asked.

"And a statement in here from the guy who picked up his route. This woman is completely innocent."

Cruz stared a moment, then flipped through some of what she had before he looked up.

He cleared his throat and said, "Maybe a reduction, but don't talk to me about dropping this."

"This isn't justifiable?" Casey said, pitching voice and eyebrows higher.

"No, not entirely. I'm sorry."

"I'll take it to trial if I have to," Casey said, clenching her hands to stop their trembling.

"You can afford that?" he asked. "You know I'll throw three ADAs at it and burn you to the ground with paperwork. No offense, but I play to win."

"Fine," she said, folding her arms. "Think of the patrons I'll get. Think of the press. Then think of the women voters."

"You don't shoot a man's balls off, I'm sorry."

"In self-defense?"

"Not in Texas," Cruz said. "A jury won't let that go, not a Texas jury."

"But rape and murder is okay as long as it's a Mexican girl?"

"My parents were Mexican," he said, the big mustache covering his mouth in its frown. "So that's that. And she was neither raped nor murdered by the victim."

"Those girls were," Casey said, jabbing her finger toward the photos.

"You say."

"You son of a bitch."

Cruz's face softened. "Look, we're the sixth most dangerous city in America. I win every election by double digits because we've got the fourth-highest conviction rate for murders. I've got her prints. I've got the gun. I've got her confession. She's either pleading guilty and doing time for something, or she's going down like a sack of concrete."

Casey didn't say anything. She pressed her lips tight, snatched up the photos and the DNA reports, and crammed the file back into her briefcase.

"Hey," Cruz said when she reached for the door, "try to get Tom Selleck."

"What?" she said, glaring at him.

Cruz stroked his mustache. "You know, the mustache, the green eyes. If they get Susan Lucci for the sequel, then I think I gotta be Selleck."

CHAPTER
8

HALF THE SHADE UNDER THE PUMP ROOF STOOD empty, so Casey knew her team had been hard at work. She let herself in the back way, taking one step inside before she recoiled, retching. She clasped her hand to her face and peered inside. A pool of sewer water covered her office floor. A small slick of luminescent greens, purples, and blues oozed across the surface, a psychedelic scum hinting of gasoline. From the low center of the small room a floor drain coughed and bubbled.

"Stacy!" she said, covering her face the instant the word left her lips.

Across the dark pool, the door swung open and Stacy appeared.

"Oh, God, I know," she said. "The plumber's on his way. Someone clogged the toilet."

Casey saw now that the outside bathroom door was ajar and the small stream issuing from it bounced merrily along the broken pavement, glinting in the sunshine as it made its way toward the street.

Casey looked down at her soaking foot and cursed before heading to the spigot on the near side of the building. She cranked it open and washed off her foot, shoe and all, before taking the shoe off and wiggling her toes under the cold water. The clients waiting patiently in the front craned their necks and watched politely. No one said a word when she rounded the corner and let herself in to the reception area. Along the one big window that remained sat five women in the folding lawn chairs used to stage the prospective clients before they were seen by a lawyer.

In the chair closest to Stacy's counter sat Maria Delgado. She stood when she saw Casey and clasped her hands together, muttering a prayer.

"I had no idea it got into your office," Stacy said, touching Casey's arm. "The whole place smells like shit, so I had no idea. They should be here any minute to get things pumped out. It's just the bathroom and the file room in the back. And your office. Everything else is okay, except the smell. We opened all the windows we could, so it's hot. I kept the air on, too, and I told them outside not to smoke."

"Smoke?"

"The gasoline floating on the surface," Stacy said, "so it doesn't explode."

"Nice," Casey said. She looked from Stacy to Maria and back to Stacy. "Can you just get me a legal pad and a pen? I'll use the conference room. Is Tina here?"

"I sent her to get some rubber boots so we can get files," Stacy said, "but you won't need her for now. Maria speaks English."

Casey extended her hand to Maria, whose red and swollen eyes moistened anew. Casey felt the weight of the burger in her stomach like a stone as the trembling woman clutched her hand and began to thank her repeatedly before she'd even done anything.

"Let's go in here and talk," Casey said softly as she accepted the supplies from Stacy.

They passed the open door to Donna's office. Donna sat behind her desk, pinching her nose and interviewing an elderly woman. Casey removed her hand from her own face when she got inside their conference room. Casey offered Maria a chair and sat down opposite her, trying to resist the temptation to plug her nose.

When Casey finally persuaded Maria to stop thanking her, Maria said, "My sister is in jail. They took her baby. Her husband was killed."

"Okay," Casey said. "Settle down. Relax. Who put your sister in jail? Was she arrested?"

"ICE agents," Maria said. "For a week, she was in the jail. Finally they let her call me and she tells me it's tomorrow they take her to the judge. How can this be?"

"All right, wait," Casey said, jotting notes. "Immigration and Customs Enforcement agents arrested her and put her into what jail?"

"Right here," Maria said. "The county. I went to her. I saw her."

"You said she has a baby. Where is the baby?"

"Paquita, she is in a foster home. They took her."

"Maria," Casey said, setting her pen down and leaning toward the young woman, "your sister has to have more going on than just being undocumented. Is she involved with drugs?"

"Never," Maria said, shaking her head violently. "Isodora is a good girl. Always good."

"Because ICE doesn't do things like that unless there's

something going on," Casey said. "You said the husband was killed. What happened? Was he involved in something? Drugs or rebels or something?"

"He was a good man," Maria said. "Good like her. They said it was an accident, but my sister and her husband, they are not citizens. They have no green cards and then Ellie was killed, and now people know about them."

"What accident? Why would they make her leave?"

"Ms. Jordan," Maria said, her eyes filling now, "this man is very important. I am so scared."

Casey reached across the table and took her hands and said, "Tell me what happened, Maria. I have no idea what you're talking about."

"Elijandro would go sometimes with the wife of the boss," Maria said, "but he never did nothing."

"So, he had, I mean, it looked like he was involved with his boss's wife?" Casey said, forgetting now about the smell and the heat pressing in on them.

"She would come for him at night sometimes," Maria said. "Not like that. The wife, she didn't speak Spanish and she needed Ellie to do that for her. My sister, she said she knew Ellie didn't do nothing else."

Maria shrugged and her eyes darted into her lap.

"What was the accident?" Casey asked.

Maria sighed heavily and said, "Ellie was a hunter, the best. He would take people from the ranch, guests, important people. I have seen these pictures of Ellie with them. My sister, she woke up and Ellie was gone. He left a note that he was with the husband to hunt. When the policeman came, he told her there was an accident, that Ellie was dead."

Casey began to write again.

"My sister didn't believe it," Maria said. "She wouldn't believe it. Then the ICE people, they came and took Paquita and they put Isodora in the jail."

"But why would they do that just because the husband was killed in a hunting accident?" Casey asked.

"Because people know about them now," Maria said. "And my sister is illegal. It is all on TV. Did you not see it?"

Casey looked at her blankly.

"On CNN," Maria said. "On Channel Six. Everywhere."

"There was a hunting accident a week ago," Casey said, her nostrils flaring and delivering a sudden blast of the stench, "out at Lucky Star Ranch, but that's not what you're talking about."

"Yes, it is," Maria said, wringing her hands, "this is my sister's husband."

"But," Casey said, "that's Senator Chase."

"Yes, the senator," Maria said. "This is why we are very afraid. They said it was an accident, but it was the senator who killed Elijandro."

CHAPTER
9

Teuch let the half-breed foreman, Ells, push him around just as he did the others, but Teuch promised himself that if he had the chance, he'd put a bullet between Ells's beady eyes when the time came. Teuch got a good look at the main house since they were working on a bad septic line. Teuch toiled alongside a Mex named Gomez, digging out the shit hole most of the day, but all the while keeping one eye on the comings and goings of fancy people, expensive cars, and the army of staff at the big house.

After the first hour the stink stopped bothering him and the next time his red bandana slipped down off his face he let it stay there and soak up the sweat on his neck. By noon they had their shirts off and the lady of the house—a blonde bombshell with cleavage—stopped and shaded her eyes to look them over before she climbed into her Range Rover and sped off in a whirl of dust down the gravel drive. When they climbed up out of the hole just after three, Teuch dropped down beside the water bucket, his back against one of the ancient oaks. He ladled the tepid liquid onto his head, drinking from the rivulet that ran down alongside his nose.

When he looked up, he saw the half-breed staring at his chest.

Teuch looked down at the ink, a hooded demon, then offered Ells a wink. If Ells hadn't blinked, Teuch might have thought the foreman's face had turned to stone, so cold was his expression.

"You one of them Latin Kings?" the foreman asked.

Teuch grinned and shook his head. "I dropped the flag."

"I thought they say once a Latin King, always a Latin King."

Teuch shrugged, ladled a cup of water for himself, then spit out some grit.

"We don't want no bangers around here," the foreman said, scowling.

"It's just ink," Teuch said, surveying his arms and torso. "I got a lot of it."

The foreman circled him, pointed at the back of his shoulder, and said, "That's a prison tattoo. What were you in prison for?"

Teuch looked at him for a minute, sighed, then said, "Cunnilingus."

The foreman narrowed his eyes and balled up his fists.

Teuch waggled his tongue and said, "You believe they got a law like that? It ain't no crime in Mexico, but up here? A man don't know how to care for his woman is all. I know you Comanches don't do it. That's why we get at all your sisters."

The foreman took out his wallet, counted out a five and five singles, and flipped them Teuch's way. They fluttered to the dirt and the foreman pointed at the driveway leading out to the main gate.

"Get your greasy ass outta here," he said, still stone-faced. "Don't come back."

Teuch smiled and spat at the money. "I got what I need and it ain't your money."

He extended his thumb, forefinger, and pinky, the Latin King high sign, and said, "*Amor del Rey.*"

Love of the King, his gang's creed.

Then he walked toward the driveway, studying the house from the corner of his eye as he went. With his shirt over his shoulder, he ambled along down the center of the gravel drive for nearly a mile until he reached the main gate. A camera mounted atop the wall whirred and swung his way. The gates hummed open. Teuch held up his middle finger and the camera moved with him as he walked through and headed down the last stretch of driveway to the road. He hung a left and headed toward town, sticking out his thumb at every passing vehicle.

Just before five, a battered white pickup pulled over in a dusty cloud and two Mexicans wearing cowboy hats drove him to the motel. He cleaned up, then went out for some cold beer. The back window of his room looked out over the scrub brush and some power lines to the west. With his feet up on the open windowsill, he sipped at a couple of forty-ounce King Cobras while the sun bled itself to death in a bed of purple clouds.

After a time he heard ringing in his ears and a pleasant light-headedness settled in. He felt good about how far he'd come and where the immediate future would

take him. He felt a little too good actually, but he could
sober up a bit with a meal at the Applebee's he'd seen one
exit up on Route 45. The food supplies stacked up on the
dresser would go to waste, but he hadn't expected to get
as close as he had to the house on the very first day. Part
of his success with the Kings came because he knew an
opportunity when he saw one and he never hesitated to
grab it. He'd grab this one.

He packed up the few things he had and pulled on a
gray hooded sweatshirt over his T-shirt and jeans. He lay
the MAC-10 next to the canvas duffel bag on the bed and
banged into the bathroom door on his way to take a leak.

In the mirror he caught sight of himself, the sparkle
in his dark eyes, the jaunty smile full of yellow teeth beneath a pencil-thin mustache. He gave himself a wink and
bent over to wash his hands when someone began hammering on the front door. He marched across the room
and grabbed the door handle.

"The fuck, homes?" he said, yanking it open.

A tall serious cop with a ten-gallon cowboy hat, a gold
star that read CHIEF, and a six-shooter on his hip let a hardened fist fall to his side. The cop's cold blue eyes scoured
Teuch, then swept past him, casing the hotel room. Purple
twilight glowed behind him and the evening air buzzed
with crickets.

Teuch grinned at the police chief. He didn't mind deal-
ing with cops and their laughable set of rules.

"Hey, Officer," he said, laying the accent on thick, saying *off-fee-sour*.

"Mind if I come in?" the police chief asked in a manner
as polite as his tan uniform shirt with its sharp creases and
its dark brown tie.

"Oh, sorry, homes," Teuch said, holding the edge of the door and knowing that a cop denied entry couldn't use anything he found inside to put you in jail, whether it was a MAC-10, a bag of reefer, or someone's severed head, "but I'm going out for dinner so if you want to talk to me, you gotta talk outside. Let me get my keys and I'll be out."

Teuch started to close the door. He had turned for his things when the police chief kicked it open and marched into the room.

Teuch stumbled and spun and said, "You can't do that shit, man. I know my rights."

The police chief's eyes skipped to the bed, where the machine gun lay, then right back to Teuch. The tall cop drew his revolver like a silver-screen gunslinger, drawing back the hammer with his opposite hand and a click that cut through the musty air of the thirty-dollar room.

Teuch raised his hands and felt his bowels loosening. "I didn't do nothing."

"What's that for?" the police chief asked, wagging his head toward the MAC-10. "I heard you got kicked off the work crew out to the senator's place."

"Fuck the senator," Teuch said, angry at the jelly in his gut and confident in his freedom of speech.

The pistol's muzzle flashed, the explosion deafening Teuch instantly and the shot knocking him off his feet. He came down on his rump with a jolt. His head banged back into the leg of the desk. He groped at his chest, feeling no pain, but aware that his hand came up soaked in blood before everything went black.

CHAPTER
10

THE FEMALE SERGEANT ON DUTY AT THE JAIL KEPT on writing. She said visiting hours, even for attorneys, didn't begin until after lunch, but she looked up when Casey said her name.

"Not *The Casey Jordan Story* Casey Jordan, are you?"

Casey's cheeks burned. She averted her eyes and nodded.

"Oh my God," the sergeant said. "My mother and I taped that show. We watched it three times. You look so much younger than I thought you would."

The sergeant stood up and extended her beefy hand. "I am so honored."

"Thank you," Casey said, taking her hand and eyeing the name tag on her uniform, "Belinda. Do you think you could help me see Isodora a little early? I've got a million things I'm trying to get done."

The sergeant's face bloomed with a knowing smile. "I can still see Susan Lucci's face when she says, 'A woman like me can't rest when another woman is in need.' And here you are. I can't even believe it."

She picked up the phone and barked a couple of orders, regained her smile, and escorted Casey down a long hallway to a small interview room.

"Would you mind signing this?" the sergeant asked. "I swear, I never ask for autographs, but, well, my mother won't even believe me."

Casey felt her entire face go up in flames. "Sure."

The sergeant had a pad of paper and she held it out to Casey with a pen, her round cheeks red and nearly glistening. Casey asked the mother's name and signed the paper with best wishes before handing it back.

"Oh, this is perfect," the sergeant said. "Thank you so much."

"My pleasure," Casey said.

"You must get this all the time."

"Not really, but it's my pleasure."

"Well, I've got to get back to the desk," the sergeant said, stealing an appreciative glance at the autograph, "but she'll be right in."

Casey sat down and pinched the bridge of her nose. After only a couple of minutes the door opened.

The guard who escorted the bedraggled Isodora into the interview room shot Casey a dirty look from under a cap of short dark hair. The dough of her pasty white face bore permanent lines of displeasure. She pointed Isodora toward the metal chair with her scarred baton.

"Sit down," she said, and Isodora did.

Casey held the guard's gaze until the big woman stroked her shadow of a mustache, grunted, and told them they had ten minutes and that was it.

"We're not supposed to be pulling them out of meals," the guard said, continuing to glare at Casey.

"You were so kind to do it, though," Casey said.

The guard slammed the door on her way out.

Casey breathed in. The small square room smelled like a dirty mop tinged with the sour scent of vomit. Above them, the fluorescent tube flickered like a coming storm. Casey turned her attention to Isodora, her bony frame swallowed up by the orange prison jumpsuit. Behind the disheveled curtain of long dark hair hid the petite and pretty tearstained face of a woman who looked too young and too meek to be sitting in a jail.

"It's all right," Casey said, reaching across the battered table for Isodora's hand.

Isodora flinched.

"Maria sent me," Casey said. "I'm Casey Jordan."

Her red-rimmed eyes darted up through the tangle of hair and her hand relaxed under Casey's touch.

"I'm going to try to get your baby for you," Casey said with a squeeze. "Did anyone talk to you about Hutto?"

Hutto, the detention facility the Department of Homeland Security used for undocumented alien families, was a former prison run by a private company. The old fortress had generated some negative publicity, but it was still the best option for undocumented aliens with children because it allowed them to spend much of their days together.

"What's her name?" Casey said. "Your little girl?"

Isodora sucked in her lower lip and nodded tightly. Fresh tears spilled down her cheeks. "Paquita," she said in a whisper, her entire frame trembling.

"That's a pretty name," Casey said. "Let's work on this. Now you have to tell me everything, Isodora. I'm your lawyer, and that means no matter what you did, I'm going to help you.

"Did you ever have a granny? An *abuelita*? That's what I'm like. Anything you did is okay with me, but I need to know. Now, did you do something wrong?"

Isodora's face crumpled and a sob escaped her.

"I did nothing," she said, gasping out the words between great gulps of air. "They took Paquita. Elijandro is dead. I don't care where I go. Just make them give her back to me, Miss Casey. Please."

Casey swallowed and squeezed her hand again.

"You're sure there's nothing?" she asked softly. "Drugs? Bad people your husband was with? Because I can't figure out why this is happening."

"They said I'm illegal," Isodora said, still sobbing. "Undocumented."

"Okay," Casey said gently, "but there's something more. Maybe it's a mistake. It's a big government."

Gently, Casey presented a slew of possibilities— drugs, weapons, smuggling people, and bad politics—but at every suggestion Isodora swore both she and her husband had done nothing wrong. Several times she excitedly broke into Spanish and Casey had to ask her to say it again.

Finally Casey asked, "What about the senator's wife, Isodora?"

Even through the curtain of hair, Casey could see the young woman's face redden.

She shook her head and said, "No, no. He did nothing with her. He was a good husband. A good man."

"But he went with her sometimes?" Casey asked. "At night? Your sister told me."

"She had a problem and Ellie, he was such a good man. She needed him to speak Spanish. What was he to say? She was the wife. We had our own *house.*"

Isodora parted her hair and looked hard at Casey, setting her jaw. "I will tell you this. I know he did nothing. He, Elijandro, he would have this—how do you say—hives, this rash. Big red dots."

Isodora rubbed her chest. "Here he had them. When he was with me, he would have this. Always. Before we married, I used to tease him and call them *diablo se mancha*, devil spots. And when he came back after the first time he went with her, I made him show me and he didn't have it. So, you see?"

Casey nodded and said, "I see why you believed him. I'm just trying to find the reason why Senator Chase would have done this."

Isodora bit her lip and nodded, as if holding back tears.

"Maybe he thought like you," Isodora said in a whisper.

At the sound of the guard rattling the door, Casey stood up.

"All right," she said. "I'll do everything I can. I should at least be able to get you to a place where you can be with Paquita."

The guard stood frowning behind the young girl and nudged Isodora's ribs with the baton, telling her to get moving.

Casey rounded the table and pushed her face so close to the guard's that she could smell the cigarettes on the hefty woman's breath.

"You *touch* her with that thing again," Casey said in

a low growl. "You so much as wave it at her and I'll have you bounced so far out of this place you'll think you were riding a rocket."

The guard snickered and said, "Yeah, I heard all about it. A woman like you can't rest when another woman is in need. Lady, why don't you go get some sleep."

Casey opened her mouth to speak, but nothing came out and she could only watch Isodora being led away.

Instead of lodging a complaint with the sergeant, Casey simply asked when Isodora would be delivered to the courthouse for her appearance on Monday.

CHAPTER
11

C HIEF GAGE BACKED HIS CRUISER UP TO THE MOTEL
door and dragged Teuch's body out. He unfolded a thick
plastic tarp inside his trunk and dumped the body in,
slamming the trunk closed and dusting his hands as he
scanned the empty parking lot and the pockets of wan
light spilling from cheap fixtures up and down the row
of doors. He moved with the confidence of a man who'd
been a law unto himself for nearly twenty years.

He was only a deputy fresh out of community college
when the senator's old man died and the senator took over
the ranch, bumping his older sister and her no-good husband to a beach house in Galveston. It was a deflowered
high school cheerleader who gave Gage the first opportunity to distinguish himself with the senator, who was then
just a young lawyer at the attorney general's office in the
city. When she awoke in a ditch with her skirt hiked up
over her boobs she called 911 from a pay phone outside
of town, gibbering so that the dispatcher couldn't understand her.

They sent Gage out to pick her up and when he saw the black eye and realized where the whole thing was headed, he told her to shut up and drove her straight back out to the ranch. Gage showed his stuff by offering the girl the chance to make up with Chase or be taken in for possession of a small bag of cocaine he removed from his sock and tucked into the low-cut neckline of her rumpled dress and beneath the double-D cup of her bra. The senator never forgot that, and together they had ruled their own little slice of heaven in this forgotten corner of Dallas County ever since.

Inside the motel room, Gage knelt down beside the bloodstained carpet and mopped it as best he could, putting his back to the flimsy bureau, moving it along the wall toward the bathroom to hide the vast bulk of the mess. He clucked his tongue, satisfied with the camouflage of stains from other bygone accidents and crimes. The towel went into the trunk with Teuch's things, and Gage drove off into the night, tires roaring over the still-warm asphalt.

Out on Route 45, about twenty minutes and two counties to the south, Gage pulled off at a picnic area. He got out of his cruiser and rousted the lone trucker, who was stripped to his underwear and pulled over for the night, telling him he'd have to move on to the truck stop down in Corsicana. The running lights of the big rig hadn't even disappeared over the next rise before Gage had Teuch's body out on the curb. He dragged the young gangbanger by the armpits out into the scrub a ways where no one had any business being and flopped him down in the parched dirt.

Somewhere in the distance a coyote sniggered and then wailed in a high-pitched scream, the sound rolling endlessly across the flat land. A chill jiggered Gage's spine, only to be warmed by the metal curve of the hammer on the big pistol at his waist. They'd do a good job on the Mexican, the coyotes would. Gage took only one cursory glance around before drawing the pistol and taking aim at the center of the Mexican's forehead, standing well away so as not to spatter his pants with gore. Orange flame burst from the gun's barrel and the deafening roar rolled right back out across the same flat land, truncating the coyote's call. A hairy divot from the top of Teuch's head took off like a flushed snipe, disappearing into the shadows and drawing a chuckle up from Gage's belly.

The police chief returned to his car, whipping it around, gravel singing in a cloud of dust, and accelerating on down the highway. He gripped the wheel and let the surge push him back into the seat as the needle pegged 120. Gage was in no particular hurry to get away.

He just liked to drive fast.

CHAPTER
12

When she got to her office, the first call Casey made was to Norman Case, the district counsel at the Department of Homeland Security. Casey knew of him from his days as an assistant in the attorney general's office. He had the reputation of being a fair and decent lawyer and had won several high-profile drug trials for the federal government.

Casey called the office, gave her name to the secretary, and spilled out Isodora's story as quickly as she could, hoping to elicit some sympathy.

The secretary answered her with disinterest, suggesting she send a letter to the office.

Casey cleared her throat and said, "I don't know if you caught my name, Casey Jordan? I run a women's law clinic downtown, the Marcia Sales Clinic? We've been in the news."

Silence greeted her. Humiliation swelled up inside Casey's stomach.

"My client," Casey said, "if you could see her, they

took her little girl and it's all a mistake and I'm trying to
help her."

After a moment of silence, the secretary sighed and
said, "Hang on."

Casey opened her clenched fist and beat the side of her
leg with an open palm.

"Ms. Jordan?" said a man. "Norman Case. How can
I help you?"

Casey explained Isodora's situation and said, "I think
someone in your office must have mistaken her for someone else. She's undocumented, but she has no record. Her
husband was killed in a hunting accident. The thing at
Senator Chase's ranch."

"Rough," Case said. "I don't really know Chase, but
you had to feel bad for him."

Casey recalled the pathetic image of the wildly popu-
lar senator talking at a press conference about the tragedy,
tears streaming down his face, his broken voice almost
impossible to understand.

"Me, too," she said. "But I feel even worse for the dead
man's wife. She's the one I'm talking about. They took her
right off the senator's ranch. You'd think after all that—"

"I doubt the senator even knows," Case said. "Some of
the ICE people run things without a lot of cross talk. We
just process what they bring us. I'll look into it for you.
You know how it goes with these illegals. There's what?
Twelve million of them? You can't blame the left hand for
not knowing what the right is doing these days."

"I'm hoping you can release her," Casey said.

"The hearing is Monday," Case said.

"If she goes into the hearing and they think she's
someone else," Casey said, "the judge isn't going to do

anything outside the lines. Even if we can't get her set free, at least let's get her identity right and we get her to Hutto so she can be with her little girl. I'm hoping we can get it done before the weekend. She's just a baby."

"Give me her name and I'll see what I can do," Case said.

She thanked him and gave him her cell phone number, asking for whoever worked on it to call her the minute they worked through the mistake.

It was four when she realized she hadn't heard from Norman Case or anyone in his office. She ushered a pregnant young woman out of her office and scooped up the phone. This time Case's secretary was short with her. She sounded offended and said that the DHS lawyer was unavailable and that all she could do was take a message.

"He's there?"

"Yes, but he's in a meeting," the secretary said.

"Will he call me when he's done?"

"Ms. Jordan, he told me to take a message. After that, you're on your own."

"Look, just help me here. Can you just ask him if he was able to straighten out Isodora's identity? Can you please do that?"

"Do you use that trick all the time?" the secretary asked.

"What trick?"

"About the poor mother and her kid and your do-good clinic."

"What trick?"

"You play me and I make a fool out of myself to my boss, telling him you're all this and all that. Fool me once, shame on you. You won't fool me twice."

"I didn't say anything that wasn't true."

"They pay in cash, right?" the secretary said. "These drug dealers?"

Casey snorted and half-laughed. "What are you talking about?"

"You'll have to talk to Mr. Case."

"Please," Casey said. "I really don't know what you're talking about."

"Your client?" the secretary said. "They got the right person. She and her husband? Organized crime. A big gang, one of the biggest. Murder. Extortion. Drugs."

"It's a mistake," Casey said.

"You're the mistake," the secretary said.

CHAPTER
13

TEUCH DREAMED OF A JAILHOUSE HAIRCUT. THE clammy plastic cape tight on his neck. His hands pinned down on the armrests of the chair, weighted in concrete. And the buzzing as the hundred tiny blades snickered across his scalp. Tufts of dry black hair falling like fat snowflakes, sliding down the front of his face, depositing themselves in his open mouth. A mouth dry as desert dust and buzzing.

In the dream, he saw his sister-in-law, Isodora, as a child, pushing through the line of prisoners in a blaze orange jumpsuit of her own. He felt shame when her dark eyes found his. Her face crumpled and she began to shriek.

The sound woke Teuch and he saw a real child in a kid's rugby shirt, his face crumpled like Isodora's in the dream, and in his hand the pelt of a small butchered animal. Teuch moved his dry mouth. No sound came from it, but the movement sent a cloud of buzzing flies up from his face. As in the dream, his arms would not move, nor his legs, nor any part of him except the swollen silent lips. Still, he could listen from his bed in the deep brown weeds.

"Daddy! Daddy! Daddy!" The child stood frozen in terror, the pelt gripped tight, black hair woven through his fingers.

"Finish your business and get back here," a voice said. "If it's a bug, walk away. You want bologna or peanut butter?"

The father appeared, glasses fogging from the heat, plastic-wrapped sandwich in hand, mouth agog.

"Put that down!" he said, pointing at the bloody pelt. "Goddamn it!"

The boy's face spilled tears. The father reached for the pelt.

"What the hell?" he said, snatching the pelt and throwing it to the ground before he saw Teuch and the flies. "Oh my God."

The man and the boy disappeared and even though the flies returned, tickling Teuch's face, licking and feeding in the corners of his eyes and nose, he drifted back into another dream until something woke him suddenly. The man had come back without the boy, but with a cop who kicked at Teuch's foot. A dirty white cop. The long mustache on his face hid in the shadow of a tall felt hat.

"Jesus," the cop said, parting the weeds and kneeling down beside Teuch to touch his neck. "This man's alive."

CHAPTER
14

"GET MARIA DELGADO IN HERE," CASEY SAID TO STACY, banging open the door between her office and where Stacy sat.

"What got under your skin?" Stacy asked.

"I just made an ass out of myself," she said.

Stacy raised her eyebrows.

"You said I had to see her? That I shouldn't be worrying about a lunch?" Casey said. "I could *lose* my lunch when I think of her sniveling face. Crocodile tears. Do you know the sister and her husband are gangbangers? Drugs. Murder. All of it. *That's* why they want her out."

"Oh, right," Stacy said, picking up the phone and dialing. "Our government couldn't be the ones making the mistake. Not the gang who gave us Iraq."

"Don't get political," Casey said.

"Maria?" Stacy said into the phone. "It's Stacy Berg. Can you come down to the clinic?"

Stacy looked at Casey from under half-lidded eyes.

"Yes, I know it's Friday afternoon," Stacy said into the

phone. "I'm afraid it's very important. Right away. Yes. Good."

Stacy slammed the phone down and took out a nail file that she began to work at with great concentration.

———

Casey worked up her witness list for Rosalita's case while she waited for Maria. She didn't want the woman to get off easy over the phone. She wanted Maria to feel her rage. Half an hour later Stacy knocked once, threw open the door, and announced Maria. Casey pointed to a chair and didn't let her even settle in before she began.

"You didn't tell me about your brother-in-law, the gangbanger," Casey said.

"My brother-in-law?" Maria said, touching her chest. "Elijandro? Ellie is a laborer and a hunting guide."

"What else does he do?"

Maria shrugged and said, "He teaches Sunday school."

"Someone's in a gang," Casey said. "The Torres brothers? The Latin Kings?"

Maria's eyes widened and she said, "Ellie's brother."

"Who?"

"My sister's husband," Maria said. "His brother. Teuch is his name. Teuch Torres. He's a Latin King, but Ellie, he doesn't—didn't—even talk to him. Teuch is very bad."

"Yes, he is," Casey said. "Why didn't you tell me about him?"

"He lives in San Antonio. My sister met him only twice. Once at Paquita's baptism, then right after that for the last time. I was there. Ellie took us down to Christmas dinner at his mother's. She is a housekeeper there. Teuch and Ellie got into a fight. They have no business together at all. Nada. They don't even speak."

"Well," Casey said, lowering her voice, "ICE made the connection. I'll do my best, look for some kind of precedent. I'm sorry I was a little rough. I just felt ridiculous."

"I never thought about Teuch," Maria said. "He's so far away and they have nothing to do with him. There are many people with the name Torres. I don't know how they would find him and put him with Elijandro. I am worried that they would do this."

"I'm worried, too," Casey said.

———

Casey worked alone and didn't realize how late it was until her stomach growled and she looked at her watch. Stacy and Donna had gone on a double date with their new boyfriends, one a guy who owned a shoe factory and the other a financial planner. They'd been talking about it for over a week, so Casey encouraged them to leave while she prepared for Isodora's hearing on Monday by herself. Sharon never stayed late, especially on Friday. She had two kids at home and a husband who expected dinner on the table at six.

Casey closed the book in front of her with a clump and rubbed her eyes. The room had grown dark around her but for the glow of the computer screen and the small lamp on her desk. Outside she heard the crunch of tires on the broken pavement and she sat up straight. José's warning about Domingo Mondo jumped to mind. The wife,

Soledad, had been whipped across her backside regularly
with an electric cord.

Casey heard a car door slam and she reached for the desk
drawer by her knee. She opened it, removing the nickel-
plated .38 José had insisted she keep there. Comforted by the
cold shape of the metal in her hand, she dug into her purse,
searching for her cell phone. Feet scuffed across the parking
lot and came to rest outside the metal door.

Casey flipped open the phone and saw she'd missed
three calls from José. Her heart took off at a gallop. The
phone had been left on vibrate. She'd missed José's warning calls.

A fist hammered the metal door.

Casey hit dial on José's number.

The door shuddered under another pounding.

José answered his phone.

"It's me," Casey said. "I think he's here."

"Who? Where?" José asked.

"Domingo Mondo."

"Aren't you at your office?" José asked.

"Yes, and I think he's right outside."

CHAPTER
15

Silence hung between them a moment until José said, "That's me. I'm outside."

"Jesus. You?"

He rapped twice on the door and said, "Me. Three times now."

He rapped three times.

"You're not pointing that .38 at me, are you?" he asked.

Casey looked at the gun in her hand and lowered it quietly into the drawer. "Of course not."

"Can I come in?"

Casey hung up the phone and went to the door, calling to him and putting her ear up to it just because she couldn't help herself. When he said his name, she threw the bolt and swung open the door. His big white smile glowed at her from the shadows of the streetlight. He'd slicked his dark hair back behind his ears and wore a clean white shirt, dark jeans, and cowboy boots that showed no wear.

"What are you doing here?" she asked.

"I tried to call."

"I know, I thought to warn me about Mondo. That made it worse."

"I'm glad you're being safe," he said. "I just put the redheaded wife to bed—so to speak. That little Roadway Inn down by the highway. I thought I'd see if you were around. Did you eat yet?"

Casey shook her head. "Are you shaking?" he asked, lightly taking hold of her wrist. "I'm sorry I scared you like that. I tried to call and then I saw the light on, so I stopped."

"I'm fine," she said, pulling away. "I'd love to get something, though. We could talk about Rosalita and a new case I've got that I think I'm going to need your help on."

"You like fried oysters?" he asked.

"Sure."

"Come on. Follow me. Del Frisco's has the best."

Casey shut down her computer, packed her notes into her briefcase, and followed him out into the back lot. She noticed for the first time the slight bow in his muscular legs. When he turned to say something, she blushed and looked away. He stood there, waiting for her to get into the Mercedes and start the engine before he nodded and climbed into his pickup. She followed him onto the Toll-way and they headed north almost to the Belt Line.

Casey handed her keys to a valet.

"You know the hubcaps is gone on this, right?" the valet said.

"I try not to be too flashy," she said.

"Just 'cause I don't want anyone saying nothing."

"Try to keep it away from that Bentley over there," she said, angling her head toward the lot and the enormous car with its sparkling grill. "I don't want those wide doors chipping my paint when some P. Diddy guy swings it open."

Casey left the valet pinching his lip and stepped toward the door José held open for her.

"Very fancy," she said, looking around at the dark wood, the candles, and the linen tablecloths.

"I try to spend as much as I can, so if something happens to me my wife won't get a dime."

"You have a daughter, don't you?"

"And a life insurance trust in her name," he said, following Casey inside, "so if I do die, she'll be all set. The trustee is my mom and you know she won't let the ex see a penny of it. Cash, cars, my watch."

He rattled the stainless steel Submariner.

"Anything liquid," he said, "and even though it goes to my girl, she'll have her mitts all over it."

José had called ahead for a table and the hostess took them to it right away.

"I'm sorry. You don't want to hear crap like that," he said, leaning over his open menu. "That's no way to start a da—a dinner."

"This isn't a date, is it?" Casey said. "Is that what you were going to say?"

"I like working with you," he said. "I don't want to screw that up."

"You think I can afford to fire you?"

José rubbed his chin and said, "I think you'd fire yourself if you got the itch."

"Can I ask you a strange question?"

"Would you mind a strange answer?"

"Do men ever get a rash from sex?"

"Down in Juarez you're apt to, but I don't frequent those kinds of places."

"Not that kind of rash. I mean, like breaking out in hives on your chest."

"Can I wait until I've had a couple oysters?"

"I'm being serious," Casey said. "I had a client tell me her husband always breaks out in a rash. That's how she knows he hasn't been sleeping with his boss's wife."

"This sounds more like my paying clients," he said.

"I don't buy it," Casey said, ignoring his smirk. "Some women just don't want to know. You heard about Senator Chase and that hunting accident?"

"It was all over. Everywhere."

"This part wasn't."

Casey told him the story, as much as she knew. José's dark eyebrows dipped farther and farther toward his nose as she went on. When the champagne came, the waiter popped the cork and she stopped talking.

The waiter filled their glasses. José raised his and said, "I didn't mean to be goofy about it. Cheers, anyway."

"I wouldn't believe it if I hadn't gotten that kind of reaction from Norman Case," she said before taking a sip and nodding at her glass. "That's good. He's supposed to be a straight shooter."

"You think Chase killed this guy over the wife?"

"If it was an accident," Casey said, "why the rush to get Isodora out of the country?"

"Embarrassment?" José said. "Isn't Chase big on sending every Mexican without a swimming pool back across the border?"

"He didn't support the Immigration Bill, but who did?"

"It's how he didn't support it."

"I didn't follow it that close," Casey said.

"I did," José said, sipping his champagne. "I ever tell you I got a degree in poli-sci from Angelo State? Anyway, that man's a xenophobe."

"But these people lived on his ranch."

"Funny how they do that," José said, forcing a smile, "use these people like slaves until someone catches them. Then they say they didn't know and start calling them thieves and talk about breaking into the country."

"How can we find out?" Casey asked.

"It'll be hard to prove that it wasn't an accident," José said. "They said the guy jumped right up in front of him. No one else was there."

"Pretend the wife was with Elijandro," Casey said, eyeing the plate of deep-fried oysters the waiter set down. "Go at it like that and how do you prove it wasn't an accident?"

"You dig in," José said, stabbing an oyster and drowning it in hot sauce. "You ask questions. You start from the start. Eventually work your way around to the wife, but I'd save that. First you got the arrest report. Autopsy. Visit the scene. Even if it is in the *Triángulo de Bermudas*."

"Even I speak that Spanish," Casey said. "The Bermuda Triangle's in the Caribbean."

"We have our own here," José said. "The Mexicans around here are real superstitious about that corner of the county. There's a chief of police who don't like Mexicans and supposedly people have disappeared going through there."

"What do you mean? Arrested? Kidnapped?"

José shrugged. "Don't know, but when I was doing some undercover work right before I left the force there were these two bangers who almost went to war over a missing container full of people. One of the guys ran the route and the other's cousins were in the thing and it just disappeared."

"Maybe they didn't make it across the border," Casey said. "Or they got lost in the desert someplace."

"Right," José said, swallowing his oyster and holding his fork in the air. "Only the truck driver made a call from just outside Wilmer, so they made it across. That was the last time anyone had a line on the truck. Twenty people. Poof. Vanished.

"Don't worry though," he said with a grin.

"Why not?"

" 'Cause I'm not superstitious."

CHAPTER
16

On Monday morning, Casey waited for Isodora on the fourth floor, in the central hallway by the immigration courtrooms. The court schedule was posted on a thick column in the middle of the hall, and a small crowd, composed mostly of family members, clustered around it. The din of Spanish-speaking voices echoed up and down the sterile hallway with a rhythm and life that reminded Casey of something caged. She detected only two other attorneys, both men, who stood out in their suits and ties. She pressed through the crowd and rolled her eyes when she saw that Isodora was the second-from-the-last case in courtroom number three.

A few minutes later, Maria appeared, out of breath and explaining that an accident had made her bus late.

"You'll get her out, Ms. Jordan?" she asked.

"It depends on what the judge had for breakfast," Casey said.

"Breakfast?"

"It's just a saying," Casey said, eyeing a commotion

by the elevators. "It means these judges can pretty much do what they want. Sometimes it depends on their mood. You brought the money?"

"Everything I could get," she said, pulling an envelope fat with faded small bills from her purse. "Almost eleven hundred."

The elevators at the far end of the hall disgorged the prisoners, who marched forward in orange jumpsuits, handcuffed and chained together like a troop from death row. Casey twisted her lips in disgust, walking to meet the advancing prisoners. She scanned the bunch for Isodora and finally found her, the last of the female prisoners before the men came led by a four-hundred-pound Latino with tattoos and a greasy ponytail. The pretty young Isodora hung her head, and when she did look up, her big brown eyes sagged with despair.

"Will I get my baby, Miss Casey?" she asked.

"I'm going to try, Isodora," Casey said, falling in alongside her client on their way to the courtroom. "What can you tell me about your husband's brother?"

"Teuch?"

"You know him, then."

Isodora shrugged. "He's nothing like my husband."

"He's a gang member?"

"He's a King. The Latin Kings," Isodora said, shuffling along under the clinking of chains.

"And you and your husband aren't in business with him in any way?" Casey asked as they stopped just outside the courtroom.

Isodora's eyebrows shot up. "Never. They didn't speak."

Casey raised a finger into the air and said, "You say it to the judge, just like that."

The court had no wood paneling or carved balus-trades. It was a big empty room filled up with rows of simple metal benches facing a dais with a desk flanked by the American and Texas flags. Behind the desk, a plastic ICE seal had been screwed into the wall. On the floor, to either side of the dais, rested a table for the government and another for the defense, each with three metal chairs. The ICE agent sat down at the government table. On the defense side, a young Hispanic interpreter already waited.

The prisoners were shuttled into the front row and the agents escorting them clanked and rattled the chains as they separated them one from another, the women on one side and the men on the other. Casey found a seat in the back with Maria among the family members and the two other lawyers.

The judge came in through a side door, followed by a sharply dressed young woman wearing her hair in a tight dark bun. Casey knew that she would be the ICE assistant chief counsel.

The judge, a thin, elderly man in a robe that had faded from black to dark green, peered down his nose, adjusting his glasses as he studied his morning slate of cases. With very little interest, the judge clicked on a small tape recorder, set it on his desk, and began calling the prisoners to the defense table to give an accounting of themselves. None of them spoke English and the judge directed his attention to the young man sitting beside them, the interpreter, glancing only occasionally at the prisoners and the family members appearing on their behalf.

During this process, the young woman with the tight hair would chirp respectfully at the judge from the other side of the room about the government's position. The two of them, despite their differences in age and appearance, worked together like cogs in a machine, grinding slowly through the roomful of prisoners. While the judge showed no emotion, Casey took it as a good sign that many of the prisoners were released to their friends and relatives, even though some—like the enormous man wearing the ponytail—were left to sit and scowl in their handcuffs.

When the judge called Isodora's name, Casey stood and approached the front of the room to address the court beside her client.

"May it please the court, Your Honor," Casey said, using her best courtroom etiquette, "I'd like to ask for a hearing to seek adjustment of status for my client. In the meantime, I'd like to respectfully ask the court to release my client to her own recognizance."

"Without bail?" the judge asked, leafing through the file without looking up at her.

"My client has undergone extreme hardship, Your Honor," Casey said. "Her husband was just killed in a hunting accident. You may have heard of the—"

"You don't think that has anything to do with this?" the judge asked, glaring down at her with a furrowed brow, his mouth a paper cut.

"No, Your Honor," Casey said. "I just wanted you to know the circumstances. My client has a child, who is a United States citizen who is currently in foster care."

"Ms. Jordan," the judge said. "Do you need me to extend to you the courtesy of explaining the law that you're supposed to already know? You've been in this court before. You know how I feel about this whole anchor baby nonsense. I won't have it."

"The little girl is only two, Your Honor," Casey said in

a pleading tone. "She needs her mother and I think I could show the court extreme hardship that would convince it to adjust her undocumented status."

The ICE lawyer leaned toward the judge from the corner of her table and said something in a low tone, pointing to the file in front of him. The judge put his head down and began to read, moving his lips as he did.

"Well, it's your lucky day," he said, looking up. "Even under the circumstances."

The judge looked back down and selected a paper from the file, which he studied as he spoke. "The government is willing to offer Ms. Torres a voluntary departure."

"Circumstances?" Casey said.

The judge scowled at her. "Your client has links to organized crime, Ms. Jordan. She's a Homeland Security person of interest and the state is giving her a generous offer."

"She has nothing to do with her brother-in-law, Your Honor. I'd like you to hear her on that subject."

"At a minimum, they have the same last name," he said. "As you can see, we have a lot on the docket, Ms. Jordan."

"What's our alternative, Your Honor? Can I get a hearing?"

The judge raised his eyebrows and glanced over at the young woman lawyer from ICE before holding the paper up at Casey. "Of course you can have your hearing. That's your right, isn't it? Probably by the end of the week. That will end with an order of deportation, unless I'm a fool, and I'm not. After that, you can appeal to the Immigration Board in writing. And, right now, those rulings are running about eighteen months. In the meantime, under the circumstances, I can't see your client being reunited with her child."

"She met the brother-in-law only twice in her life," Casey said.

"You can argue that at your hearing," the judge said, looking at the next file, "not here."

"Your Honor," Casey said, raising her voice, "the court can't keep a mother and her child apart for that amount of time without doing irreparable harm."

"The *court* isn't keeping them apart, Ms. Jordan," said the judge, scrunching up his wizened face. "The offer of a voluntary deportation is extremely generous. Maybe you don't know that."

Casey's cheeks burned. She turned to Isodora just in time to see two tears spill from the corners of her eyes.

"My baby, please," she said.

"If we go along, they're going to put you on the next plane out of here," Casey said in a low tone. "Maybe today."

"To Mexico?" she asked.

Casey nodded.

"But Paquita is American, Miss Casey."

"I know," Casey said. "But she can't help you stay here until she's twenty-one. And if we take the hearing and they *order* your deportation, you can't get back in legally, ever."

"I just want my baby."

"Maybe I can work on some kind of visa," Casey said, trying to overcome the sinking feeling that nothing would bring this woman back. "There are other ways to get you back. Maybe a green card."

Isodora clasped her hands together, looked down, and nodded yes.

"Ms. Jordan," the judge said, "you may be getting paid by the hour, but the court isn't."

"We'll take the voluntary deportation, Your Honor," Casey said.

The ICE lawyer looked up at the judge, beaming.

CHAPTER
17

"WHAT HAPPENED?" MARIA ASKED IN THE HALLWAY outside the courtroom.

"We did the best we could," Casey said, watching Isodora as she trudged away down the hall behind the fat man while the three other prisoners she'd come in with sauntered alongside them.

"They didn't let her talk," Maria said.

"They didn't stop her," Casey said. "They offered her a deal and she took it. She wants to be with her baby, Maria. You can't blame her for that."

"Everyone I know," Maria said, "they say she will be let go until her hearing. Now she must leave? This is not right."

"Maybe," Casey said.

"I know this."

"I'm going to try and find out if it's not right," Casey said. "Excuse me."

Casey broke off from Maria and strode down a side hall, working her way through a small maze toward the

ICE counsel offices. When Casey turned the corner past the judges' offices, she actually caught sight of the back of the ICE lawyer's tight hair bun up ahead.

Casey took off at a jog, catching the young lawyer just as she reached for the handle to the door of the ICE counsel offices.

"I wanted to thank you," Casey said with her broadest smile.

The lawyer gazed without commitment.

"For offering up the voluntary," Casey said.

"It's the best thing for the child," she said.

"Look, we don't want to embarrass the senator, either," Casey said. "I just wanted you to share that with everyone. That's never been my or my client's intent."

The lawyer stammered for a moment before she raised her eyebrows and said, "I'm sorry?"

"Having undocumented workers there, on his ranch," Casey said. "I'm sure he didn't know. Some people don't understand how hard it is to find good help."

The lawyer blinked and bit down on her lower lip.

"I know we can't really talk about it," Casey said, pressing the tips of her fingers into the young woman's shoulder. "But, unofficially, just pass the word, so they don't worry."

"The staff at his liaison office is great," the lawyer said. "I'm sure they'll be glad to hear it."

CHAPTER
18

JOSÉ DIDN'T ANSWER HIS CELL PHONE. CASEY TRIED paging him, but that didn't work, either. She went into the reception area and asked Stacy if she'd heard from him.

"Since when does he answer to me?" Stacy asked. "You're the one having dinners with him."

"How'd you know about dinner?" Casey asked, her cheeks warming.

"I got my sources," Stacy said.

Casey glanced at a young woman sitting by the window, waiting for her appointment, and angled her head, signaling Stacy into her office for some privacy.

"Don't worry," Stacy said. "She can't understand you. So how was it?"

"First time I ever had fried oysters," Casey said, glancing at the young woman.

"Not the food," Stacy said, "José. How was *it*?"

"There was no it," Casey said. "Are you kidding? We had dinner, talked shop, and said good night."

"No kiss?"

"You watch too much TV. Anyone ever tell you that?"

"I would've kissed him," Stacy said. "He's gorgeous, and you probably ran for your car, didn't invite him over for a drink, a walk, a talk, nothing. What about Saturday?"

"He had plans with his daughter," Casey said. "I don't know, I think he's just being nice."

"You've got to be more aggressive. He's hot for you. What? You think he's hanging around here, shagging deadbeat dads and disappearing witnesses for the fun of it? Tina? She baited her hook the other day with that dress and the push-up bra and he didn't even look twice. He's gaga for you."

"Okay, seriously, that's enough," Casey said.

Stacy shrugged. "What do you need him for now, then?"

"Forget it," Casey said. "Nothing I can't do myself, anyway."

"Don't be so touchy."

Casey disappeared into her office, gently closing the door. She tried José again, then headed out the back and got into the Benz. She didn't want to give the Wilmer police chief time to prepare for her, so instead of making a phone call, she headed to the southeast corner of the county.

The drive to Wilmer south on 45 took less than half an hour. After announcing herself to a young woman behind the desk, Casey waited in a chair by the door. The receptionist glanced up at her often enough that Casey began to brace herself for a Movie of the Week comment. None came.

When Chief Gage emerged from the back, he was so tall the crew cut on his bullet head nearly chafed the doorframe. Casey felt the same one-way familiarity that she presumed the receptionist had with her.

She'd seen Gage's face on TV when Senator Chase's hunting accident filled the first block of almost every newscast for three days. Gage issued the official statement closing the case as an accident. He'd done the press conference in a hat proportional to his own height, and still it was his face that Casey remembered well, the black caterpillar eyebrows, the lantern jaw, and the icy blue eyes of a Siberian husky.

Casey shook his skillet-size hand, and he led her down a short hall to a large windowed office looking out on the full bloom of a pecan tree. A thick sheet of glass raised up by four elephant tusks served as his desk, and the heads of other trophy animals graced the high walls: a panther, a bison, a warthog, and an elk, among others. Framed eight-by-ten pictures of the chief with numerous celebrities made a complete ring around the office, one next to the other breaking only for the window: Clint Eastwood, George W. Bush, Sylvester Stallone, Billy Ray Cyrus. Antique handguns and their corresponding bullets hung in an oak case beneath a Dahl ram's head, and a cabinet of rifles stood in the corner. Beneath Casey's high-heeled shoes, the skin of a zebra covered the wood plank floorboards.

Casey sat down across from the chief in a wooden chair with a cane seat that rasped and creaked under every shift. She surveyed the room one last time, quickly, and noticed an absence of books. When she returned her eyes she found the chief staring intently.

"How can I help you, Ms. Jordan?" the chief said. He picked a bayonet up off a pile of papers on his desk and leaned back, turning it over slowly in his fingers.

"I'm interested in Senator Chase's accident," she said.

"Terrible thing," he said, fingering the tip of the blade as if to test its sharpness.

"I'm wondering how you knew it was an accident," Casey said.

Gage curled his lips, picked at his teeth with the bayonet, and said, "That's old news."

"Unless you represent the victim's widow," Casey said. "That's me. Strangely, the government is in a rush to get her out of Dodge."

"Maybe the government finally got tired of paying for their kids to go to our schools," Gage said. "But that ain't my business. My business is keeping this town quiet, things running smooth. What's your business, miss?"

Casey cleared her throat and said, "Your investigation of Elijandro Torres's death. How it was conducted."

Gage ridged his brow and considered her for a minute before pursing his lips to choke back a snicker and saying, "No, miss, that's not your business."

"I'd like to see the police report," Casey said. "And the coroner's."

Gage stood up and pointed the bayonet at the door. "People in this town pay me to keep them safe, miss. I got work to do."

"Your records are public information."

"And you can submit your request in writing," Gage said, waggling the bayonet at the door.

Casey got up and the chief followed her all the way out through the reception area, standing in the doorway with his arms folded across the broad expanse of his chest.

Casey had her cell phone going before she even got onto the highway, but hadn't gone a mile on 45 before she saw flashing lights in her rearview mirror.

"I've got to go," she said to Stacy, "just get that request going. I want these people to have that fax in their hands before I get back to the office, and call Jessica Teal at the coroner's. Tell her I need a copy of Elijandro's autopsy."

Casey pulled over and watched in her side mirror as Gage emerged from the police cruiser and fixed the big hat on his head. He wore mirrored sunglasses. At the back corner of the car he stopped, raised up a booted foot, and heel-kicked the taillight, rocking her car.

"Christ," Casey said, shaking her head as the chief ambled alongside her. She rolled down her window and gripped the wheel, her palms slick now with sweat in spite of the blowing AC.

Gage pointed at a green rectangular sign fifty yards up the road.

"You see that?" he asked.

It read WILMER CITY LIMIT.

"Yes," Casey said through clenched teeth.

"Good," Gage said. "I noticed you got a brake light out. I'm gonna let you go this time. We're awful friendly here in Wilmer. Just a quiet little place in the corner of the county. I aim to keep it as such. You have a good day now, miss."

The chief tipped his hat and walked away.

CHAPTER
19

WHEN SHE GOT BACK TO HER OFFICE, CASEY FOUND José sitting behind her desk.

"Hi," he said.

"Where the hell have you been?" she asked. "What are you doing at my desk? You look like a thug."

José rubbed at the stubble on his cheek and stood up. His baggy jeans sagged toward the floor, barely clinging to his hips by a thick leather belt. His flannel shirt had no sleeves, exposing bronze cannonball arms wrapped in barbed-wire tattoos.

"Nice to see you, too," he said, yanking the bandana off his head, rounding the desk, and reaching for the door.

"I'm sorry," she said. "Wait."

He did. They sat down and she told him about Isodora's court appearance, the ICE lawyer, and Gage, leaving out the part about the taillight. As she explained, his face relaxed.

"You should have let me do that," he said.

"I tried you."

"I was doing a favor for a friend on the force," he said, looking down at his street garb as an explanation. "I had to leave everything in the truck. Not the kind of people you want to get hold of your cell phone."

"I should have waited, but Jesus," she said, "they held her baby hostage. An all-time low, even for the US government. It's all tied up in Chase's accident, which I'm starting to feel pretty certain wasn't an accident."

"Gage isn't the type of guy who'd react well to your questions whether he's hiding something or not."

"Cop talk?"

"I'm not defending him," José said, massaging his thick arm. "I'm not saying Chase didn't kill the man and Gage didn't cover it up. Hey, I think the Cubans got Kennedy. I'm just saying, he's not the type to pander to a woman lawyer who tangles up the justice system to spare a couple of *muchachas* from a beating."

"But he'd relate to you," she said skeptically.

"He'd react differently," José said. "Let me at least try to talk to him and get a feel for it."

"Fine."

"You're not mad," he said.

"Maybe at myself," she said with a sigh. "You're right. I shouldn't have gone down there. All I did was give him a chance to cover everything up."

"He'll have to give you the police report. Meantime, let me play good cop and see if I can get something out of him," José said, rising from his chair and reaching for the door.

"José," she said, "this guy's an asshole."

He turned and winked at her. "I've never met one of those."

He left and closed the door. She stared, listening to the sound of the big diesel engine whirring to life, until her intercom beeped and Stacy told her she had a call from Jessica Teal, her contact in the coroner's office.

"We didn't do an autopsy," Jessica said without a greeting.

"You had to have," Casey said, "it was in Dallas County."

"Not always," Jessica said. "It's up to the police. We can't do an autopsy on everyone who dies. If they determine the cause of death is accidental and a doctor signs the death certificate, that's it. We wouldn't see it."

"Didn't you hear about it?" Casey asked.

"I did, but I assumed it must have been pretty obvious if the police were calling it an accident without us, a high-profile thing like that. Everyone here figured they were trying to minimize the impact on the senator. Bad enough the guy was an illegal, after the senator's tirades about them. Press has been amazingly quiet on that, though. Either they bought the story about the guy not being a regular around the ranch or the senator called in some serious markers."

"Can we dig him up?" Casey asked.

Jessica was silent for a moment before she asked, "Do you have a reason?"

"The wife thinks it wasn't an accident," Casey said.

"I didn't see anything about a wife in the news," Jessica said.

"She's an illegal, too," Casey said. "They're putting her on a plane in about an hour. It's a long story, but the ICE got rid of her faster than a Colombian drug dealer."

"What's ICE?"

"Immigration and Customs Enforcement. It's part of Homeland Security."

"So we're safe now that this Mexican widow will be back on the other side of the border," Jessica said.

"Your tax dollars at work."

"We'll need the wife to exhume the body. That and a court order."

"Is there a form or something for the wife?" Casey asked.

"I can get you one."

Casey looked at her watch and said, "Can you fax it right now?"

"Sure."

Casey hung up. She told Stacy to get the fax to her as soon as it came in and dialed José.

"If you had to get to the airport at this time of day in less than an hour, what would you do?" she asked him.

"Book a later flight."

"If you *had* to."

"I'd call my buddy who I just dipped down into the barrio for and have him send a couple motorcycle cops to meet you at the on-ramp."

"Can you?"

"For you?" he said. "You only have to ask once. I practically feel a rash coming on."

"God."

"I'll have them there before you hit the ramp at Stemmons," José said. "Keep your phone on."

"How will they know it's me?" she asked.

"They're not gonna miss that fancy ride. Get going."

She ducked into the other room and watched Stacy pulling the coroner's fax from the machine, grabbed it, and dashed out to her Mercedes.

CHAPTER
20

TEUCH CRACKED AN EYE. THROUGH THE COVER OF his lashes he watched a man in a white lab coat clip an X-ray up onto the large light box before stepping back to address a semicircle of younger people, also in lab coats. They crowded around him like the chicks of a hen. Teuch thought he saw the name STEPHEN on a brass nameplate pinned to his coat.

"Dr. Noton," one of the chicks asked, "is there any damage to the premotor area?"

Teuch's eyes flickered, causing him to lose focus for a moment.

"We cauterized only the prefrontal," the doctor called Noton said.

"Have you ever seen damage to that area that didn't scramble the personality?"

Noton pushed up the plastic glasses on his nose with his thumb and said, "Mostly scrambled. Sometimes over easy, though. Sometimes it's an altered personality, or just an amplified one. It's tough to know with a John Doe. We don't have any reference points."

"The police don't know anything?"

Noton shook his head.

"But he'll be functional?" the same person asked. "Walking. Talking."

"Eventually," Noton said. "I've seen people with massive frontal lobe damage walk out of the hospital in less than a week. Others? It can take years before they're functional enough to live on their own."

Teuch flexed his fingers and toes under the sheet and smiled inwardly, knowing from the clarity of his thoughts that he'd be one of the ones walking out in less than a week.

Noton reached for a tray and lifted a shiny half-dome up for all to see. "Anyway, who wouldn't want a titanium skull?"

A couple of them chuckled politely.

"Doctor," another one asked, "I thought you had to wait at least three days after a thoracic surgery to patch a skull."

"The bullet went right through the chest," Noton said, looking up and scratching his cheek. "They opened him up and got right out. Dr. Kilkoyne did the surgery if you want to talk with her about it. Said she never saw anything like it. Bullet hit at just the right angle, ran along the rib, and out under the arm. Human armor."

"Lucky guy, right?"

"Very," Noton said. "Whoever he is."

"Will the police be back?" someone asked.

Noton shrugged. "When he comes to, they will."

Teuch let his lids settle closed. He thought about opossums and how they survived. These doctors would grow careless. And then, when the time was right, John Doe would be gone.

He had work to do.

CHAPTER
21

After he lined up Casey's motorcycle escort, José paid a visit to Ken Trent, his former captain. José was hoping for a connection to Gage that might put him in a favorable light with the big chief.

"Guy's a grade A flaming asshole," Ken said, leaning back in his chair.

"Tell me what you really think," José said.

"The two of you'll get along swell."

"Seriously, someone must know him," José said. "Even assholes have friends."

"Tell you who might be able to help," Ken said. "Dave Wayson, you know him?"

"The narco guy who got into the Secret Service?" José asked.

"He got the detail out on the senator's ranch when the first lady came for that square dance fund-raiser they did for some Bible group. Mention my name to Wayson. My wife's brother was the one who helped him get into the Secret Service. He'll help you."

Ken jotted down Dave's number and handed it across his desk to José.

"Did he get to know Gage?" José asked, sticking the number into his pocket.

"Podunk cops like Gage fall in love with the Secret Service guys. Makes them feel like they're on the inside."

"What kind of bullshit is that?"

"I don't know," Ken said, "I'm making it up as I go, but it's the only thing I can come up with."

José laughed and stood to go.

"That poker game is still running every Tuesday," Ken said, walking him to the door. "You should get there."

"I know," José said, shaking his old friend's hand. "I keep saying I will and one day I'll surprise you."

"How's things on the home front?"

"Cold and deep as the *Titanic*."

"Not her, your little girl," Ken said.

José turned and smiled. "Honestly? I'd be married to that two-timing bitch ten more years if it got me another little girl like Kenna. She's the silver lining. Platinum, really."

"Good," Ken said.

José wanted to get home to change his clothes before seeing Gage. On the way he dialed Wayson, who answered his phone on the first ring, out of breath, as if he had been expecting someone important. He sounded disappointed at the sound of José's voice until José mentioned Ken's name. Then Wayson perked right up.

"Cold fish, that guy," Wayson said in reference to Gage. "I actually went down there after the whole first-lady visit to help him out with some protocols for the senator."

"Gage is protecting the senator?" José asked. "From who?"

"You know how some of these politicians get," Wayson said. "The people around them kiss their ass so hard half of them think their next stop is the White House. Makes 'em feel important to have a couple guys running around with earpieces when they sit down at a restaurant."

"Would you mind giving him a call?" José asked. "Ken said I could count on you. What I'd really like is if you could tell him there's some noise about the whole hunting accident, this woman defense lawyer bugging people about it. Tell him that her investigator, me, is a good shit, ex–Dallas PD, one of the guys, and the best way to get everyone home by dinner is to be nice and help me out a little. Tell him I think the whole thing is crap. Can you do that?"

"I'll tell him you're Santa Claus if you want," Wayson said. "Once I got down there—on my day off, I might add—the guy acted like I was lucky to be helping him. A weird cat. Big as a redwood, too, with that creepy old Frankenstein head. I was nice, though. Figured I was there, anyway."

José had a one-bedroom in a downtown building that had seen better days. He parked the truck in his lot across the street, then ran up to change. When he opened the door, he bumped into the couch, forgetting that he'd left the living room a mess from his daughter's visit two days before. They'd shuffled the furniture and draped blankets over everything, pinning them down with unopened soup cans to construct an extensive fort. Several different tunnels led to the main room of the fort, where the two of them had eaten hamburgers and French fries and where they'd watched *Air Bud* from a nest of pillows, ultimately falling asleep.

At Kenna's request, José had left the whole mess intact

and moved his personal base of operations to the bedroom, where clothes and paperwork made up a soup of
dishevelment. The gang clothes came off and went into
the pile in the corner by the window. He sniffed the air,
thinking the smell came from the clothes, but realizing the culprit lurked somewhere out in the little galley
kitchen. He found his regular jeans on the bed and tucked
in his T-shirt, wondering at the extra flesh that had been
accumulating around his middle.

Desperate fingers plumbed the fat for the washboard
within. In his mind, he did a simple calculation of the
doughnuts and beer he could cut out to bring it back. He
swung the bedroom door to a close, stood sideways, and
sucked it in. After a determined nod, he replaced the
cutoff flannel with the last garment hanging in his tiny
closet, a loose-fitting white dress shirt that in his respect-
able years had always been teamed up with a blazer and
tie. For shoes, he simply laced up the Timberland boots
he'd worn open-tongued in the barrio.

Sitting on the bed, he dialed information for the
Wilmer Police Department. While he didn't speak to
Gage, the chief's secretary told him if he could get there
before five-thirty, the chief would be able to see him. On
the way out, José emptied the garbage to remove the bad
smell. While Kenna never minded the clutter, he didn't
want her to spend her visits in squalor.

Because of traffic, the drive to Wilmer took nearly
forty-five minutes. Gage was in the office, and after twenty
minutes he appeared in the lobby with a frown as big as
his head. He extended a hand and José shook it, matching
his grip and then weakening the way a dog will roll to its
back in order not to fight, until Gage's lips evened out.

"Wayson says you're okay," Gage said, studying José carefully as if he still wasn't sure, "otherwise you'd be shit out of luck."

"I understand you met my lovely client," José said, shaking his head in the knowing way of good old boys.

Gage continued to study him. José held the chief's gaze, aware that the success of his trip hung in the balance. Finally, the enormous cop snorted and turned without speaking. José followed the chief back into his office as though he'd been politely invited.

"I got a redheaded bitch for a sister-in-law," Gage said, sitting back in his chair, taking up his bayonet paperweight and throwing his big boots onto the desk. "One's enough."

"I hcar you," José said, eager to prove they were of the same mind. "She's not fun, but she's plugged into a lot of those society people, pretty much my pipeline for work. So, when she asked me to come down here and look into this guy's death, what could I say? I spoke to Wayson. He said all good things about you, and I figured we could work together on this one. You know what I mean?"

Gage smiled, pointed his bayonet, and said, "I always called you guys PTs instead of PIs. Peeping Toms. Must make a hell of a pot of money to stop being a cop for that."

"Right," José said, forcing a smile. "Anyway, I don't want to bother you any, but she's got this Mex girl raising her skirts."

"You look half Mex yourself," Gage said, using the point on his teeth.

"Dad's family came over in 1821," José said without missing a beat. "So he said he figured he'd get a little leeway."

"And you do," Gage said with a magnanimous wave of the blade. "Not too many Texans who don't have a Mex up their family tree somewhere. What do you wanna do? She'll get the goddamn report anyway. Not quick, but she'll get it."

"Nothing really," José said. "Maybe take me out to where it happened so I can say I was there, saw it, and the whole thing couldn't have been nothing but an accident."

"And that'll make her happy?" Gage said, his face giving nothing away.

"She's a lawyer," José said. "I'm a cop—or I was. She'll be happy."

"You can even take her the report," Gage said, swinging his feet off the desk and rising up. "Let her know it's all Momma's cooking. Save me a stamp."

Gage took a folder from the top of his pile and handed it over to José, who took it, half-rolled it, and swatted it against his leg as he got up, too.

"Let's go," Gage said, taking his hat off the antler of a dead deer mounted on the wall and fixing it on his head. "We'll have you home for dinner."

CHAPTER
22

ISODORA WORE A WHITE COTTON SHIFT, HER OWN clothes. She held Paquita tight, rocking her back and forth as she stood on the tarmac waiting in the long line of Mexicans boarding the unmarked gray plane. When she saw Casey, her face lit up and she angled her little girl's face so Casey could see her.

"She's beautiful," Casey said.

"Thank you so much, Miss Casey," Isodora said.

"I feel like I didn't do anything," Casey said.

"I have her. That's all I need."

"What will you do in Monterrey? Do you have family there?"

"No, but Maria gave me some money," Isodora said. "I'll find something. I heard a man talking about a new soap factory outside the city. Maybe I can get work."

"Who'll watch Paquita?"

A worried look crossed Isodora's face and she shook her head, signaling that she hadn't thought that far.

"I want you to sign this for me, Isodora," Casey said,

handing her the fax and a pen. "I'm not giving up. When you get to a place, I want you to call me. Call collect."

Casey took the signed release back and handed Isodora a card that she examined, then tucked into the small bag hanging from her shoulder.

"You won't forget?" Casey said.

"Will you?" Isodora asked.

One of the ICE agents yelled something and they turned to see the tail of the line disappearing up the metal steps.

"No," Casey said, and watched her go.

———

Despite her law clinic's steady downward spiral in property value and the embarrassing condition of her car, Casey had been able to hang on to the one luxury that mattered. When she first came to Dallas, she'd purchased a condo out in Las Colinas, across from the Omni Hotel. Beyond the grass and the tree-lined sidewalks, two long buildings with brick storefronts snuggled up to the canal that ran between them. Brick pavers and wrought-iron balconies jutting from the expensive condos above gave Casey the feeling of Venice the moment she saw the place.

The refuge of the six-story buildings blocked out the sound of the passing freeway and allowed the songs of mockingbirds, blue jays, and house finches and the occasional complaint of a mallard down on the water to float in through the curtains, waking Casey just before sunrise. She had purchased the spacious two-bedroom unit with cash, opting out of a mortgage so she'd always have a place to call her own.

Because of the fine hotel just across the wide boulevard, the small, almost secret neighborhood had more good and different restaurants than it deserved, including a Japanese steak house, a fine Italian restaurant with black-tie waiters, a small sports bar, a French bistro on the canal, and a Lone Star Texas chili joint, as well as the unusually good food at the Omni.

By the time she returned from the airport through the rush-hour traffic, Casey was ready for the chili joint and a couple of cold bottles of Budweiser. She showered, put on a V-neck T-shirt and jeans, and headed out the back door. Hers was one of the few units to have a small private stairway leading out onto the canal. As she left, she gave the door to her condo a half-hearted shove closed. She followed the brick sidewalk under a walking bridge, then rounded a corner, entering a wide alleyway that led to the restaurant.

Noise from the chili joint washed over her. The place was jammed, but the hostess recognized her and led her to a corner table not too far from the open doors where luckier diners sat out on the patio under red and white umbrellas. On the opposite side of the room, a long-haired blond cowboy with a drooping mustache strummed away on an acoustic guitar. When he looked up and noticed Casey, he crooned "Tequila Sunrise" without taking his deep blue eyes off of her. She couldn't help smiling, but it was to herself, not him. She dialed José, hoping to catch him and invite him for a drink, but got no answer.

When the chair across from her scraped along the plank floor, she looked up to see the cowboy singer before turning back to her steak.

"I like your music," she said, "but you don't want my husband to walk in here right now. He's the jealous type."

"Just trying to be friendly," the cowboy said, nodding at her empty beer bottle. "Can I buy you another?"

"I'm serious. He's a cop."

"No harm meant," the cowboy singer said, raising his hands in surrender and getting up.

"None taken," she said.

After a thick mug of coffee and a brownie with ice cream that she shouldn't have had, Casey tried José one last time before paying the bill and heading for the door. The sounds from the restaurant had died down, and when she rounded the corner Casey could hear the steady plunk of water dripping from some unknown source into the still water of the canal. Clouds of bugs flickered under the street lamps and the dark pockets between lights along with the dripping water made Casey shiver and pick up her pace.

When she got to her door, she realized that not only hadn't she closed it tight, but she hadn't left a single light on inside. She halted on the stoop and eased the door open, peering into the blackness, straining to see the stairway she knew to be there.

That's when someone reached out from the dark entryway and grabbed her arm.

CHAPTER
23

YOU WANT ME TO RIDE WITH YOU?" JOSÉ ASKED, following him out the door.

"Better off taking yourself," Gage said. "We got to pass the highway, and when we're done you'll want to just keep going."

The chief told his secretary that he'd see her tomorrow, and then told José he'd pull around front to meet him. José climbed into his truck and stuck the handheld GPS into the front left pocket of his jeans, covering it with the tail of his shirt. He waited along the street until he saw Gage whiz past in a brown-and-beige cruiser. He took off after him, spinning his wheel and stamping on the gas, and wondered the whole way if the chief was trying to have some fun with him.

When they got to the open gates of the workers' entrance to the ranch, Gage left his car off to the side of the drive and climbed in with José. José could see from Gage's face, even behind the mirrored glasses, that he was all business.

"No sense wasting my shocks when I don't have to," Gage said, pointing for José to proceed.

They passed a handful of faded barns. Behind them, and through a gap in the trees, José caught just a glimpse of at least a dozen long rows of tenant houses. In the gap, two emaciated little girls in soiled white dresses jumped a dirty piece of rope.

José slowed his truck, and while he could no longer see the tenant shacks or the girls, the smell of raw sewage seeped into the cab through the crack in his window.

"That's a lot of shacks over there," he said, angling his head back toward the barns and sniffing.

Gage glanced toward the shantytown, then focused ahead before he said, "Big ranch. Lots of hands. None of my business. None of yours."

"Couple thousand head of cattle or something?" José said. "Cotton, too?"

Gage grinned at him. "You are a detective."

"Observant," José said. "Sometimes places like that, with that many workers, are breeding grounds for trouble."

"What, like César Chávez kind of strike stuff?" Gage asked.

"I was thinking gangs and drugs."

"Mosquitoes on a puddle," Gage said with a shrug. "All you do is spray it every once in a while, keep things cleaned up."

José let up on the brake and kept going.

For several miles they traveled over rough and rutted roads until they came to a rare cluster of low hills scarred with farm fields and topped by hardwood. José recognized the widely spaced rows of bright green sprouts distending from the brown furrows as corn when they climbed out and hiked up the hillside toward the crown.

About fifty yards from the upper edge of the field, Gage stopped and eyed first one tree line, then the other, as if to triangulate his position, then started for the wood that ran up the hillside. José carried the file with him and leafed through the report as he followed Gage into the wood. Late-day copper light filtered through the young leaves. Pollen floated past, glittering like stardust, and insects buzzed and darted about, cutting tiny arcs through the beams.

"Says Elijandro sat in front of the senator," José said, tapping the report, "about twenty feet and off to his left."

"Bird was out there," Gage said, pointing back at the place where they'd stood in the nascent corn. "Senator Chase sat here, and the guide sat there. Decoys were lower down, but the bird came to a strut up there, through that gap, right in line with the guide."

Gage pointed past a large oak, then swung his hand to the left, pointing a line over the top of a low stump closer to the field.

"And Elijandro—the guide—jumped up when the senator shot?" José said, his eyes darting about the area, soaking it in.

"Bird was right out there," Gage said, directing a thick finger toward the field and following his own finger to the spot in front of the stump. "Blew his brains all over. Rain got to it, I guess, and the bugs."

The chief toed some dead leaves, leaving a scuff mark.

"I didn't see any photos of the body in the file," José said.

"This ain't *CSI*," Gage said.

"What about the shell casing?" José asked.

Gage's eyebrows shot up. "What about it?"

"Senator right-handed? Shoots a right-handed gun?"

"I believe so. Why?"

José looked back to where the senator had sat and scanned the forest floor off to the side where the shell would have ejected. He shrugged and said, "Just details."

Pointing to the gap between the two trees that would have been the senator's aim point, José said, "That's a real narrow lane to shoot through."

"He's not much of a hunter," Gage said, "the senator. Probably got excited."

After a silence, Gage said, "Wayson said you used to be a homicide detective. This ain't that. No question about the weapon, senator's twelve-gauge. Not much reason to look for the shell casing, but help yourself if you like."

José looked up and grinned. "Nah. Just thinking out loud. I'm good. I saw the place. Pretty clear how it all happened."

"Cut and dry."

"That's what I'll tell her," José said. "Sorry to drag you out here."

"It's on my way."

José let the chief lead the way out, but before he followed, he reached into his pocket and set the GPS.

The two of them trudged back to José's truck. He dropped the chief off at his cruiser, noticing for the first time the camera mounted above the gates. As he left, he watched the cruiser disappear in his rearview mirror, guessing that the chief wasn't going home but to report in to the senator.

José took the highway a couple of exits north, then

got off and found a diner where he had a plate of hash and eggs and several cups of coffee in a booth next to the dusty window. He took his time eating and spread the police file out across the tabletop of his booth, digging into it, and burning through the last light of day.

CHAPTER
24

CASEY LURCHED AWAY, STUMBLING AND LOSING HER footing because of the unrelenting grip on her arm.

She curled her fingers into a claw and slashed up and across in the direction she thought her attacker's face must be. The nails caught something, slicing through like butter, and the man cried out without letting go.

Casey screamed.

"Casey Jordan!" he shouted. "Are you Casey Jordan?"

She could see him in the light now, not the abusive husband of Soledad Mondo but a bulky, fiftyish man with a bulbous nose, wearing a tweed sport coat, and with a bad, frizzy gray comb-over hanging half off his balding head.

"Let me go, you son of a bitch!" she shrieked, swinging again.

This time he caught her hand and grabbed hold of it tight, backing her down into the doorway, surprising her with his strength.

"Are you Casey Jordan?" he hollered.

"Yes," she said. "Let go of me!"

The man released her wrists and stepped back into the shadows, fumbling with something inside his coat pocket, maybe a knife, maybe a gun. She gasped and thought to run, or kick him in the balls, but felt stuck in cement with limbs paralyzed by their own weight.

Whatever he took out flashed in the gloomy entryway. She blinked.

"I'm serving you with court papers," he said, extending the packet and jiggling it at her while he patted his bleeding cheek.

"You hide in my entryway?" she said, not taking it. "You think you can just do that?"

"It was all open," he said.

"You're a process server?" she asked.

"Sometimes people run," he said. "You cut me. Anyway, here."

She took it and he stepped around her.

"What's this about?" she asked, wheeling on him.

He shrugged and stopped in the glow of the light, examining the blood on his fingertips and stopping up the slash marks with a handkerchief from his pocket.

"I just serve them," he said. "But I always tell people, if they think about it . . . they'll know."

Casey watched him shuffle away down the canal. She pulled the door shut tight and threw the bolt, flipping the light switch and tearing open the sleeve that held the court documents. With practiced precision, her eyes quickly found the meat of it.

Her lip curled up off her teeth and she snarled.

"You asshole," she said, thinking of her ex-husband as she went up the narrow stairs. "You sick, pathetic, washed-up asshole."

She slapped the papers down on the dark green granite of the kitchen island, went to the fridge to pour a glass of sauvignon blanc, then picked the papers back up again, shaking her head. She crossed into the living room and flopped onto the couch, snatching up the phone.

"Paige? It's me. I got a new low for you."

"The DA?" she said.

"My ex," Casey said. "He's suing me."

"You're divorced already."

"For slander."

Casey heard the rustle of her putting her hand over the phone to whisper. She said, "You told someone about his pecker?"

"The movie," Casey said, snapping open the papers. "For the goddamn movie. Listen to this: 'false portrayal of his excellent character and impeccable integrity.' Can you vomit?"

"How much?" Paige asked in a normal voice.

"What?"

"Is he suing for?"

Casey barked out a laugh. "Five million."

"Can he do that?"

"He just did."

"But can he win?"

"Of course he can't win."

"Then tear it up, honey," Paige said.

Casey didn't reply. Then she said, "I don't think, anyway."

"You're the lawyer."

"Not a First Amendment lawyer. I told them he didn't say some of the crap they put in there. How can I be liable for that?" she asked.

"You're the lawyer."

"Thanks. You keep saying that."

"Look, I'm at dinner right now," Paige said, "and they just put a big hot steak in front of Luddy and he's giving me the hairy eyeball. Want to meet us after for a drink?"

"No, I'm sorry," Casey said. "I just wanted to vent. You should have seen the creep who served me."

"Served what?"

"The papers," Casey said. "The lawsuit. They have to give it to you in person. So you can't say you didn't get it. I have to respond to the goddamn court."

"You want me to leave, honey? Come over there?"

"No, you have your dinner."

"'Cause I can. I mean it."

"You're sweet. Tell Luddy I said hi."

"I'll do that."

"Paige?"

"What, honey?"

"I'm sorry to keep bothering you, but do you know Senator Chase at all?"

"Little rooster," she said. "Drinks too much when he can. Nothing like his father, who my daddy always said was a prince. Oh, Luddy, you stop that and eat already."

"How about the wife?" Casey asked.

"Mandy? A little too good for the rest of us, I've heard. Don't know her that well."

"Could you introduce me?"

Paige laughed and said, "She *used* to be an actress, that's what they say, so I can't imagine she wouldn't want to meet you with your own Lifetime original. What does that have to do with you getting sued?"

"Nothing," Casey said. "It's a whole other story. I'll tell you when I see you."

"How about I ask her to our little fund-raising tea tomorrow?" Paige asked. "Sissy James's husband is one of the senator's biggest supporters. I'll have her ask. If she can, I'm sure she'll come for Sissy. The little rooster will make her."

"Perfect," Casey said.

CHAPTER
25

Nᴇʟʟʏ ᴍᴏᴠᴇᴅ ǫᴜɪᴇᴛʟʏ ᴛʜʀᴏᴜɢʜ ᴛʜᴇ ᴜᴘᴘᴇʀ ʜᴀʟʟ to her mistress's dressing room with an armful of clean clothes before plunging into the darkness of the closet. Tiffany lamps sprang to life, exposing rack after rack of dresses, pantsuits, skirts, tops, and gowns. The scent of cedar—an undercurrent in the dark—seemed to fade. Nelly drank in the sight. Mahogany shoe cubbies filled the back wall. A ladder on brass tracks ran the length of the room. The entire village where Nelly had been born could have been dressed thrice over by the clothes in this closet.

Silently she returned the silk undergarments to their drawers, two skirts to their hangers, a cashmere sweater to its shelf, and a lace teddy to its dainty hook. Mrs. Chase liked her clothes replaced by the end of the day and she liked the work to be done while she dined. Nelly suspected that that way it seemed as though a fairy revived the soiled clothes magically, and not that dirty Mexicans like her had touched the pretty things.

Nelly checked the plastic watch she wore on the in-side of her wrist, almost seven-thirty and the end of her fourteen-hour day. Still, she was grateful to be inside the house where the broad tile roof, the thick wood beams, and two AC units the size of small cars kept the place cool and comfortable. Also, she'd last worked in the household of a woman who made Mrs. Chase look like a saint.

On her way through the dressing room she froze and cocked her head, straining for sounds from the bedroom. The tick of an expanding vent sent her scampering for the hall. She'd been skittish since the night of the argument, the night after the ranch hand died. That evening she'd been putting away her mistress's clothes when she heard shouting from the bedroom. Instead of sprinting away, as she did now, she'd frozen inside the closet, only to be frightened more when the lights went out.

The fight between the senator and his wife moved from the bedroom into her dressing room, with him haunting her, deriding her, his words slurring from drink. Nelly heard the things he'd said about Ellie, the hand who had died. She heard her mistress turn on the senator with venom in her voice. The bickering escalated into a torrent of screams and the smack of his palm on her cheek.

That's when her mistress darted into the closet, flip-ping on the light and exposing Nelly, who covered her face, cowering at the sight of the senator's bulging eyes and the flash of his teeth.

"Get out, you little Mexican sneak!" he'd shouted, stabbing his finger toward the door and raising the bottle in his other hand as if he might strike her with it.

"Leave her," the wife said, "she doesn't even under-stand."

That's what her mistress had said, and she scurried
out, bumping her knee on the doorframe, yanking the
door closed behind her so that it slammed, and sprinting
out of the house and down the path that led to her own
little place in the rows of shacks.

That's what her mistress said, but she and Nelly both
knew that wasn't true. Nelly spoke some English, and
understood even more than she spoke. She played along,
though. She'd never been one to do much talking anyway. But then Bill Ells, the ranch foreman, appeared
in the basement laundry room; he knew enough about
Nelly from the others not to believe her ignorance of the
language. He spoke soothingly to her, though, and even
made her smile. She hadn't minded admitting to him,
just between the two of them, that the senator had said
some bad things about the hand who had died.

Then, of course, she told him she would never speak
about it to anyone.

Now she descended the back stairs, past the kitchen
with its commotion of banging pots, jabbering cooks and
servers, and the smells of grilling meat, fresh bread, and
spices. She trudged outside into the hot night and followed
the flagstone walkway around the garages and stables
toward the dirt path that led to the low rows of shacks.
When she rounded the stables she saw a police cruiser that
made her pause. The chief's car wasn't a strange sight, but
he usually parked it in the guest parking lot beneath the
three towering oaks on the other side of the big house.

The darkened stable door burned in an orange glow
and she saw his face, big as a pumpkin beneath the towering hat. The chief touched his cigarette to the flame, blew
out the match, then walked her way. She stood fixed in her

spot, her eyes searching for meaning in his, but the faint glow of the orange ember gave nothing away.

He stopped at the car and rested his hand on the light rack atop the roof.

"You're Nelly," he said.

She inclined her head without a sound.

Gage nodded and opened the back door, flooding the ground with the dome light. Gage pointed to her and then into the backseat. "*Por qué?*" she asked.

"You got to speak American to me," he said, grinning so that the cigarette angled toward the stars.

"What do you want?"

"That's better," he said. "You and me need to talk a little is all."

"Talk?"

Gage angled his head at the backseat. Nelly's stomach heaved and she brought her hand to her mouth, but got in. Stones rattled off the car's undercarriage as Gage spun the car around and sped off down the back drive. They took a left out of the ranch and accelerated down the country road. Nelly's stomach heaved again when they raced up the ramp to the highway going south, away from the town, the police station, and any legitimate purpose she could think of.

"*Dónde vamos?*" she asked, the words barely trickling from her lips.

"I told you, speako Americano," Gage said, grinning at her in the rearview mirror as though holding back a full slate of laughter.

"Where are we going?"

"You'll be all right," he said. "You'll be with your people."

Ten minutes later Gage got off the highway and went down another rural road. He turned off into a gated drive and stopped. A man wearing jeans and a cowboy hat and carrying a machine gun walked up out of the culvert and spoke in a low voice to Gage before unlocking the arm of the gate and swinging it open. Nelly jammed a knuckle into her mouth, stifling a cry. They jounced along the rutted track and around a bend, and came to a stop in a cloud of dust before a tractor trailer.

They got out to the sound of crickets and the low whine of the big truck's engine. Diesel fumes mixed with the dust, choking her. Gage reached for her arm. Nelly screamed, winced, and turned away, but he got hold and she felt the thick fingers clamp down.

"You're all right," he said, lifting her nearly off her feet and propelling her to the back of the truck, his words hardly betraying the strain from his effort. "You're just gonna take a little ride."

Her feet skimmed the dirt, kicking up gravel as Gage marched her the length of a rusted orange container. In the back, a man wearing a Hawaiian shirt and a thick beard swung open the doors, aiming a machine gun of his own inside. A laser beam of light from the scope stabbed the dark hole like a long red needle. A warm stench floated up out of the truck and Nelly heard sniffling and groans and realized the floor of the trailer was littered with human forms.

The man in the flowered shirt stepped back and rested his gun on the ground. He took Nelly's other arm and together with Gage hoisted her up and into the back. She stumbled over one person and stepped on another, who shouted a halfhearted curse. Nelly's stomach heaved again, this time spouting a thin stream of vomit that her hands couldn't completely contain. The smell of her own filth lost itself in the pervasive stench. She spun to see Gage and the other man swinging shut the metal doors. The latch clanged home.

The truck's brakes hissed and shrieked, and the container of human beings lurched forward, slowly gaining speed.

CHAPTER
26

JOSÉ LEFT HIS TRUCK A GOOD BIT UP THE ROAD FROM the workers' entrance to the ranch, taking care to drive it well into the scrub along the embankment of the bridge that crossed the Trinity. From the backseat of his truck he removed a backpack that held night-vision goggles, a powerful flashlight, a good hunting knife, a rain poncho, and a couple of packages of dried nuts. He hoisted the pack and climbed out onto the road, hiking back toward the entrance, but plunging in through the scrub to avoid the gates and come out on the drive far enough up the way to avoid the camera.

Using the GPS, he navigated the dirt roads until he found the hillside and stopped for a moment to catch his breath and wipe the sweat from his brow. Up in the field, his night vision revealed three deer peering down at him until he started up through the corn and they bolted into the woods. When he reached the place where Elijandro had died, he removed the goggles and flicked on the powerful flashlight. The search for the shell casing turned up nothing and he snorted in frustration, knowing that it had to be there.

"Unless," he said aloud, finishing the sentence with the thought that Gage or the senator might have taken the shell for a reason. The question was, for what reason?

José thought about Gage's description of Elijandro's head injury, brains all over. He took out his cell phone to make a call and saw that he'd missed three calls from Casey and that she'd left a message. Instead of calling her back, he dialed Ken Trent.

"How'd it go?" Trent asked.

"You said it, a weird cat. He was fine, actually. I wanted to ask you about turkey hunting."

"Season ends tomorrow, so you'll have to wait till next year if you're wanting to go with me."

"I'm fine with a Butterball from Kroger," José said. "I wanted to know what kind of gun you use, what kind of shells."

Somewhere nearby in the black woods, a rabbit screamed like a dying banshee. José jumped.

"What the hell is that?" Trent asked.

"I think a rabbit," José said. "Coyote must have got it."

"Where are you?"

"Murder site," José said, "accident site, whatever."

"In the woods?"

"The senator's got some spread."

"Gage isn't with you."

"No, just me. I circled back."

The line went quiet. José knew how his old boss liked to size up pictures in his mind.

"I use six shot for turkeys," Trent finally said. "HEVI-Shot. Lots of people shoot fours."

"What are those? Pellets the size of a pea?" José asked, never one himself for anything more than a handgun.

"More like a BB, a little smaller even."

"How tight is that pattern at about twenty feet?"

"Fit in the palm of your hand."

"Would that punch a hole in a man's skull?"

"Make a nice divot."

"A hole?"

"Maybe. You'd have to talk to Vern Thomson about ballistics."

"It wouldn't punch through the skull and out the other side, though, would it?" José asked.

"Doubt that."

"Would a shell casing say what kind of load you had?" José asked.

"The number's right on the side," Trent said, "printed on the plastic."

"I appreciate it. One more thing."

"Yeah?"

"Would you ever hunt a turkey using a slug instead of shot?"

"Not unless you were happy with a Butterball," Trent said. "You gotta hit them in the head or the neck. Their feathers are so layered, they're like Kevlar. Slug's for a deer. You gonna tell me what's going on?"

"Long story," José said. "I'll buy you a beer. Gotta go. Thanks."

José hung up and began a different search.

He positioned himself in front of the tree where the senator had supposedly shot from and aimed the flashlight in the direction of the stump where Elijandro had sat. Beyond it, a big silver beech rose up on one side with what looked like a younger oak—about eight inches in diameter—on the other. Beyond them yawned the pitch black of the open field, where the turkey had supposedly been.

As he stepped over the stump, José shone his light down into the scuffed-up leaves and crouched. Softly he pushed aside the leaves, one at a time, filling the night air with a damp loamy smell, until he found some purple rubbery matter that he suspected was gore. He poked at it with his fingertip, verifying it to be more than clotted blood. Gage hadn't exaggerated.

Shining the beam, he stalked over to the beech tree and ran his hands over its smooth gray skin. He found nothing. He bent to the small oak with its rougher bark, went over it once, and then again more carefully. His fingers passed over a rough brown patch in a jagged crease. He took out his knife and poked the tip into the fibrous web, digging in half an inch before the point struck something metal. With his heart pounding he stepped back, shone his light, and took a photo of the tree's trunk with his phone, closing in to take a second one up close. He dug around what he now realized was a hole until the warped copper of the shotgun slug was exposed.

He took another picture, then dug the rest of it out, taking care to dig the knife into the tree and not the slug itself in order to preserve its integrity. When he had it free, he examined it under the beam of light, turning it over, but seeing nothing he could pinpoint. He fished a plastic Baggie from the backpack, dropped the slug in, and returned the bag to his pack.

José looked around, breathing hard. His heart pounded out a quick beat inside his chest. He knew that if the slug had passed through Elijandro's head, even though the human eye couldn't know it, a forensics lab could.

CHAPTER
27

José's blood cooled as the highway snaked into the high-rises of downtown Dallas. He thought about Casey and checked his phone, saw the calls he'd missed, and dialed her up.

"Are you okay?" José asked. "I saw you called."

"I'm okay now."

"What happened?" he asked.

She told him about the creep who had served her the lawsuit papers.

"We had a guy downtown once," José said, "he went to serve this husband with divorce papers. He pops out from between two cars in this parking garage and before he can say anything, the husband buries a screwdriver in the guy's chest, said he had a window in his office that he could never get open. Guy went free, too. Partly because the window story checked out, but partly because I think the jury felt like that service guy got what he deserved, sneaking around like that."

"I gave him a pretty good gash with my nails," she said. "Where are you?"

"On my way back just now," he said. "Listen, Gage showed me where it happened. I waited until it got dark and went back in there by myself. I think I've got something, a shotgun slug. I took it out of a tree. If it's what killed Elijandro, there'll be bone and blood on it."

"How does that help?" Casey asked. "No one ever said Chase didn't shoot him."

"If he shot him with this, it's going to be hard to say it was an accident," José said.

He explained to her about turkey hunting.

"A slug you use for deer," he said. "That's it."

"Deer or a man."

"Or a man," José said. "Plus, Gage is lying. His face is a billboard. Even a Podunk cop would have saved the shell casing, and he would have questioned the senator and a lot of other people around him when he saw the little gap between two trees that he was supposedly shooting at the turkey through. And this report? It looks like a third-grader wrote it. This thing is like an anthill. Looks like a mound of dirt until you kick it over."

"They didn't do an autopsy, either," Casey said. "Some local funeral director signed the death certificate and they buried him quick."

"No autopsy?" José said. "How's all this gonna look when they get Gage on the stand? This thing is way too sloppy. He's either gonna have to spill what happened or get pegged as an accomplice. Big stiff white boy like that don't want to see the inside of no Texas jail."

"You think we can get this to a trial?"

"If it weren't a US senator, I'd say no doubt about it," José said. "With Chase? We need to tread light."

Neither of them said anything for a moment and José rolled down the exit ramp and turned onto the city street that would take him home.

"You okay?" José asked, stopping at a light.

"Sure," Casey said. "Fine."

"You want me to come over?"

When she didn't respond, he cracked his neck from side to side and shifted in his seat, his hands tight on the wheel.

Then she said, "No rashes, right?"

The light turned green. He grinned, whipping his truck around, and said, "Guaranteed."

———

In the morning, José woke to find Casey standing at the edge of the bed, fully dressed, tugging on his big toe.

"Look," she said, "I don't want to ruin a good thing."

José rubbed his eyes and sat up, his bare back against the headboard, gathering the sheets around his waist.

"That bad?" he said, peeking under the sheet.

She blushed and shook her head. She'd stacked her hair up in a tight bun and even the nape of her neck flushed.

"No," she said, drawing out the word and sitting on the edge of the bed. "But we've got this thing, this case, and there's a lot to it. If we're right, and something really happened, it's going to get worse before it gets better. A lot worse. I just don't want to get bogged down."

"I'm kind of supercharged after that," José said.

"I need you," Casey said, "as an investigator. I'd like

to think we can put this to the side and keep going on the case, not get distracted."

"An occasional distraction is never a bad thing," he said, hugging his knees. "Right?"

"Maybe," she said, her expression giving nothing away. "Let's just not count on anything. If it happens, hey, okay. No expectations, that's all. You want breakfast?"

"You making it?"

"What did I just say about expectations?" she asked, arching an eyebrow, then cracking a smile. "There's a café on the canal."

After breakfast, José took his slug downtown to Dante Villa, a guy he knew in the police lab, while Casey visited her friend at the morgue.

———

José stood over Dante's shoulder as he punched up the digital image on his computer.

"You got a winner," Dante said. "Trace amounts of blood and bone."

"Is it old?"

"Not so old. A few weeks, I'm gonna guess."

"Can you do a DNA profile without anyone knowing?" José asked.

"You want to match it to something?"

"Eventually. Can you keep it semiofficial?"

"I can slip it in with some files I've got going, sure," Dante said, cleaning his glasses on a corner of his lab coat. "Preserve the chain of evidence, if that's what you mean. You might have to pay for the test. That way no one can bitch at me for doing it later on. Can I ask what you're going to do with all this?"

"This is one where, honestly," José said, "you're not going to want to know. If it turns back to bite me in the ass, you're better off sticking to the science."

"Something I'll see in the paper?"

José said, "More like CNN."

CHAPTER
28

"TEXAS ISN'T LIKE A LOT OF PLACES," JESSICA SAID, passing a file across her desk to Casey. "We like autonomy, right? So you get some off-the-map town like Wilmer that can have the local funeral director designated as its coroner and even though we're half an hour up the road and technically they're in our jurisdiction, they call the shots."

Casey opened the file and examined the death certificate, her eyes coming to rest on the words "hunting accident."

"Meaning what?" Casey asked.

"Meaning, you see that guy Blake Morris's signature? Morris and Sons funeral directors? He's the ME."

"But he's not an ME, right?"

"In Wilmer he is."

"Without any investigation?" Casey asked.

Jessica shook her head. "I didn't say that. I'm sure they'll say he *investigated*. He probably looked at the body, heard the senator's story, the cops talked to the wife, who said your guy went out hunting with the senator, and bingo, case closed."

"That's not an investigation," Casey said.

"Texas style," Jessica said. "Hey, at least they did that. I told you, technically, they could have just had some doctor sign the death certificate."

"Instead, they had some funeral director do the same damn thing," Casey said.

Jessica shrugged.

"But you can open it up, right?" Casey asked. "Look more thoroughly?"

"You know any judges?"

"Most of them," Casey said.

"Any of them like you?"

"Why do you say it like that?"

"You know I like you," Jessica said, "but some people think you're a little pushy."

"Okay, I'll just sit on the curb and wait for someone to come by and ask me if I need any help."

"Don't take it that way, I'm just saying."

"Judge Remy," Casey said, "she'll help."

"We need her to order the exhumation," Jessica said, dangling the papers over her desk. "The wife's signature goes a long way, but the court still has to weigh in. She might want the DA to get behind it. Anyway, you get Remy to sign this, and we're in."

CHAPTER
29

EARRINGS THE SIZE OF FISHING LURES WERE A feminine counterbalance to the steely gray in Judge Remy's short spiked hair. Her bright green eyes rested in her sagging gray face like two jewels. Around the judge's neck silver reading glasses hung from a pewter chain. When Casey finished the story, the judge used her glasses to examine some of the documents in Casey's file.

"Where is the DA on this?" she asked in a gentle Texas drawl that belied her reputation for harsh sentences.

"I presume he'll be behind it one hundred percent," Casey said.

"Presume?"

"We aren't drinking buddies," Casey said.

"Neither are *we*," the judge said, removing the glasses from her nose and waving them between Casey and herself before she let them fall into the folds of her robe, "but I get it."

Casey smiled.

"You like skydiving?" the judge asked.

"I haven't," Casey said, "but I would. If I had a parachute."

"You ever packed a chute?" the judge asked.

"No."

"You don't pack the chute just right, you end up mush. You don't just jump out of a plane unless you're really ready."

"I'm not the one who needs to be ready," Casey said, edging forward in her chair. "I think Chase is the one who's going to take a fall here."

"Really?" the judge asked, narrowing her eyes.

Casey nodded.

Judge Remy compressed her lips into a frown, took a pen from her desk, and with a flourish signed the order. She held it out, but when Casey took hold, the judge didn't let go. Casey felt the tension running like a current through the taut sheet of paper. Casey met the judge's eyes, the glint now shadowed by something dire.

"This man knows how to pack a chute," the judge said quietly. "I see the son of a bitch on FOX News about every other week talking about shutting down the borders. He'll play the sympathetic, persecuted public figure, a victim of the rabid liberal media and an ambitious glory hound. That's you. And after his opening move, he'll come after you with everything he has, every mistake you've ever made. They'll dig and they'll pry and they'll worm their way underneath your skin until they find something unpleasant and they'll bring it to the surface and spit it up for everyone to see.

"And they will see, because the whores with the cameras and the microphones will be like locusts on this one.

You think Lifetime made you look like an ass? This'll be a Hollywood double feature."

The judge let go of the order and Casey nearly fell back into her chair.

"You'll be tangled in your lines with the earth coming up at you like a hammer," the judge said. "And he'll be floating to the ground."

Casey set her jaw.

"That said? I'm behind you," the judge said, then poked her chin at the order in Casey's hands. "Obviously."

CHAPTER
30

I've done a lot of shit," José said, "but I never dug up no bodies."

"Stick with me," Casey said, trying to concentrate on the last sentence of the answer to Jordan's slander complaint before she shut down her computer. "It's a bowl of cherries."

"Can I come?"

"What?" Casey said, looking up.

"When you dig him up?"

"I imagine when I get this Morris guy from the funeral home on the line that his first call is going to be to Gage," Casey said, e-mailing the answer to her complaint to Stacy and shutting down the machine, "so I'd like it a lot if you would."

"There goes the beginnings of a beautiful friendship, though," José said with a sigh. "Don't be surprised if I'm off his Christmas-card list when I show up with you and that court order.

"You don't look like you're ready for *Tales from the Crypt*."

"I'm not," Casey said, standing and smoothing the folds of her sundress. "The dig is for tomorrow."

"Picnic you going on?"

"Tea party."

"Oh, well, let me just shuffle on out of here then," José said, sidestepping toward her back door. "I was gonna cancel my meeting with the redhead's husband for you."

"I appreciate it," Casey said, closing up her computer and packing it into her briefcase.

José sniffed the air. "They got that plumbing going okay, I see."

"Woman's kid flushed down a toy duck," Casey said, shaking her head. "The plumber cost us more than a filing number for a federal appeal."

"That something you go on with a guy or something?" José asked. "Tea party, I mean."

Casey suppressed a smile. "José? Are you jealous?"

José stuffed his thick fists into the front pockets of his jeans, but did not look away. "Not one bit."

"It's a fund-raiser for the clinic at Paige Ludden's. Also, Chase's wife might be there."

José raised his eyebrows. "Want me to have a chat with her?"

"It's not like a barbeque," Casey said. "It's ladies, flowers, and little cucumber sandwiches."

"I could wait by her car. Kind of jump out of the bushes like a process server."

Casey shouldered her bag and hollered out to Stacy to print and file the answer to the slander complaint and that she was leaving.

Stacy appeared in the doorway with her arms folded

across her chest and said, "We got a call from Isodora, collect."

"Isodora, you're kidding," Casey said. "Why didn't you get me?"

"You were the one who said not to disturb you for any reason."

"She called from Monterrey? Did she leave a number?"

"A church in a place she called Higueras. I did Google Earth. It's northeast of Monterrey. Remote. Over some mountains and down in some river valley. I asked for a number but she said it wasn't her phone and she didn't know."

"What church?"

"She didn't say," Stacy said, "she said 'the church.' "

"Christ," Casey said, "you should have gotten me."

Stacy narrowed her eyes and said, "Some of us listen to what people say."

Stacy turned and walked out.

Casey followed, stopping at the doorway, and said, "I want you to get Sharon and the two of you start calling down there. I want you to find her and figure out a way I can speak with her."

Stacy busied herself with some files, slamming open a drawer and stuffing them in with the same vigor she used to cram the trash down in an overloaded bin.

"Stacy?" Casey said. "We set on that?"

"I'll get to it," Stacy said, and turned her back.

"Great," Casey said to herself in a mutter, turning and heading for the back door only to be blocked by José. He took a gentle hold of her elbows.

"You want me in this with you, right? I mean, like a team?"

"Some team," she said. "You see the crap I have to put up with. She could make ten thousand more at a downtown firm, so I have to eat the attitude."

"She did do what you asked," he said quietly. "What about me?"

"What about you?" she asked.

José shrugged and said, "Chase's wife. You're the lawyer. I'm supposed to be the investigator."

She looked up at him, and the little nervous tic skittered across his eyelid.

She asked, "Did I ever tell you I was a prosecutor with an eighty-seven-percent conviction record? I didn't get that depending on Barney Fife and company to lock down my evidence."

"Barney Fife?" he said, aping a wince.

"Not you," she said. "Them. The Austin police. I know how to interrogate a witness, is all. Especially a cheating wife."

"Cheating wives," he said. "That I know about."

Casey furrowed her brow, wanting to apologize, but thinking that would make it even worse.

"Let's tag-team the wife," she said. "Let me see if I can work the inside and you keep the thumbscrews in your back pocket."

"What about after?" he asked.

"The wheel?"

"No. After your tea?" José said. "No expectations, but maybe something between us? Some kind of spontaneous distraction? A spontaneous combustion type of thing? You know, since we've got the dig tomorrow, anyway, and we'll be going down there together."

"A planned *spontaneous* combustion?" she asked, arching a brow. "That's arson, right?"

José shrugged. "I never made an arson case, so I can't help there."

"I think it is," she said, rigid and stepping around him, afraid of what she'd say if she brushed up against the muscles in his arm, wanting to, not wanting to. "Let's keep it legal. Come on."

"Of course," he said. "Please. Don't mind me."

"I don't," she said, offering a smile before she went out the door so he'd know there were no hard feelings. "Honest."

CHAPTER
31

THE CAST-IRON GATES CLANGED OPEN AND CASEY let the Benz roll through between the fieldstone pillars of medieval proportions. The house, centered on a ten-acre rise in an oval hilltop of grass, dwarfed even the gates. The dome over the central body had been shipped in pieces from a Bulgarian church. That and the three-story fluted columns always made Casey think of the US Capitol building. Luddy had inherited it all from his mother's side and the house, Grace Manor, bore his grandmother's name.

More than a dozen cars hugged the low wall of the circular fountain in front—Jaguars, Mercedeses, two Rolls-Royce sedans—and Casey grimaced at her watch. Cobblestones rumbled beneath her as she sped up the hill and into the circle, where she screeched to a halt and jumped out. With her car blocking the drive, she threw her keys on the seat before dashing up the steps.

A stiff-faced butler led her through the house and into the garden, where the crowd twittered and buzzed beneath a white tent hemmed in by fragrant yellow roses. Notes from a string quartet floated on a merciful breeze and Casey could see the glaze of sweat on her friend's pink cheeks despite the cool glass of champagne that she sipped disinterestedly.

"I am so sorry," Casey said, bussing her friend's cheek.

"Pish," Paige said, indirectly announcing Casey's arrival in her most Southern and charming way, "a working girl like you? We're all jealous as high school lovers, just wishing we didn't have all that we got going on so we could be in the trenches with you, honey. Come right here, you beautiful thing. Too hot for tea after all, and I decided all on my own to break right into the *back* of Luddy's cellar. Sissy? Here she is, darling."

Paige floated through them, a butterfly flickering, pollinating, and sipping up their contributions like nectar with Casey in tow. Casey let her speech lilt into the drawl of forgotten balls and fetes from another life. Stacy's skeptical face and her expression, "You make me vomit," came into Casey's mind, but she smiled the smile of a grateful beneficiary, shaking the hand of a woman old enough that she wore white gloves and a hat with both a netted veil and flowers.

From Chase's wife, Mandy, Casey received no more than a vacant stare and a forced half-smile that left Paige's fingers in a vise around her wrist as she dragged Casey on to the next woman, whispering hotly in her ear that Mandy was the most extraordinary bitch she'd ever shared a back lawn with. Casey glanced back at the tall blonde in the bright red dress, standing out like a hooker in a girls' choir, and wondered if the woman had the same surgeon as Paige.

Before they'd finished, Casey realized the glass of champagne Paige had armed her with had been emptied and refilled twice, brightening Casey's appreciation of the sights, sounds, smells, and money that the tea party had provided.

Paige finally sat her down in a white rattan love seat before bringing two fresh glasses and resting her own feet beside her, fanning herself with a sigh.

"Honey, you are just a charm," Paige said.

"I didn't do a thing."

"Oh, pish, all that habeas corpus and right-to-appeal jargon? They loved it. They *just* loved it. You made my job easy."

"You are so good," Casey said, touching her arm.

"It's the least," Paige said, sipping her champagne and shaking her head, "the very least."

"Oh, God," Casey said, jumping up. "I'll be back. There she goes."

Looking past the table piled high with dainty sandwiches, Casey just caught the flash of red as Mandy Chase slipped into the house, deserting the party with no respect for convention. Casey stumbled on the walk, her heel catching between two flagstones and breaking off. She heard someone behind her offer up a little gasp from beneath the tent, but paid no mind, churning ahead on one shoe and kicking it off somewhere near the fireplace as she shot through the house.

Mandy Chase had just given up trying to get around Casey's beat-up Benz blocking the circle and began to carefully back the white Range Rover out. Casey closed the distance and patted the window. The senator's wife jammed on her brakes and jerked her head around, covering her mouth in astonished fright before glowering at Casey and running the window down.

"I could have killed you," Mandy Chase said.

"I'm sorry," Casey said. "I wanted to talk to you."

Mandy raised her chin. "I'm late for an appointment. You met me. My husband will send whatever kind of funding Colby James asks him to send. You should know how this works. Now, you'll have to excuse me."

Mandy gripped the wheel and swung her head back over her shoulder.

"Wait," Casey said, walking quickly as the SUV began to roll back. "I have to talk to you about Elijandro Torres."

This time, Mandy's shocked look was coupled with a stomp on the gas. She spun the wheel and backed right onto the lawn. Casey kept up, hanging on to the window frame, even as Mandy slammed the Range Rover into drive.

"I know you were sleeping with him," Casey said, raising her voice above the engine.

"Go to hell," Mandy said, her face twisted with rage.

She swatted Casey's hand like a fly, then beat it with her fist, pounding the fingers. Casey cried out, let go, and cursed as the Range Rover shot off down the driveway and disappeared through the gates.

CHAPTER
32

THE NEXT MORNING CASEY RODE BESIDE JOSÉ IN HIS truck. Jessica, from the medical examiner's office, followed them in a white county van along with a forensic investigator. On their way down to Wilmer, Casey told the story of the senator's wife.

"So much for working the inside," José said.

"So much for spontaneous combustion," she said.

"What's that got to do with it?"

"You're mocking my approach to Mandy Chase," she said. "That's my comeback."

"To mock my approach to romance?" he asked.

"I thought it sounded good."

"It doesn't," José said. "You make it sound like you don't care. You can't mess with a man's confidence that way."

"Your confidence runneth over."

"Anyway, you didn't expect the wife to just confess that her screwing with Elijandro is what got him killed, did you?" he asked.

"Maybe show some reaction."

"She cursed you and almost ran you over."

"Something a little more emotional. Tears? A gasp?"

"Maybe he didn't mean that much to her," José said. "She just moves on to the next one. Some women are like that."

She glanced over at him, but his eyes kept to the road, the long lashes curling skyward.

"Next time, you'll try," she said.

"Neither of us are going to be too welcome anywhere in Wilmer after this," he said. "Did you tell Gage I'm coming to the dig?"

"I thought it best to surprise him."

"I was thinking," José said. "If we're right, and they're lying about Elijandro jumping up in front of the senator, then an autopsy might help prove it."

"Prove what?"

"That Elijandro was just sitting there, waiting for a turkey," José said. "If he just sat there and took a bullet to the back of the head, forensics is going to be able to show that from the angle of the bullet."

"One more crack in their story," Casey said.

They pulled off the highway and Casey read from her BlackBerry, directing him toward a cemetery on the south end of the small town. Beside the entrance, marked by two yellow brick columns stained with bird droppings, a man in a dark suit stood next to an old station wagon with wood-paneled sides. Dark plastic glasses sat crooked on a mostly bald head vaguely bearing the shape of a lightbulb. In the backseat of the car, two Mexicans sat without sound or movement in jeans and grubby white T-shirts.

José's truck rumbled up alongside the undertaker

with the ME van behind them. Casey rolled her window down.

"Mr. Morris?"

Morris glared up at her and removed a cupped hand from behind his back. In it he'd concealed a cigarette that he sucked on hard before nodding, tucking it away, and blowing out the smoke.

"When the chief gets here, you can follow me," he said without looking at Casey.

Jessica got out of the van, walked up, and said, "Ready?"

"I just told her," the undertaker said, "when the chief gets here."

"We don't need to wait for the chief," Jessica said. "I'm with the ME's office."

The undertaker studied her for a moment, then said, "You might not need to wait, but I do."

Casey shook her head at Jessica to go along with this and they both returned to their vehicles.

Casey sat looking out over the low stone markers lined in rows beneath a smattering of red cedars that lent the feel of a golf course to the place. When Gage's cruiser arrived five minutes later, the big chief got out wearing his mirrored sunglasses, spoke to Morris, and got back into his car without looking their way. Casey studied the big man's mouth, certain his lower lip protruded in a pout. Morris cranked up the old wagon and rolled in through the gates. Gage followed him, then came José and the county van. The little caravan wound its way through the stones and the trees until they reached a slope many acres into the cemetery.

Here the path turned to dirt. The grass and trees

ended, as did the shiny granite headstones. They traveled only a short way over the rough ground before the wagon stopped and Morris got out, followed now by the two Mexicans, who bore spades they removed from the back of the wagon. The investigator with Jessica, a heavyset man with dark wavy hair, also removed some tools from the van to assist.

Insects buzzed and a hot breeze wafted the high, parched grass. A band of cicadas added to the sound of heat, singing from a twisted mesquite tree on the edge of the cut grass where the paying customers rested. Morris pointed out a spot of freshly turned dirt marked by one of the hundreds of gravestones that looked like small loaves of bread laid down in the weeds. The group stood around the grave and when Gage saw José, he surprised Casey by offering him a small smile.

"I've got this," Jessica said, offering up a copy of the court order to Gage.

The chief held up his hand. "All set. I got mine faxed to me yesterday."

Casey waited for the big man to explode. She searched his face, unable to fathom how he could go along without making any protestation or at least showing discomfort or disdain.

To the Mexicans, Gage said, "Get digging. I got work needs getting to."

Jessica's ME investigator spoke up and said, "When they get close, I'd like to do the last part of it."

The undertaker spoke to the men in Spanish and they nodded their heads without stopping their work.

"They'll need to dig a bigger hole than that," Casey

said under her breath, not wanting to betray her ignorance. She'd never seen an exhumation before.

The Mexicans stopped suddenly and spoke to the undertaker, who waved Jessica's investigator forward as though offering him a seat in a fine restaurant.

"How about a little more than that," the investigator said, pointing with the small trowel he held, the jowls of his heavy face trembling at the sight of the small hole.

The undertaker shrugged and sent the Mexicans back at it. Three more strokes and one of the shovels struck metal with a clang. The Mexicans stepped back and looked at the investigator, who stood.

"What?" he said, peering into the small, shallow hole.

"Pay dirt," the undertaker said. "Want them to finish it up, or you looking to use that spoon?"

The investigator knelt at the hole's edge and scraped away some dirt.

"This is an . . ." the investigator said, puffing and continuing to dig.

Casey peered over his shoulder as the trowel scratched away. She saw the circular gleam of stainless steel.

"Urn," the investigator said, finishing his sentence and looking back over his shoulder at Casey and Jessica. He wiggled the trowel and extracted what looked like a martini mixer. "It's an urn."

"So much for DNA," Jessica said.

Everyone looked at Morris, who stood smoking and looking off at the other graves, unconcerned. Gage fought back a smirk.

Casey stepped toward the chief and said, "You people cremated him?"

"What the wife wanted," Gage said, removing a piece of paper from his front pocket, unfolding it, and handing it to Casey. "Signed it right there."

Casey looked down at the creased paper and saw Isodora's signature.

"You like playing games?" Casey asked, looking back at the chief.

"Yeah," Gage said with a puff of laughter. "When I win."

CHAPTER
33

"DO I LOOK LIKE A TURNIP?" THE DA ASKED. "IF THIS were Brad Pitt, maybe you could get the *National Enquirer* to run with it. You want me to convene a grand jury on a US senator?"

Casey glanced at José, who sat with her across from Dustin Cruz's desk.

"We're not looking for an indictment yet," José said. "We just think that if you investigate, that's where this is going."

Cruz looked at José and blinked, as if noticing him for the first time.

"Did she tell you about the last conversation we had in this office?" Cruz asked José.

José looked at him and cocked his head.

"Last time," Cruz said, "she sat there telling me about how the press was going to react to me prosecuting a young woman for murder. Forget that I've got a confession. *She's* going to make the killer look like the victim with a bunch of talk about old rape cases, and stink me up for women voters.

"Remember that conversation?" Cruz asked, turning to Casey. "Rosalita Suarez?"

"She's an innocent woman," Casey said with a shrug, "and my client."

"So that means you can fight dirty?" Cruz said. "Go to the media?"

"We're not here about that," José said, spreading his fingers and raising his hand. "This is different."

"*This* is a US senator," Cruz said, his thick eyebrows arching.

"Exactly," José said. "Your office could investigate this thing and get people to talk. They've got a hundred or so Mexicans out there, people in the house, on the grounds, the ranch—you could get in there with some subpoenas and get things going. Hell, the undertaker, the police chief, the wife even, get them on record, build a case."

Cruz huffed through his nose. "You think that makes me hungry to stick my neck out? Let's say you can prove the dead guy was banging the wife, which you can't. You got headlines, but not much else. Let's say you get a DNA match with the blood on the shotgun slug, so what? They already said he shot the guy. They said it was an accident."

"With a deer slug?" José said. "They were hunting turkeys."

Cruz made a face. "That's what? Maybe fifty-fifty that a jury will even follow you?"

"What about cremating the body like that?" José said. "Destroying the evidence?"

"The wife signed off," Cruz said.

"She had no idea what she even signed," Casey said.

"Look," Cruz said with a grim smile, "Chase's no Sunday-school teacher, but you go to kill the king, you better damn well make sure you do it. That's advice for *you* two. I have no interest in this. None."

"Looking for a spot on the federal bench?" Casey said, blurting out her words.

Cruz forced a smile and said, "Nice thought. Wrong party. I'm not a fan of Chase. All those white-toothed television commercials with a bunch of happy kids around him don't fool me for a second.

"I'm just not stupid," he continued, narrowing his eyes at Casey, "and maybe the enemy of my enemy is my friend? You ever heard that one?"

CHAPTER
34

Casey and José climbed back into his truck and headed for the coffee shop where their day had begun so she could get her car. The sun beat down on the metal snake of traffic, glinting off windshields, pulverizing the blacktop so that it quavered in the heat.

Traffic on the highway suddenly slowed to a crawl. Up ahead, Casey could see the flashing lights from the accident that had slowed things down. As they closed in, she saw the belly of a tractor trailer turned on its side. Pallets of disposable diapers had spilled from the truck onto the road and median, like snow from a land of giants.

A burst of white foam and smoke drew her eyes back to the wreck. A fireman sprayed down the naked engine of the big truck. The cab of the rig had plowed a compact car into the guardrail. Emergency workers scrambled to extract what looked like a body from the accordion of steel.

Casey noticed a new Audi sedan pull out of the line of traffic and off to the side. A man in a tailored brown suit hurried out of the car and rushed toward the open bay of an ambulance. A woman strapped into a stretcher, bleeding all over the sheets but fully conscious, strained to see the crumpled car. The man in the suit, whom Casey knew instinctively to be a lawyer, bent over the woman and handed her a card. Casey's stomach turned.

"And they bitch when lawyers get a bad rap," she said under her breath.

"What a mess," José said, easing the truck into the only lane moving through.

"The person in the car or the diapers?" Casey asked.

"The senator and the dead ranch hand," José said, stepping on the accelerator as the traffic opened up.

"That, too," she said, nodding.

"If I'm working this case," he said, glancing her way, "and I presume that's what I'm still doing—"

"Yes, please. I'm not giving up."

"The wife is the key," he said.

"The problem we'll have with the wife is spousal privilege," Casey said, using her thumb and forefinger to take hold of her lower lip. "She can't testify against him."

"At all?"

"Not unless someone else was present," Casey said. "Anything said in front of a third party loses the privilege. You said they have a hundred or more people working out there. Servants all around?"

"More like slaves," José said. "Doesn't it make you sick, a guy like Chase who's always bitching about a secure border, talking about these people like they're criminals? Where would he get his staff with a secure border? He wouldn't be out there hiring Caucasians. He might have to pay them minimum wage, more even."

"In my old life," Casey said, "in my ex-husband's world, everyone knew that if you wanted the inside scoop, you asked the servants."

"I doubt we'll get invited for dinner," José said, "but I can poke around the immigrant community out there and see if there's a way in. I wish I still had my badge, something that would make people more apt to talk."

Casey sat silently for a few minutes, thinking, the tension building up in her like steam in a kettle.

When they got off the exit for her car, the words burst from a seam in her mouth in a hot jet. "We can make them talk."

"Someone deputize you without telling me?" he asked.

"We can bring them in on our own," she said, forcing the words to slow. "Or threaten to."

"Oh. Kidnap them?" José said with a shitty grin.

"No. I'm serious. Subpoena them."

"How?"

"We agree Chase murdered Isodora's husband, right?"

"My gut says it was no accident," José said. "But you just heard the DA; he's not going to even look into it, let alone investigate. Where are you going to get a subpoena?"

"I'll prosecute him myself," Casey said, breathing short, shallow breaths of excitement.

"You're a defense lawyer."

"I used to be a prosecutor," she snapped.

"Now all you have to do is get elected."

"No, listen. I'm talking about a civil court," she said. "Remember that accident back there? Did you see the lawyer giving that lady his card?"

"I saw the body and the blood," he said.

"The woman they loaded into the ambulance had a

lawyer working her before she even knew her husband was dead," she said. "I saw him get out of his car and swoop down on her like a vulture. He'll be looking to file a wrongful death suit."

"I thought 'ambulance chaser' was a joke," José said.

"It's big money," she said, ticking off the reasons. "Loss of a lifetime of earnings for the family, pain and suffering for the survivor. That's where you get your multimillion-dollar damages."

"What's that got to do with this?"

"We *sue* Chase for wrongful death," she said.

"With no proof at all?"

"That's the beauty. All you need is a reasonable belief," Casey said. "Civil court is a whole different ball game."

"You can subpoena people?" José asked.

"Same as a criminal case. I can get even a halfway-decent judge to order the cooperation of anyone we say we need to prove our case."

"And if they just won't talk?" José asked.

"They can go to jail for contempt," Casey said.

"Didn't OJ get sued by the family?" José asked, pulling into the parking lot of the coffee shop. "But wasn't it after he got off?"

Casey's stomach went tight.

"Can you do it before?" José asked, shutting off the engine.

Casey sat silent for a moment, tugging on her lip, nodding.

"Why not?" she said.

"So this isn't exactly textbook," José said slowly, a touch of irony creeping into his voice.

Casey sat, thinking. She'd been here before, out on a limb, doing things others hadn't and making waves. Her stomach soured. It hadn't always turned out well.

Still, she said, "But there's no reason we couldn't do it."

"If you're going to invent some new legal strategy," José said, "maybe you should save it for some Latin King drug dealer. We're talking about a US senator. This isn't going to be done quietly. They'll bring everything at you."

"But if I do it," Casey said, tightening her face and turning to him, "if I try Chase for Elijandro's death in civil court and I can get all the evidence out, then Cruz will be wishing he took the case."

José nodded. He reached out and covered her clenched hand. Softly, he said, "I don't want them making a fool out of you."

"So I let him go?" Casey said, raising her voice, stiffening her back with indignation. "Is that it? He's a US senator, so he's above the law? Bullshit. Not if I can help it. It's unconventional, but there isn't a goddamn reason why I can't do it. Trust me. This I know."

José patted her hand, studying her, then gripped it tight and offered a small smile of collaboration.

"Okay, I'd ask you to dinner tonight," he said, "but I think I'm going to head out to Chase's ranch to speak some Spanish, talk to the help."

"And I've got to get Isodora," Casey said, grinning at him, relieved and bubbling again, ready to act. "Jessica said if we get DNA from her and the baby, your lab guy can use it to show that the blood on the bullet is Elijandro's. And she'll need to sign an application to the surrogate court so we can get this suit started."

"What does she need to apply for?"

"When you have a wrongful death," Casey said, talking fast, slipping comfortably into the familiar territory of the law, "the court has to assign an administrator to sue on behalf of whoever died. It's a formality, but it's got to be done so I can get things going. Besides, I've got an idea on how I can use this to get her back into the country."

"But she's where? Sharon said Higueras? Higueras, where?"

"Outside Monterrey. A ways outside in the middle of nowhere."

"With no phone number," José said.

"At a church," Casey said. "In a town where the only information Sharon came up with on the Internet was a blurb on the name of the newest mayor, Ignacio de Jesus Gonzalez Gonzalez. That's it."

"Can't be too many churches in a town where the mayor has the same last name twice."

"I'm going to check the flights into Monterrey."

"Whoa. You're not going down there?" José said. "It's not like just dropping into the barrio, five blocks over and you're sitting at a Starbucks. You're talking rural Mexico. *Federales*, road bandits, gangs, maybe even soldiers out there with all those rebel problems. You don't just tour the countryside."

"I'm sure I'll be fine," she said.

"You know the only thing they found from the last woman I knew who drove around the countryside in Mexico?" José asked. "Her shoe."

"Maybe she liked it so much she decided to stay," Casey said.

"With her blood in it."

"Is this your way of offering to go?" she asked.

"I'm telling *you* not to."

"Well, I am," Casey said, swinging open the door and climbing out of his truck, breathless with excitement. "That's the next step. I've got the right lawsuit, now I need the client."

"Send someone," José said. "I don't want to, but I'll do it."

"I'm going," she said. "I sent her there, and now I'm going to find her and bring her back. You're welcome to join me."

She shut the door and started for her car.

José rolled his window down and said, "Okay, book me a ticket, will you?"

Casey tossed her briefcase into the front seat, smiled, and said, "Yes. I'll see you tomorrow. Good luck at the ranch. And José?"

"Yes?"

"Thank you."

CHAPTER
35

JOSÉ NESTLED THE BIG WHITE TRUCK INTO THE SAME spot he'd used before, in the trees under the shadow of the bridge embankment. This time he walked out onto the bridge to study his spot, assuring himself that no passerby could detect the truck coming from the other direction. Below, the water slipped silently past, a river of murk unwilling to give back a reflection of the brilliant night sky above. Trees rose up from the river's edge, casting a black pall about them thicker than tar. Satisfied, José started off, scuffing his boots along on the gravel shoulder until he saw the glow of oncoming headlights and dropped down into the ditch and beyond that into the dusty scrub.

The car sped past, washing away the sound of the night things all around him, then ebbing away until the chorus of bugs and rodents and frogs rang clearly again, like the piercing sound of an alarm. He took to the roadside and made it to the service entrance of the ranch without pause. To avoid the cameras he ducked back into the brush, glad for his GPS in the confusing tangle of twigs and vines, and coming out well down the drive, where he crunched away at the gravel until ominous shapes of the barns washed by a single halogen light on a pole in the yard sent his blood pumping a bit faster. Between the buildings and beyond, small lights winked at him through the trees. He stood for a time in the shadow of the biggest barn, out of the white light, his nose overwhelmed with the smell of manure and rotted and fermenting feed grain. Inside, animals of some kind shifted in their stalls, issuing an occasional grunt. On a grassy knoll above the barns rested an old farmhouse with light shining from a single downstairs window.

José moved cautiously away from the barns and through the gap in the trees, following a dirt path that opened into the clearing where row upon row of sagging shacks rested like corn stubble, truncated, broken, and listing. From the chinks between the wallboards and the occasional open door or window, a gauzy yellow light permeated the migrant camp.

Off to one side of the path sat three low buildings. A shift in the night air brought with it their stench, identifying the three buildings as latrines. He covered his face and took shallow breaths until he passed the latrines and stood on the lip of the dirt lane leading down into the cluster of hovels. In the shadows of the crooked roofs, shapes of people came to life for him. The low chatter and occasional ripple of laughter broke free from the other sounds of the night, giving the camp a festive quality.

He descended the slight incline and allowed his feet to carry him into their midst, but the festive humor melted away with each new step. Silence accompanied him like a contagion and it was remarkable to him how quickly, in this feeble light, they had sensed the presence of an outsider. He stopped in front of one shack, entirely dark, where an older man sat on an upended piece of firewood, whittling away at what smelled like a raw green willow branch, the fresh shavings littering the dirt like a light snow.

In Spanish, José explained that he was with the law and needed to ask some questions.

The old man started and stared up, the creases in his weathered face as deep as rock fissures. In Spanish, he asked, "The chief send you?"

"You mean Gage?" José asked.

The old man nodded and said, "He's the law here."

"There's a bigger law than Gage," José said. "I'm with that law."

The old man contemplated this for a while, then shook his head and returned to his whittling, and spoke no more.

José glanced around and saw that others had been listening, and when he began to move down the row, people disappeared like frogs along a creek bed so that by the time he reached the end there were no more workers to interrogate. He started back up the next row and met with the same form of denial until he noticed the flickering silhouette of a dark-haired woman in the open window of a shack, where several candles burned on a small table within.

José approached her and asked if she'd speak to him.

In an urgent whisper and speaking in English, she said, "Walk down the next row, then leave the way you came. I'll meet you by the barns."

Then, she shouted, "*Gabacho!*"

The wooden window slammed in his face.

José did as he'd been told, remembering to hold his breath as he passed the latrines. As he waited in the shadow of the biggest barn, he wondered if her urgent words might not have been a ruse to get rid of him. A few minutes later, however, she hurried out of the trees, looked around, and dragged him by the arm inside the barn. Livestock that José recognized as veal calves snorted and shifted, straining their hair rope tethers and scuffing the hay-strewn floor. The smell ranked second only to the latrines, but José soon forgot about it. Enough light from the halogen lamp outside fell in through a window that José could make out the woman's face and he realized she wasn't as young as her long dark hair had made him think.

"They're saying you're with the FBI," the woman said. "My name is Amelia. Are you looking for Nelly?"

"I'm working on a case for a lawyer who's trying to help a Mexican woman," José said. "I used to be a cop, but I'm not anymore. I'm not with the FBI. Who's Nelly?"

"A girl," Amelia said, her face wincing with pain. "A friend. I told her to run. I've been here for many years. I know what happens. When someone causes trouble, they disappear. Some say they leave here on their own. I think differently."

"Wait, wait," José said, holding up a hand. "What are you talking about?"

"Nelly heard them fighting," Amelia said. "The senator and his wife. Everyone knew Elijandro went with the wife, and not just once. He was a beautiful man. It could only end badly. Nelly is Mrs. Chase's maid. She heard them the night after the senator killed Elijandro. Nelly told me she heard the senator tell his wife that Elijandro asked for it, and I told her she must run. But Nelly had nothing and nowhere to go. She didn't believe. She listened to the others who make fun of me and call me a witch. If it makes me a witch because I know, then I'm a witch.

"She was a good girl," Amelia said. "Young and sweet, and I don't know what they did to her, but I know it's not good. No one comes back."

"Who disappears?" José asked. "This happened before?"

"The senator and his friends are very rich," Amelia said. "They do things the way rich people do, using drugs and prostitutes without fear of the law. I have always taken care of the senator's children, so I've never seen these things, but others have. They talk a little about the bad things they've seen and then they're just gone. Who is there to look for them? So we forget and pretend it didn't happen, pretend they went home or moved to Atlanta or Chicago, some big city far away. That happens, too, anyway. People leave, but there are always others to replace them, always people hungry for work. And here, people have a place to live, a place where the agents can never come because the senator makes the laws. We understand this from Mexico, how things work."

"Like razor blades," José said, more to himself than to her. "One nicks you and you throw it away for a new one. Aren't you afraid to tell me all this?"

Amelia sighed. "The little girl is the youngest and she goes away to boarding school at the end of the summer. A blade can go dull, too. I will be told to leave. This I know. What's the difference if I leave now?"

"You mean, right now?" José asked.

"I have four thousand dollars," she said, patting the rucksack she wore over her shoulder.

"How long you worked here?" he asked.

"Sixteen years."

"And you saved that?"

"It's more money than anyone here has ever seen."

"You can trust me," he said, cocking his head at a sound outside that didn't fit, a sound signaling a shift in energy, something afoot. "I'll find a place you can be safe."

"I know," she said. "No one like you has ever come before. I used to wonder why, then I stopped, but now you're here, a white Mexican with the law and I see the way you move. You're not afraid of them. You're not afraid of anyone, and I think that must be good."

"Don't say that," José said, cracking the door they'd come through and studying the empty barnyard. "Where I come from, the day you stop being afraid is the day you get yourself killed."

From the shantytown below came the shouts of men and the tilted beams of flashlights punching through the trees. A dog barked from the farmhouse on the rise. Spotlights flashed on. Worse still was the whining engine of a car coming up the service road and the clatter of stones against its underbelly.

José grabbed Amelia by the wrist, flung open the door, and ran.

CHAPTER
36

JOSÉ SWIVELED HIS HEAD AS THEY RAN, SIZING UP the best direction to escape. They dashed down the road he'd taken to get to Jessup's Knob. Behind them the rise glowed with the coming headlights. He jumped down into a ditch, pulling Amelia with him just as the head-lights shone down on them. The lights swung away, then José heard the car jam into reverse and rev its engine, and the headlights again lit up the road before the car started to move their way.

José swiped the dust from his mouth with the back of one hand as he dragged Amelia up the other side of the ditch and across a scrubby lot before they plunged into dusty and brittle undergrowth. When they were twenty yards in, the car slid to a stop out on the road and José heard its doors being flung open. More men shouted from the direction of the barns, and José used the sound to re-gain his bearings and change directions so that they'd be headed away, toward the road and his truck.

José heard the angry zip of the bullet a split second

before the sound of the shot roared past and he dove to the ground, pulling Amelia down and covering her with his body. Two more bullets zipped through the branches, snapping twigs, their shots bursting out.

"They're shooting," Amelia said, her voice and its hysterical timbre muffled by his shoulder.

"Come on," José said, crawling now through the tangle, branches clawing his face.

No more shots came, but José waited for some time before he dared rise to a crouch and quicken their pace. He had no idea how to get to the main road, and the bark of the dog at the house made him nervous they'd be tracked.

———

Gradually the way became more clear until they found themselves darting between the thick trunks of old oaks in the wan light of a clouded moon. When they reached the edge of a wide pasture and the ripe smell of cattle, José stopped and took Amelia by the shoulders.

"Are you all right?" he asked in a whisper.

He could feel her shaking beneath his grip, but she bit her lower lip and nodded. José listened and heard nothing.

"I think we're okay," he said. "Do you know where this is?"

Amelia looked out over the animals, still as boulders, some staring in their direction. She shook her head.

José raised the wire and slipped through the fence, moving out into the pasture. From there, he could see off to his left a yellow glow on the horizon above the trees. He knew it must be the lights from Dallas, giving him the direction they needed to go to get back to the road. He scanned the open ground and listened with a hand cupped to his ear for sounds of men or dogs, heard nothing but the small rustle of wind and leaves, and retrieved Amelia.

They kept to the fence line, breached it, and found themselves again in a wood open enough for easy going. When they came out the other side, a slight slope lay in front of them with a scrub line hedging the road beyond. On the other side of the road open wasteland stretched as far as he could see under the false twilight of the city. Nothing rode the small breeze but a distant chorus of coyotes. The broad sky above pressed down on the earth, heavy with dull shapeless clouds backlit by the half-moon.

Earth and stones skittered along in front of them as they descended to the scrub line. José blazed a path through that and they found themselves on the desolate road where the power line above snapped randomly at a transformer box. José walked looking over his shoulder, but nothing disturbed them all the way to the bridge. His skin began to crawl as he peered down over the bank at where he knew his truck waited.

"Stay here," he said in a low voice to Amelia, planting her by the shoulders beneath the shadow of a roadside shrub while he scrabbled down the bank.

As he closed the gap, the vague white shape of the truck appeared as if by magic in the heart of the darkness. Looking left and right, he held forth his hands like a blind man, feeling for its metal, finding it, and hurrying into the cab. The dome light came to life like an old friend, easing the rhythm of his heart. He fired the engine and let the big machine climb the hill, stopping briefly for Amelia, then spun the wheels in the dirt in his eagerness to gain the road.

The sigh had no sooner left his chest than headlights seared through the cab. He glanced instinctively, blinded, but aware of the sudden burst of flashing lights from their midst. The siren barked. José pulled over and dug the cell phone from his pocket. The trembling of his fingers surprised and annoyed him, but his eyes kept returning to the big side mirror and the shape of the enormous cop as Gage got out and fitted the big hat atop his head. In the mirror beyond Amelia on the other side of the truck, José saw a second shape emerge from the other side of Gage's car.

The phone rang and he got Ken Trent's voice mail. José punched in Ken's home phone and put the call through. Gage had reached the back corner of his truck and he rested a hand on the pistol at his hip. The gun came out and José reached for the nine-millimeter Glock under his arm, but the idea of a shoot-out with a cop short-circuited his brain and he simply sat with the cell phone hidden beside his leg as Gage tapped the barrel of the pistol against his window. José put the window down.

"You're getting to be like a bad penny," Gage said, the skin along his jawline taut and shifting in the glare of the flashing red lights, "turning up all the time in places you're not likely wanted."

"Someone took a shot at us," José said. "You get a call?"

"Got a call about someone trespassing," Gage said. "Maybe a kidnapping. That you?"

Gage flicked his eyes at Amelia.

"She's with me," José said.

"I'm going to have to ask you to get out of the truck," Gage said. "You, too, miss."

The shadow of the second man fell across Amelia's

window and José knew they would take her. He heard a tiny voice and spoke up.

"Ken?" he said, seeing from the illuminated face of his phone that the call had gone through. "Hang on, it's me, José."

He raised the phone so Gage could see it. "I've got Ken Trent on the line here, from Dallas PD. You want to talk to him?"

"Shut that down," Gage said, growling.

"Ken, I'm with Chief Gage down in Wilmer," José said, raising his voice so Ken would be sure to hear him, even with the phone so far from his face. "He's got a gun on me. Maybe you could talk some sense into him, Ken."

He hefted the glowing cell phone at Gage and said, "Ken's my old captain, Dallas PD."

Gage's face twisted. Through his teeth, he said, "Put the phone down. I'm telling you to get the fuck out of the truck."

Gage thumbed back the hammer on his shiny Colt .45. The metallic click knotted José's stomach. He placed the phone on the dash and held up his hands, saying a small prayer that his old friend had heard him and hadn't simply hung up the phone. Gage yanked open the door.

"I'm cooperating with him, Ken," José said to the phone as he got out. "I'm out at Senator Chase's place with a worker named Amelia."

Gage reached into the truck and pitched the phone down on the pavement, stamping on it and grinding the plastic into the gravel with his boot heel.

"Bad connection?" Gage asked, grinning.

"But he knows I'm here," José said. "And he knows

you're here. So I don't get to disappear in the night like Nelly."

Something shifted in Gage's eye, like a guttering flame.

"Amelia, too," José said. "She's with me. Ask her. She's not going anywhere, either."

Amelia sat rigid in the truck, her hands clutching the seat and her eyes locked on the windshield even with the shadow of the other man lurking in her window.

"She works for the Chases," Gage said. "We'll be taking her home."

"No," José said, holding the chief's pale eyes with his own. "She's with me. You can't get rid of me, and you can't get rid of her, either, not without a whole lot of TV cameras lighting up the town."

José kept his hands in the air and Gage raised his pistol, easing it toward José's face in the flashing lights from the cop car until the cold barrel ticked the tip of his nose. José never flinched, even when Gage jerked the gun, clicking free the hammer, and returned it to its closed position.

The chief leaned into the open truck, and said, "You want to come with me, don't you, girl? You got work back at the ranch waiting for you."

"You do what you want, Amelia," José said.

She looked over at them, eyes wide and lips crushed together. She shook her head.

"I don't want to go," she said, cringing as if she expected a slap.

Gage jabbed a thick finger at her.

"You walk away, you're walking away from a job and a place to stay. You leave now, you're leaving for good," he said. "You want that?"

Amelia's eyes lost focus. She stared straight ahead, but nodded her head yes.

"Everything you say," Gage said, "everything you do, you'll answer for it. That's the law, no matter what this slick spic tells you."

Gage stepped away and José climbed back into his truck. The shadow beside Amelia melted away and José watched Gage's huge figure as he holstered his gun, then diminished in the side mirror. José pulled away from the cop car with its flashing lights and blinding high beams and out onto the open road.

When they reached the highway and headed north, Amelia said, "They will kill me."

José glanced at her, then returned his attention to the road. After a minute he said, "Not if they can't find you."

CHAPTER
37

Casey finished her run and didn't bother to towel off before she fired up her computer, got the phone number of the first boyfriend she'd had after her divorce, and called him at his new home in Washington, DC.

"Tommy? Casey Jordan."

She heard him clear his throat. In a groggy voice he said, "It's six o'clock."

"I know," she said, speaking fast. "I'm sorry. I had a client deported. Well, she went voluntarily, but that was because they were holding her two-year-old daughter. She's near Monterrey. That's where they sent her and I need your help to get her back."

"Is this really Casey?" he asked. Tommy Gillespie worked for the State Department, a mid-level administrator, and a former standout baseball player at A&M. While unmarried, blond, and handsome, he was too young for Casey and too committed to a career that kept him bouncing from place to place.

"I know I haven't been good about staying in touch," she said. "But I think about you."

"I saw that thing on TV," he said.

Casey felt her cheeks warm.

"Yeah, it was pretty good," he said. "Happy ending and everything. The girl I'm seeing, she got a little choked up. She actually wanted to call you, but I told her no."

"I thought the whole thing was stupid," Casey said.

"Well, she liked it."

"I didn't mean it like that," Casey said. "Anyway, can you help me?"

"I'll try."

Casey explained what happened to Isodora, then told him about the lawsuit she had already put in motion.

"I remember the DA had a witness for a case I tried in Austin a few years ago," she said. "The guy was an illegal from Mexico. I didn't want him testifying and I tried to make something of his status to the judge, but it was all by the book. They went to the State Department and got him some kind of a visa I guess you have for people involved in legal matters."

"Sure," he said. "A visitor's visa for business, a B-1."

"Well, this is a lawsuit," Casey said.

"You think we could do business in this country without lawsuits? Litigation is covered under a B-1. It's no big deal."

"And it supersedes this voluntary deportation?"

"Sure," he said.

"What if she's on some kind of watch list?"

"Is this like that time you asked me if I liked to see justice being served and I ended up as an expert witness in that crazy trial with the woman who stole her kids?"

"Those kids were hers, and you know it," Casey said. "The senator in this case called in some favors. Evidently, the dead husband has a brother who's a Latin King. They painted her with the organized-crime thing."

"I'd like it if every bit of information got referenced and cross-checked between agencies by now, but the truth is, there's a lot less information sharing than you'd think," Tommy said. "I'm not saying you could fly her in. TSA is linked up pretty good. But if you bring her back in a car with a B-1 from the State Department? Customs won't think twice. A visa's a visa."

"Perfect."

"Not for me if someone catches it, but it works for you."

"So how do we do this?" Casey asked.

"I'll have it drawn up and faxed to you for your signature and your input of information on the lawsuit," Tommy said. "You send it back and I'll have it waiting for her in—where'd you say she was? Monterrey?"

"Yes."

"At the consulate there," he said.

"Can you get it done by tomorrow?" she asked.

"Tomorrow?" he asked.

"I need to get this done," she said. "Can you have it waiting at the consulate in Monterrey?"

Tommy chuckled and said, "You're so bashful."

"Please."

"Okay," Tommy said. "One favor."

"Name it."

"My girlfriend, Lauren? Just give her cell phone a call and leave a message. Say anything. 'Hi, this is Casey. Tommy says you're great.' She's in love with you."

"Jesus, Tommy."

"Hey, I'm the one manipulating the federal government."

"I thought it was standard to issue a B-1 for a litigation?"

"Yeah, and it takes about six months to process. You're going to get it in about six hours."

CHAPTER
38

Casey looked out the window and gripped José's knee as a thermal column buffeted their plane. They banked wide, circling to land, and she could see the cluster of downtown buildings and high-rises, dark and lifeless under a heavy pancake of brown-and-yellow smog. From factory stacks, plumes of blackened air flowed upward like hellish geysers, while orange flames licked at the soot, burning off vents of methane. The signs of industry and progress promised cheap goods, processed food, and electric power, all the same comforts offered across the border to the north. Jagged mountains looked on from a distance, dead as slag.

"My God," Casey said.

She tightened her belt and was glad she had when they hit the runway hard enough to bounce and rattle the bins in the small pantry. José pried her fingers from his knee.

"Sorry," she said.

"I didn't know you hated flying," he said. "You turned white."

"Flying is fine. Crash landings I don't like."

José teased her about her pallor all the way to the car rental counter, where he argued with the woman in Spanish for a time before turning to Casey and explaining in frustration that the luxury sedan they thought they had reserved was actually a jeep.

"That's not too bad," Casey said. "Like a small SUV."

"I don't think it's that kind of jeep," he said, scooping the keys off the counter and signing his name.

José led her outside to the parking spot that matched the number on his keys.

"At least it's got a roll bar," Casey said, rounding the machine and eyeing the patches of chipped red paint that showed the original color to be a drab army green. She looked down at her Donna Karan pantsuit, sighed, took the jacket off, and tucked it into her shoulder bag before stowing the bag behind her seat, rolling up her sleeves, and getting in.

"If it was any hotter I think the tires would melt," José said, tossing his own bag onto the floor beneath the tiny back bench seat and stripping off his outer denim shirt to reveal a snug V-neck T-shirt tucked in to the narrow waist of his jeans.

"We'll get a nice breeze," she said, undoing the scarf around her neck and using it to fasten down her hair.

"Like a hair dryer," he said, gazing up through a pair of Oakley sunglasses at a sun that burned orange through the dirty haze.

José navigated with a map he kept pinned beneath his leg, weaving through traffic and down side streets until they found the American consulate, where Isodora's and her daughter's visas were waiting as promised for Casey to

pick up. The sun crested, angry and red at its apex as they
finally broke free from the city. Its final destitute slums
spilled to the edge of a barren brown landscape littered
with rocks, garbage, and bleached animal bones. Despite
the deafening wind, the oppressive heat had Casey sweating by the time they turned off the main highway and
began a long climb into the mountains on a road of stone
and oil, baked and broken by the heat. A slick milky mud
in the bottom of the potholes spoke of a recent rain. Otherwise, dry dust coated all, prickly pear, mesquite, cactus,
and jeep.

At first, José eased the jeep over the rougher terrain,
but after a time they simply held tight and he plowed over
it all. As they climbed, the sun lost its colorful hue and
glared blindly down, a hot white eye. Casey looked back
at the dust cloud that extended like a bushy tail, disappearing into the smog below. The only traffic they met
was a battered white minivan, empty except for two
bearded men with eyes hidden behind sunglasses. When
they stopped for José to ponder a fork in the road, her
teeth felt loose and finding solid ground beneath her feet
had an unnatural quality she had never noticed before.

José must have guessed right because after another
five twisting miles they topped a rise that looked down
over a river valley punctuated by a town of mud, slat, and
adobe buildings set adjacent to a modern factory. Metal
piping wrapped itself around a white building that took
up nearly half the space of the entire town. A lifeline of
high-tension power lines stretched from the factory upstream, presumably to a dam, along a trickle of mountain-
blue water that glittered like a ribbon of steel.

Where the blue sky and water met the factory, nature

came undone. Dual metal stacks churned out a diabolical plume of their own, rivaling their city cousins, and several foaming discharges left the stream shabby with filth. The plumes, which rose like twin spires, quickly dispersed to the south, following the strangled yellow river and cloaking the valley in an unending cloud of sulfur, carbon dioxide, and soot.

"Isodora said something about a soap factory," Casey said, climbing back in beside him.

"That's a hell of a mess to make soap," José said, taking his foot off the brake and beginning the bumpy descent.

They rolled to town on the factory road, passing storefronts haunted by gaunt dirty keepers who stared at the jeep. Women in soiled white dresses, mostly hatless, made up the sparse foot traffic in the streets. The church spire stood taller than anything this side of the factory. With the dark smoke as its backdrop, the ancient bronze cross glowed pale green. A blackened bell lurked in the tower like a watchful eye. The rim beneath the tower's arched opening wept with the mess of pigeons. José parked the jeep and they mounted stone steps worn smooth by countless feet.

He pushed open one of the massive wood doors clasped in iron and allowed Casey to enter first. Cool air and the smells of incense and burned candles welcomed her. Above the altar glowed a single arched pane of stained glass. Widows in black sat scattered about, hunched over or kneeling with their gnarled hands clasped. Chanting over them, a priest in a white hat invoked God in Spanish too rapid and low for Casey to catch even a word. From the corner of her eye she saw José cross himself and briefly dip his chin. From the wall, faded images of saints looked down from their frescoes and the bullet holes, chips, and cracks bestowed upon them from a time before Texas earned its statehood. Casey and José stood waiting for Mass to end, then swam upstream against the current of black crepe to meet the priest.

José spoke Spanish to the priest, whose eyes flickered between José and Casey before he inclined his head toward Casey as if to greet her. When José mentioned Isodora's name, the priest considered them thoughtfully for a minute with dark smoldering eyes, then launched into an explanation that painted a bitter look on José's face.

"What?" Casey asked.

"When the factory came, they used pamphlets to spread word of jobs all across the countryside, all the way down to Costa Rica. Those the factory pays get paid double what you could get anywhere else, but the acid burns the workers' skin and the men drop dead young from cancer. But with the money the factory pays, every time a man or woman goes down, there are hundreds more waiting in these huts out back for the chance to take their place."

"What huts?" Casey asked.

José shrugged and said, "I don't know. He said 'huts,' like a hovel."

Casey swallowed and asked about Isodora.

"She showed up the way a lot of them do," José said quietly. "They hire a ride to Higueras from the airport. Crooked drivers bring them to the ridge, rob them of everything they own, and send them walking down into town. By the time they get here, the crooks are long gone."

The priest chattered in an undertone.

"Isodora did better than most," José said. "He says they left the baby alone and for that he praises God."

Casey's mouth dropped open. She directed her gaze at the priest, who nodded appreciatively and said something she didn't understand.

"He says lots of small towns across Mexico have American factories in them and he thanks God they all have churches to help the people," José said. "He says as bad as the soap factory is, there's worse."

"Worse?" Casey asked. "How?"

José raised an eyebrow. He turned and spoke with the priest, back and forth for a minute or so. The priest grew quite animated before José finally turned back to Casey.

José frowned and said, "He says some of the peasants who come in from the north say there's a drug factory where they use people for experiments."

"Drugs like cocaine and heroin?" Casey asked.

"No," José said, "I think like Lipitor and Paxil. He says they bring them in by the truckload from the States."

"Human guinea pigs?" Casey said. "Trucking people from America? That's crazy. That can't be true. It's some wives' tale."

"Yeah, well, this isn't the US," José said. "Crazy there and crazy here are two different things."

"It's the twenty-first century, though," Casey said.

José just stared at her.

Casey turned to the priest and studied him until he crossed himself, nodded, and motioned for them to follow him.

Several acres of packed dirt made up the church's backyard. Like mushrooms after a rain, hundreds of crate-wood and cardboard huts populated the ground where two main paths led to latrines by the back. An eight-foot white-washed wall encompassed the yard, protecting the people from more thieves, but offering no shield against the factory managers who would rob them of their health. In the dust, children in soiled frocks squealed with delight, playing games with chicken bones, stones, and greasy lengths of rawhide while babies shrieked with hunger beneath the folds of their mothers' Indian blankets.

As the priest swished past in his robes, the destitute people quieted and bent their heads. Halfway down the track to the left they pulled up short beside a muddy hut roofed with a rusted sheet of corrugated metal. A small army of flies milled about on a sunlit patch of the dirt-stained wall, fearlessly vying for a drink from human eyes, noses, and mouths. Casey gasped and thrashed the air, ceasing only when they had entered the hut to find Isodora lying atop a pile of rags in the corner, staring blankly at the ceiling with a tearstained face. She cradled the baby in her arms, its sleep rendered fitful by a small cloud of flies.

"Oh, my God, Isodora," Casey said.

She swept at the flies on the baby and pulled the young mother close, holding her tight and feeling for a sign of life from the baby. Her eyes found José and even though her tears distorted his face, she knew he shared her horror. She reached for him and he gripped her hand in his own.

"Come on, Isodora," she said, helping her up. "We're taking you home."

CHAPTER
39

ON THEIR WAY OUT OF TOWN, JOSÉ PULLED OVER at a roadside stand selling pieces of grilled chicken and orange soda in old Fanta bottles, scratched and scarred from years of reuse. The boy behind the cinder-block counter who took their money could only have been six or seven. His arms were little more than stubby claws and Casey stared back behind them at the plumes of smoke, wondering. They sat on a metal bench in the shade of the shack. Isodora tore into the meat, pulling away pieces and slipping them into her little girl's eager mouth.

They wiped their fingers on bits of newspaper and climbed into the jeep. Casey rode in back so that Isodora could huddle up behind the windshield with her baby. José slowed for the worst of the bumps and after a while the baby stopped crying and faded off to sleep. They hit the main highway going north at about three in the afternoon. The hot pavement shed its heat, waffling the air. Casey longed for the relative coolness of the dusty and broken country roads. Blue mountains turned green and

the road climbed into a pass. At its peak, the air cooled
and a field of deep blue smiled down at them from beyond
the treetops. The oasis quickly faded as they descended
into the waiting reds, browns, and yellows of the wasteland beyond.

The mountains were soon nothing but distant purple
shadows, cloaked in hot haze. Tractor trailers made up
most of the traffic on the road. Occasionally they passed
a car or a pickup truck whose driver would stare at the unlikely group. José pulled over for gas outside a small town
built from corrugated metal and crumbling concrete. He
came out from paying at the station carrying a plastic bag
filled with sweaty water bottles. They chugged the water
and got back onto the highway. Soon, on the horizon ahead,
a brown-and-yellow cloud appeared. Off toward the east, a
bruised sky brooded and flickered with lightning.

José pulled off the highway, stood up with his hands
on the windshield, and studied the sky. Big tractor trailers whooshed by without slowing, whipping them with
streams of grit and dust.

"Weather usually comes west to east," he said, glancing back at Casey and giving her a knowing nod toward
Isodora and her baby. "Why it's coming from the wrong
direction and what it means, I don't know. I think we can
beat it. If it looks bad, we'll have to get off and find a
hotel, fast. What do you think?"

"Let's try," Casey said. "I'd like to at least make it
across the border before we stop."

José fell back into his seat and ground the gears,
bringing the jeep back up to speed. They crept toward
the brown cloud of smoke and soon saw that its source
lay just beyond a low rise of hills where the land began

to dip toward the Rio Grande. They had nearly reached Nuevo Laredo when Casey sniffed the air and poked José's shoulder.

"You smell that?" Casey said, shouting above the whine of the jeep and the flap of air.

José nodded. "Stinks like hell."

"I can taste it," Casey said, studying the hills and just making out the glint of a metal stack.

The road soon rose and in a cleft between two hills, the factory made itself known on the plain below. Power lines running alongside the road detoured down to it and a wide stone road ran perpendicular to the highway. Shiny metal gates guarding the road and the fence, all of fourteen feet and capped with loops of concertina wire, stretched off into the distance, marking the boundaries of the place. Casey squinted and stared at a single pale blue sign whose words she could not read. Beyond, the storm rolled toward them. Above, the heavy brown swell of filthy air swirled and grew.

José pulled off the road and rose from his seat. Casey stood on the back of her seat, a full foot higher than José.

"The priest said a factory up north," she said, her face directed into the coming wind. "You don't think?"

Thunder rumbled from a distance.

"I think most times people wouldn't smell it like this," José said, "but the wind's just right, coming out of the east with this storm. A drug factory? Why not? That smell, God, it's awful."

Casey had her hand over her mouth and nose. She took out her cell phone to take a picture. As she did, the bark of a siren made her jump. A black police car with white doors had pulled off the highway behind them, its blue-

and-red lights flashing. Two *federales* in blue uniforms
and shiny midnight hats jumped out and scrambled up
alongside the jeep with their hands on the holsters of their
guns.

They barked out orders that Casey didn't understand.
She looked to José, who glared back at the cop closest to
him. Isodora clutched her baby tight and whined.

"What the hell do they want?" Casey said.

Before José could answer, the cops drew their guns
and began to shout.

CHAPTER
40

THE COP BEHIND CASEY SNATCHED THE PHONE FROM her hand and dropped it to the ground before he stomped and ground it, crackling, beneath his heel. José had his hands in the air and Casey did the same. José talked calmly to the cop pointing a gun at him.

"José?" Casey said, her voice frantic.

"Relax," he said. "Get out slow and keep your hands up."

José stepped out of the jeep and away with his hands in the air. Casey did the same and Isodora climbed out, too.

"Where's your ID?" José asked.

"My purse," Casey said, nodding. "It's on the floor."

José spoke to the cops. The second cop fished Casey's purse from the floor of the jeep while the first kept his gun trained on José. Isodora stood beside Casey with the baby in the gritty roadside dust. The cop threw the purse on the hood and rifled through it, finding Casey's passport as well as Isodora's visa. He found Casey's wallet and extracted the cash, holding it up for his partner, who offered only a stony nod. The second cop then removed José's wallet and passport from the front pocket of his jeans, studied the picture, and took his cash as well.

The cops patted them down, then José went back and forth with them for several minutes as they examined the documents. At one point the first cop looked Isodora's way and barked a question at her. Startled, she replied in barely audible Spanish. They turned their attention back to José and their conversation got heated before eventually cooling. Finally José lowered his hands and stepped toward the jeep.

"Come on," he said to Casey. "Come on, Isodora. Get in the jeep."

"Didn't you tell them you were a cop?" Casey asked in a low voice as they climbed aboard the jeep. Some of her hair had escaped and the hot wind whisked it across her face until she tucked it back.

"That's why they were so nice about it," José said, reaching back to give Isodora's leg a reassuring pat before he started the engine.

"What? Not shooting us?" she asked.

"They let us go," José said, looking back. "That's what counts."

"Swell."

"Said that's a military facility," José said. "No stopping. No pictures. They saw your phone."

"Military, my ass," she said. "Making what? Biological weapons? They're burning off something and it isn't gunmetal."

José put the jeep in gear and said, "They wanted to know about Isodora."

"What did you say?"

"The truth," José said. "Her husband died and we're taking her back to testify in a lawsuit."

"That's all you said?" Casey asked.

"No, I told them we were out to destroy a US senator," José said, flashing her a look. "Come on."

"They gave me the creeps," Casey said. "And that place? That place is something bad."

José glanced to his right, then returned his attention to the road.

"Looks like we're going to beat the storm," he said. "It's still a ways off."

———

Fifteen minutes later the Nuevo Laredo traffic got heavy. That's when José pointed out the helicopter.

"What? You think it's following us?" Casey said.

"It's not a traffic copter," José said. "It's not TV. It's police, or some kind of government job."

"Because I took a picture that I now don't even have? Come on."

José shrugged. "Maybe nothing to do with us. I've been watching it for about the last five minutes, though. It hasn't gone very far."

By the time they got through the heavy traffic in town, the helicopter had disappeared.

"Big Brother went home," Casey said.

"Guess so."

"Better to be aware than not," Casey said.

"That's what I thought."

The customs agent barely looked at their papers before swigging her Dict Coke and waving them through, one small segment in the snake of trucks and cars waiting to enter the United States. The wind had picked up enough for them to find a branch of their rental company just off Route 35 at Laredo Airport, drop off the jeep, and pick up a four-door sedan with air-conditioning that they could drop off in Dallas. No sooner had they pulled back onto the highway than the sky opened up, dousing the windshield with buckets and lighting up the darkened sky all around them with flashes of chain lightning.

José drove while the rest of them dozed. He took them to Casey's place, where they all had eggs and bacon, even the baby. Then Isodora and the baby disappeared into Casey's guest room, and Casey took two longneck bottles of Budweiser from the fridge and sat down on the couch next to José.

"Long day," he said.

"Longer for you. Thanks for driving."

They swigged their beer.

"What was all that back there?" Casey asked.

José shrugged. "Nothing to do with us."

"Soap we buy," Casey said. "Beer bottles. Drugs. They make the same stuff they used to make here, only over there they don't have the EPA to worry about."

"Or the unions," José said.

"Jesus, the air and the water," she said. "I keep thinking about that little boy's arms. The one at the chicken stand. The whole thing feels like it's right back at our doorstep. Isodora. Her husband. Chase. Those factories. All the people who kill themselves to get here. But mostly that little boy."

"Things happen," José said. "You're tired."

"Did you think they were going to kill us?" she asked. "Those cops."

José shook his head. "Didn't feel like it. If it did, I would have made a stand."

"What do you mean?"

He gave a quick frown. "You sense it's going down, you don't cooperate. You take a stand. Give it your best. I'll be damned if someone's ever going to put a bullet in the back of my head."

"And you think you'd get a feeling?" she asked.

"I know."

"You know my feeling?" she asked.

He shook his head.

"I feel like that storm we saw moving in, nasty."

"It got us, but not the worst of it," he said.

"I know, but I still feel like that," she said. "Like it's coming. Something."

She looked at him for a while and they drank their beer.

"Let's go to bed," she said.

" 'Let's' as in *let us*?" he said. "As in us?"

"Let us."

CHAPTER
41

Teuch woke and worked his jaw. His stomach ached, but he was hungry for only one thing. He listened to the sounds around him, the beep of the heart monitor, the hissing rise and fall of a respirator from the next bed, the low chatter of nurses at the station outside. His eyelids glowed intermittently. He cracked them open, just a bit, and marveled at the yellow light flickering in the barren window, wondering what tricks his damaged brain played, until he heard the faint rumble of thunder.

He shifted his legs under the covers and flexed his fingers, letting the muscles fire in sequence until his shoulders shrugged beneath the sheet. Above him, the IV dripped steadily and he studied the morphine dispenser, wondering how bad the pain would be without it. He stared at the crack in the curtain surrounding his bed, listened again, then removed his hand from the sheets, feeling the edges of the bandage that covered his head like a helmet. The blood on the lip of the bandage had become crusty, a good thing, since it meant the bleeding underneath had stopped.

From the mindless talk of the nurses during the day he knew it was Saturday and knew that meant a reduced staff on every front. He breathed deep and slipped from the bed, glad for the sensation of the cool floor beneath his bare feet. Sitting on the edge of the bed, he studied the IV, carefully peeling back the tape before tugging the needle free from the vein in his arm. He swung his legs over the other side of the bed now, careful not to pull the sensor clip free from his fingertip, and gently pushed open the curtain to learn that the person in the next bed was an old man with tufts of snow-white hair and a wrinkled face, toothless and wearing a grimace of pain.

Teuch studied the setup until he had it figured. He took hold of the man's hand with its long nails and soft pale skin and closed the fingers around the respirator tube. He studied the cracked-open door for a moment, then yanked the man's hand, tearing the tube free from his mouth and setting off a wild scream of alarms inside the room as well as out in the hallway.

He ducked behind the curtain and quickly tugged the sensor free from his fingertip, setting off a smaller alarm of his own. Two nurses rushed into the old man's space. The lights in the room went on. Another patient on the other side of the room groaned in agony. Teuch fished open the curtain at the foot of his bed and slipped past the nurses bent in wild motion over the dying old man. His legs felt rubbery protruding from the thin cotton robe and he gripped the rail along the wall, working his way down the hall. In front of him a door swung open and a bleary-

eyed young doctor dashed toward him. Teuch pointed
back at the room.

"He's dying!" Teuch said, and the doctor sprinted past.

Teuch didn't look back. He hurried for the exit door
at the end of the hall, nearly falling flat as it swung open
into a stairwell. A single flight down and he came to a
metal door with a red bar, an exit, clearly marked for an
emergency.

Teuch leaned against it and spilled out onto a concrete
walk, another alarm now piercing the night. Above, the
dark sky guttered with lightning. Rumbling thunder filled
the air with the damp smell of coming rain. Teuch glanced
around at the three-story brick building, the sign that read
ENNIS MEDICAL CENTER, the surrounding trees and grass,
and the nearby lights from the town. He began to jog away
from the building, the wind blowing grit into his face,
blood from the disrupted IV drizzling down the length of
his hand to spot the concrete. Stray papers rattled past and
the pale blue robe seemed to glow even under the waving
shadows of the trees along the parking lot.

Behind him, the wailing emergency alarm began
to fade.

His hunger did not.

CHAPTER
42

THE NEXT MORNING, CASEY CALLED THE BANK FIRST thing. The clinic had a little over seventeen thousand left in its account. With everything shut down, and some new donations on the immediate horizon, Casey made the decision to wire ten thousand dollars to the priest who ran the church in Higueras. She unfolded the piece of paper he'd given her and gave the specifics to her banker.

When she hung up the phone, José nodded at her and quietly said, "Nice."

José proposed he take Isodora and the baby to his aunt's house in the barrio. She had plenty of room and one guest, Amelia, already.

"Why would anyone be looking for Isodora?" Casey asked.

"I don't know," he said. "They probably aren't, but if they were, her sister's is the first place they'd check."

An hour after he left, José called Casey to say that they were comfortable and safe with his aunt.

"And," he said, "so you don't think I'm paranoid, I'm not even going to tell you about the helicopter."

"You saw a helicopter?" she asked.

José laughed and said, "No, I heard it when I got out of the car. I'm kidding, though. I heard that, a garbage truck, a 747, and a fire engine."

José had plans with his daughter for the weekend and didn't have to drop her back with her mother until Monday morning. He was supposed to start a paying job after he dropped her off, but promised instead to put it aside in order to make contact with Chase's wife. Casey got herself a new cell phone and spent the rest of her weekend at the office, catching up on paperwork, preparing not only the request for an administrator for Elijandro's estate from the surrogate court, but the entire wrongful death complaint to be filed with the county the moment she had the letter of administration. Sharon spent four hours with Casey on Saturday and Donna did the same on Sunday. With Isodora's signatures, she had everything ready to file, but the clock read twelve-eleven a.m. before she got into bed.

Monday morning came too soon and Casey drove down the beltway earlier than normal, planning all the things she had to do to file Isodora's case, jumpy from coffee and the excitement of taking on the senator. The crowd had already begun to form outside her office as usual. Casey waved cheerfully and pulled around back, letting herself in and getting right on her computer.

They were twenty minutes into their Monday-morning staff meeting when someone began to pound on the office door.

Casey rolled her eyes and said to Stacy, "Go educate whoever the hell that is, will you?"

"Happily."

When Stacy returned, she came with two men in dark suits and crew cuts. The shorter of the two flashed a badge.

"Special Agent Greg Lewis with the EPA," he said. "Is one of you Casey Jordan?"

"I am."

Lewis slipped a document out of his coat pocket and handed it to her. "I've got a court order here. We're closing you down."

"You're not closing anyone down," Casey said.

"For violation of the Resource Conservation and Recovery Act, ma'am."

"You're out of your mind," Casey said.

"This facility had a toxic release last Tuesday that you not only failed to report but where you ordered your employees back to work."

"Someone clogged the goddamned toilet," Casey said, glaring at Stacy.

Stacy wrinkled her nose in a silent snarl to say she had nothing to do with it.

"Right," Lewis said. "We'd like to talk to you about knowingly endangering the safety and health of your employees. I'm going to ask you to come with us and everyone else to vacate the premises."

"You're kidding," Casey said, standing and snatching the court order from the agent.

"Wish I were, ma'am," Lewis said. "Now, if you'll come with me."

"You're arresting me?"

"Not yet, ma'am," agent Lewis said. "We just want to talk at this point."

"Talk to my lawyer."

"You have to leave the premises, ma'am," he said, exhaling through a circular hole in his lips. "We're closing you down."

"You mean Senator Chase is closing us down," Casey said.

Lewis stared blankly.

"Ma'am, it'd be best if you came with us," Lewis's partner said.

"What if we won't leave?" Casey asked.

Lewis looked sideways at his partner, who pressed his lips tight and shook his head as though he'd predicted the outcome.

"Then we will arrest you and everyone in here, ma'am," Lewis said, turning to her and drawing back his suit jacket to expose a chrome set of handcuffs as well as a semiautomatic pistol. "But we'll start with you."

Casey gritted her teeth and stared.

"We'll get our things," she said finally.

"No," Lewis said, holding a hand in the air. "This is a contaminated site, ma'am. No one can take anything with them. Those are the rules."

Casey bit the inside of her mouth, but said, "Fine, we'll go."

The agents turned. Casey began to follow them into the lobby. She passed close to Stacy and said, "Buy me some time."

"What?"

"I need those files," Casey said, hissing. "Do something."

Casey kept going, staying right behind the agents. The shorter one opened the front door, the old service station bell tinkling. Casey saw the dark green government sedan and that the clinic's potential clients had already fled the scene.

Lewis looked back at her and his face went white when Stacy screamed.

Casey turned and saw her office manager flopped down in the doorway, writhing and clutching her chest.

"Oh my God," Casey said. "A heart attack."

She let the agents push past her.

"I'll call 911," she said, then ducked into her office and threw the bolt.

Her heart hammered at the inside of her ribs and her breath came in short strangled gasps. Her hands trembled as she pulled files from the shelf, spilling others across the floor. She tossed them down on top of the computer and yanked it free from the wall socket. Through the metal door she could hear the commotion, but she didn't know if it came from Stacy or the agents realizing what had happened.

With an armful of papers, files, and the computer, she flung open the back door and dashed to her car. No keys.

She set her work down and sprinted back inside. Someone pounded on the other side of the door, rattling the hardware. Her purse hung over the back of her chair. She snatched it and took off, fumbling for the keys as she ran.

She found them, dropped them, and heard a shout from in front of the clinic. She groped for the keys, scratching her knuckles on the broken pavement.

"Ms. Jordan!" Agent Lewis said, rounding the building.

Casey glanced up. Her fingers found the key. She stuck it into the lock and turned.

"Ms. Jordan, stop," Lewis said, starting to jog.

Casey grabbed the papers and the computer. Lewis closed the distance to twenty feet and lengthened his stride.

"Stop right there!"

She tossed everything across to the passenger seat, then jumped in and slammed the door. Lewis grabbed the door handle. She smacked down the lock and started the car.

Lewis pounded on the glass and Casey jammed the car in reverse, nearly running him under her front wheel.

Lewis had his gun out.

She threw it into drive.

He pounded the glass with the butt of the gun and she knew it would shatter. She closed her eyes and stomped on the gas. Lewis swung the gun in a wide arc, hit the roof with a bang that made her think gunshot, then cartwheeled over, losing his grip and spilling to the ground as she fishtailed out of the lot, burning her wheels on the street until they got their grip and she shot through the intersection like a bullet.

CHAPTER
43

José had an aunt in West Dallas, one of those types who refuse to leave the home she raised her own kids in, even if the kids, like the area, had gone bad. She went to Mass every day and she kept her small place clean. As a cop, José had pushed the drugs and the gangs up around the corner and off her street, and stowed a Smith & Wesson snub-noosed .38, the same as his own, in the nightstand next to her bed. When he showed up with Amelia, his aunt didn't ask a thing, just took her in with a smile.

José stopped by early Monday morning before heading to Wilmer. He ate a plate of eggs and peppers while the two women sipped strong coffee, and he went over Amelia's story again so everything Nelly had overheard would be fresh in his mind. He knew he'd be lucky to get a chance with Mandy Chase, and that if he did, he wouldn't get a second one.

With a full stomach and plenty of ideas, he drove down to Wilmer in the rental sedan they'd picked up in Laredo. He knew Gage would recognize his truck and he didn't trust his luck with the chief a second time. It wasn't yet seven-thirty and José figured a woman like Mandy Chase wasn't likely to get up—let alone out—much before ten. He pulled the car off the road a good two hundred yards from the entrance to Lucky Star and dumped two sugars and four half-and-halfs into his coffee. He hadn't finished stirring his drink before the white Range Rover that he knew belonged to the wife came bursting out of gates in a cloud of dust and hit the road with a slight swerve before racing off toward town.

José capped his coffee and set off after her, keeping enough distance to avoid suspicion. He followed her onto Route 45, north toward Dallas. When she got off at a South Side exit, José squinted and looked around, unable to make sense of a rich senator's wife traveling to the wrong side of town. The white SUV was easy to follow, even from a distance. When it turned into the back lot of a run-down building with boarded-up windows, José could only think of another rich wife he'd been hired to follow the previous year. She'd come to this part of town to buy her meth.

He watched from across the street as Mandy Chase got out of the Range Rover wearing jeans and a T-shirt, with her hair bound up in a purple scarf, and wearing a pair of large dark sunglasses. She glanced around, then walked hurriedly past a handful of battered cars parked in the lot and slipped into the back door of the three-story brick building.

José studied the area, waiting and watching for some time. When he got out of the car, he felt for the gun under his arm and then the one tucked into the waist of his pants before crossing the street. Clouds hid the sun, but the day was already warm and dank with humidity. Cars whooshed past on the nearby highway and the smell of spent fuel choked the air. In the gutters and scattered across the busted pavement of the lot lay flattened cans, broken glass, used condoms, and the wrappers of a hundred different forms of junk food. José circled the building and watched from the corner as a thin stream of ratty-looking people, mostly men, entered the front of the brick building through a battered wooden door.

Next to the building, a decrepit brick church stood in near-ruin, its faded walls tainted by vandals and graffiti. José returned to the back of the building and listened at the door Mandy Chase had gone into. The random clank of metal mixed into the occasional bark of orders between people confused him. The door opened easily and the heavy smell of cooking greeted him: frying potatoes, crackling grease, fake eggs, and white toast singed brown and black.

José stood at the back of a large kitchen, where several people worked over industrial-size pots with two-foot utensils. Mandy Chase was nowhere in sight. An older black man with tight white curls of hair and plastic-rimmed glasses looked up from his work, wiping the sweat from his face on the white sleeve of his uniform before asking José if he could help him.

"Looking for Mandy Chase," José said uncertainly.

The man flashed a yellow-toothed smile and the wrinkles at the corners of his eyes deepened.

"Miss Mandy?" the cook said, grinning even harder. "She'll be out there."

José followed the direction of the man's bony finger, through a set of swinging double doors and into a large hall, thick with the din of nearly a hundred homeless and mentally ill people sitting on benches along three long rows of tables. At the front of the hall, Mandy Chase stood alongside several older black women ladling out food to the line of tattered people. Armed with a giant spoon, she offered up a smile as well as a couple of words to go with her scoops of rubbery yellow eggs whipped to life from a powder.

José walked in back of the other helpers until he came to Mandy. Up close, he could see the dark roots of her blonde hair and the mottled skin on her long neck from too much sun. Still, she was strikingly beautiful and as out of place as a daisy blooming from broken asphalt.

"Anything I can do to help?" he asked.

"Oh," she said, glancing at him with a scoop of eggs balanced on her spoon, "good. Can you get more trays from the kitchen?"

"Sure," José said.

To the man who'd directed him in the first place, he said, "Mandy sent me for more trays."

"Helping out? Good," the old man said, pointing to a station beside a stainless-steel sink where a younger man worked over a mountain of dishes with a steamy spray nozzle. "Right over there, and you might as well take them plates, too. They're hungry today. Weather coming and I think they sense it."

José placed two stacks of mismatched plates, warm and wet from the water, onto a stack of damp gray trays and carried them out to the service line. He set them down alongside the bins of bent and tarnished silverware and returned to Mandy's side.

"Set," he said. "Anything else?"

"Mr. Jenkins," she said, raising her voice so the tooth-less man in front of her could hear, "it's good to see you. How's your cat?"

"Linda?" the old man asked, opening his coat to reveal a pouch slung across his naked chest, where an emaciated tabby cat stared out with bulging yellow eyes.

"There she is," Mandy said, scooping out another clump of eggs for the cat. "Get her fed, Mr. Jenkins. She's too thin."

Mr. Jenkins worked his gums and gave Mandy a nod before closing his coat and passing on.

Mandy glanced up at José and said, "You're new."

"I'm not really a volunteer," José said. "But it's nice to see you helping people."

Mandy's face clouded over. She stopped spooning and studied his face.

"José O'Brien," he said, extending a hand. "I used to be with Dallas PD."

"He sent you?" she said, her face crimping with dis-gust, her big brown eyes wincing.

"Who would 'he' be?" José asked.

Mandy turned sharply away, set her jaw, and contin-ued with her work.

"Leave me alone, Mr. O'Brien," she said, bitter.

"Your husband?" José asked. "I'm not with him. Not even close. He having you followed after your little thing with Elijandro?"

She ignored him, her shoulders drew back, and the cords in her neck showed. José waited for her to turn back, but she didn't.

"I thought," José said, "when I saw you here, doing this, no cameras, no reporters, just a bunch of broken-down homeless people, that maybe you're not the rich-bitch wife of a megalomaniac senator."

After a pause, through clenched teeth she said, "That's exactly what I am, so leave me the hell alone."

"I'm not with your husband," he said.

"Everyone is with my husband," she said, scooping out eggs. "Go to hell."

"You knew Elijandro had a wife," José said. "I'm helping *her*. Elijandro had a little girl, too. They've got nothing. Now, some lawyer might have told you that what your husband said about Ellie can't come out in court, but that won't hold up. We know about Nelly hearing the two of you fight."

Mandy looked at him sharply.

"Even without Nelly," José said quietly, "I've got a witness who knows Nelly was there and what she heard and I'm told that's just as good. So we're gonna subpoena you, and even the senator can't make that go away."

"What about Nelly?" she asked.

José shook his head and said, "She's gone, like you probably know. Look, I didn't think it was going to go like this, then I see you dishing out eggs here and I think maybe you give a shit about someone other than yourself. I've seen wives dipping in with the help before and they're usually not working the soup line in their off-hours."

"*Dipping in?*" Mandy said, shaking her head. "You're pathetic. If you're not with my husband, you should be. Send him your résumé, Mr. O'Brien."

"Your husband is not a good man," José said.

Mandy turned and looked him in the eye, her own glass-blue irises burning with hatred as she said, "You have no idea."

"Tell me," José said. "Help me. Help Elijandro's little girl."

"I tell you, it'll be the end of my problems, that's for sure," she said.

"How so?"

She looked deep into his eyes and said, " 'Cause I'll be dead."

CHAPTER
44

CASEY RACED TO THE COURTHOUSE. SHE PARKED ON the deck in back, riffled through her files to find the request for a letter of administration and the complaint, and hurried into the surrogate court clerk's offices. She had to make a couple of calls and use some favors to get the judge out of a conference to sign the letter of administration, but after half an hour she had it and went straight to the county court clerk. After a short wait in line she handed over the complaint along with the letter of administration, cut a check, and got back an index number. Cases were typically assigned the same day, so she left her cell phone number and asked to be called the moment a judge was assigned. With the papers filed, there was now nothing Chase could do to stop her.

That done, she returned to the car and dialed Sharon's cell phone to find out how the scene with the EPA agents had ended.

"Jesus, you should have seen that guy's face," Sharon said. "I thought his head was going to explode. He said you almost ran him over. His pants were torn, knee bleeding all over. I can't believe you."

"They asked me to leave," Casey said. "I left. They can't arrest you for that."

"A couple city cops showed up," Sharon said. "They listened for a while and headed for the doughnut shop around the corner."

"I got the papers filed, anyway."

"What do we do now?" Sharon asked.

"Call the others. Tell them to think of it like a mini vacation. Let me sort this out," Casey said, "see how our senator enjoys the media crawling up his ass."

CHAPTER
45

JOSÉ DIDN'T ANSWER HIS PHONE, BUT THAT WAS NOTH-ing new. She left him a message about the EPA, then called Tim Smith, an environmental attorney from Baker Botts, one of the three big firms in Dallas.

"You better make plans to relocate your office," Smith said, "at least for the near future."

"It's bullshit," Casey said.

"Even if it's totally unfounded," Smith said, "and from what you tell me, it's not."

"A little oil in the pipes?" Casey said.

"Probably got a plume," Smith said. "Most old stations have them. Gas leaking from the tanks for fifty years. Let me guess, some magnanimous developer donated the property."

"So?"

"I saw one of these out by Tech," Smith said. "Rich alumni owns a piece of land, gives it to the school, takes a huge tax write-off, and surprise, the school goes to put up a building and finds out the site has PCBs off the charts.

The alum says he didn't know. He doesn't own it any-more, and the school has to clean it up. EPA? They don't care. You own it, you clean it. Doesn't matter some farmer dumped oil down a dry well sixty years ago, you fix it. That's the game."

"I'm a nonprofit," she said.

"You could go belly-up," he said. "State comes in, cleans it, and auctions the land. Change the name of your charity and you can buy it back cheap. About a five-year process, though. My wife's a Realtor with some nice downtown office space if you want her number."

Casey's head spun.

"They said something about me sending people to work, some Resource Recovery Act. I've heard of it, but what is it?"

"Hardball," Smith said. "Trying to scare you."

"How so?"

"It's a crime to knowingly expose employees to toxic substances," Smith said.

"Is there anything to it?"

"Very tough for them," he said. "It's just a position. Sixty, seventy percent of the time you can plea down."

"Plea down?"

"It's rare you get jail time with petroleum products," he said. "It's not like it's arsenic."

"Jail?" she asked. "Not really, right?"

"Highly unlikely," he said.

"But possible?" she asked. "You're kidding."

"I wish you hadn't pulled that stunt with running away."

"I wasn't under arrest."

"You made them look bad, grabbing your stuff and

slipping out the back like that," he said. "These federal agents get touchy."

"They're with the *EPA*," she said.

"That's what they get touchy about. They carry guns, too, you know. Pension after twenty years. All that."

"Just do your best," Casey said, "and let me know."

"No worries. I'll handle it."

Casey hung up and headed for her Realtor's office to find a place where she and her team could work.

CHAPTER
46

Y OU'RE AFRAID OF HIM?" JOSÉ ASKED.

Mandy pressed her lips together and let the spoon clatter into the bottom of the empty egg pan. She turned toward the kitchen and José followed.

Mandy laid the pan into the sink, untied her apron, and hung it on a nail.

"I'm all finished, Frank," she said to the wrinkled cook. "I'll see you next week."

From the front pocket of her jeans she removed a folded check that she stuffed into the pocket of Frank's apron.

The old man smiled at her, touched his cap, and said, "You're awful good to these folks, Miss Mandy."

"I'm happy to help, Frank," she said, and turned away.

With her hand on the back door, Mandy turned to José and said, "I'll talk to you, but not here. You go out the front. I've seen them out here before, watching. Is there a place we can meet that has two entrances?"

"There's a place up on Lamar near Grand," José said.

"Pilar's Kitchen. I'll go in through the kitchen and meet you at a back table."

Mandy started to open the door. José grabbed her arm and said, "This isn't some little trick, right?"

"If I wanted you gone," she said, yanking her arm free, "all I'd have to do is say abracadabra. I have some things to pick up, but I'll meet you there in half an hour."

José watched her go, then turned and melted in with the steady flow of sated homeless out the front door. After a careful look around, he circled the block for his car. He took a couple of side streets, signaling one way, turning another, and checking his rearview mirror. By the time he reached Pilar's he was convinced that no one had followed him.

He took a deep breath and tried to make it past the overflowing garbage cans in the alley, nearly denying himself a mouthful of the ripe stink. The back screen door opened with a screech and several of the help glanced up from their handiwork of pans and dishes, but none spoke. The cook, dressed in a dirty white T-shirt and a paper hat, removed his cigarette, but only gave José a nod before turning back to his pan. Pilar nearly knocked José down as she banged her big hips through the double doors with a tray overloaded with more dirty dishes bleeding egg yolk and dripping with refried beans.

Pilar's scowl turned into a grin when she realized it was José who'd bumped her. When he told her to keep her eyes open for a blonde coming in through the front and asked Pilar to send her into the back room, the big cook waggled her eyebrows.

"Just business, Pilar," he said, pecking her cheek and slipping past. "Let me know if any gringos come in the front, too."

"Gringos like you?" she asked, catching the door with her foot.

"They'll be lighter-skinned than me," he said.

José sat at a corner table. Pilar reappeared in a colorful flow of silk that only heightened her immense bulk, slapped a cup of coffee on the table in front of José, and disappeared into the front room of the restaurant.

It wasn't more than ten minutes before Pilar returned in a flourish of silk, waving Mandy to the seat opposite him and plunking down another mug of coffee. As the big cook sashayed away, Mandy leaned around the corner to follow Pilar with her eyes.

"Flamboyant," José said, "but solid."

"Yes."

"Your husband have you followed regularly?"

"From time to time," Mandy said, blowing steam across the rim of her mug before sipping.

"You acted pretty indignant when I hinted about you and Ellie."

"Ellie was a good husband, Mr. O'Brien," she said. "A good man."

"What are you?" he asked.

She leaned forward, looking hard at him with those big eyes.

"People disappear," she said in a low whisper. "Mexican people."

"The Triangle?" José said, clenching his coffee mug and narrowing his eyes.

"You know?"

"I've heard things about folks down in that corner of the county for a couple of years now. We're a superstitious people, though, us Latinos."

"People always come and go at the ranch," she said, "fundraisers, advisers, lobbyists. There's one I see more than others, Monte Street, pinstriped suits with pink shirts and red ties, that type. My husband calls him 'Money,' Money Street. I heard them one night out in the gazebo, smoking cigars and talking about people the way you talk about livestock. Dollars per head."

She looked up to see that José understood.

"There's an abandoned quarry, up Blindsay Road not far from the ranch," she said. "I heard them talking about it and the next night I went out there to see. There was a tractor trailer full of people and a handful of men with guns."

"Your husband, importing illegals?" José said.

Mandy shook her head. "I don't know. I couldn't believe that was it, the way he goes on about immigration. I got close enough to hear, but they spoke Spanish, and I don't.

"I knew Ellie from the dove shoots. The one hunt wives do. I liked Ellie. There was something about him. He gave you a good feeling. Honest. Strong. I asked him to help and he did. We went out there a couple times and didn't see anything and I think he started to think I was crazy, so I went myself for a while. I think they only use the quarry once every few weeks. Anyway, I went and got Ellie and we got close and he heard some things that scared the hell out of him. He wouldn't talk about it, just kept shaking his head. So I wasn't paying attention when I pulled out of the side entrance to the quarry, and I almost ran Chief Gage off the road. I pulled out on the road right in front of him. He must have seen me with Ellie."

"Something any good Texan will kill for," José said. He studied Mandy's face, the lines at the corners of her eyes and mouth tugging her into middle age.

"My husband and I have done our own things for a long time," she said. "Everyone knows about his strippers and little coke whores. I stayed for my kids, but it wasn't a nunnery."

"He didn't care?"

She shook her head. "He doesn't give a damn about me. It's for whatever they do at that quarry. That's why he killed Ellie, and to let me know I better stay out of it."

"Ellie didn't tell you anything?"

"The only thing he said was that those trucks weren't bringing people into the country."

"What were they doing?"

"Taking them back. To Mexico."

"Your husband is shipping illegals out of the country?" José said, wrinkling his brow. "Like some vigilante deporting them?"

Mandy swigged her coffee and swallowed. "No. They take them back there for something else."

"Ellie didn't say what?"

Mandy shook her head. "He said people had been going missing for some time. Some people thought it was just a superstition. Whatever he heard, he didn't want to talk about it. I don't think he heard enough to know anything for certain and he wasn't the type to speculate. All I know is that from the look on his face, it wasn't anything good."

CHAPTER
47

CASEY WAS LOOKING AT SPACE IN AN ABANDONED adult bookstore not far from her condemned office when her cell phone rang. She began to gush about her plan to nail Chase when she heard Judge Remy's voice, but the judge cut her off and suggested Casey save what she had to say for her chambers in fifteen minutes. Casey nudged a dusty package of French ticklers with the toe of her shoe and said she'd be there in ten.

"Not for me," she said to the Realtor, offering a weak smile, snapping her phone shut, and heading for the door.

Her Mercedes coughed alive and the crunch of broken glass barely registered as she pulled away from the garbage-strewn curb. When she got to the judge's chambers, Casey extended a hand.

"Please sit," the judge said, "I've got a settlement conference in five minutes. I'm glad you could see me in person. Here's your complaint; the clerk hand-delivered it *after* he spoke with the admin judge, who called me to see if I was okay to handle this."

"I'm glad you agreed."

"I'm not in a position to say no," she said, "not after signing that exhumation. I stuck my neck out, so the admin figured he'd give me the short straw on this. No one wants a trial with a senator. It would have been nice if you could have warned me."

Casey sat, stiff-backed, and said, "There are fourteen judges. Cases are supposed to be random."

Remy scrunched her face and tilted her head. "Do you think this is some old lady slipping on a bunch of grapes at the Kroger? You're suing a United States senator. You think they just spin the wheel?"

"How did they even know about the exhumation?" Casey asked.

"That's my point," Remy said. "People seem to know a lot, even though nothing's been reported in the papers."

"Well, it will," Casey said. "I've got a press conference tomorrow morning. He already shut down my office. The EPA showed up with guns, in case you think I don't know I'm suing a US senator."

"That's what I wanted to talk to you about," she said. "They'll come sniffing up my skirt, too. Don't think I got this case as a favor, it's not. I don't need the face time and I don't want it. I wanted to tell you, straight out, before this stink bomb explodes. Everything goes by the book. I will have my chute open."

Casey fished some papers from her briefcase on the floor and held them up one at a time. "I have orders of deposition for the senator and his wife. The undertaker. His two assistants. The police chief. The ranch foreman. Subpoenas for the Wilmer police investigation papers and the phone records of the senator's home, office, and cell phone."

The corner of the judge's lip twitched. "We typically wait for the answer to come back, then send a bill of particulars for what you want."

Casey nodded her head and removed another document. "Except when the plaintiff has a reasonable suspicion of spoliation of the evidence or a conspiracy between domestic partners to use the marital privilege as a shield, *Cleveland v. Norris* and *Kronkite v. The State of Texas.* I have the briefs."

The judge plucked up her reading glasses and took the briefs, examining one, then the other before pointing them at Casey.

"I can trust you on this?"

"It's not a gray area," Casey said. "One of my associates wrote her UT bar review article on *Kronkite.*"

The judge inhaled deeply and exhaled through her nose, shaking her head, but signed the orders, one after another, with a flourish.

"Here we go," she said, rising up.

CHAPTER
48

TEUCH STRUGGLED UPRIGHT IN THE NARROW BED, clawing free from the tangled sheets but unable to shake the fog of pain. Sunlight poured in through the cracked and dusty window, exposing the dried blood on his pillow. Teuch groaned and went to take hold of his head, but he no sooner touched the stiff and pungent dressings than a searing jolt of pain shot through his skull. The springs in the cot beside his squeaked and a fat man with a dirty but ample mustache produced a bottle of peppermint schnapps and wagged it Teuch's way.

"You need one?" the man asked, then took a swig himself that peppered the dank air with a hint of candy freshness.

Sweat beaded on Teuch's upper lip and he made a grab for the bottle.

"Easy," the man said in a whine, "I was givin' it to you."

Teuch slugged down what remained in the bottle, then returned the empty to the bum along with a look evil enough to cut off any complaint. Teuch staggered to his feet and tugged at the drawstrings to keep the worn and baggy sweat-pants from slipping off his naked hips. Barefoot, he made his way through the rows of cots, most of them sagging beneath sleeping men. Teuch steadied himself on the human lumps without regard for the indignant cries and moans.

After a good pee, Teuch made his way into the front room, where a wizened man in a security cap slept behind the desk. Teuch remembered the old-timer from his arrival the previous night. After the drunk with the peppermint schnapps found Teuch collapsed under a bridge, delirious from exhaustion and pain, he and a friend had carried Teuch to the shelter. The old guard had brought out a cardboard box full of old clothes. With the help of the drunk, the guard had changed Teuch before dropping him into bed. Now, with his mind at least partially cleared, Teuch needed to find a phone.

He slapped the old man's face, sending a stream of drool down his cheek as he blustered to life.

"A phone," Teuch said. "I need it."

The guard's eyes widened behind his thick glasses, and he swiped away the drool and collected his senses.

"When the nuns get here," he said, angling his head at the door halfway down the wall behind him. "Out that door. They got one. I ain't."

Teuch winced at a fresh wave of pain.

"When?" he said through gritted teeth.

The guard peered at him. "You oughta sit down."

"When?" Teuch said, growling from his throat.

"A couple minutes," the guard said, examining his watch. "No more."

Teuch staggered over to the door and began to hammer on it with the meat of his fist.

"No need for that," he heard the guard call from his desk.

The door flung inward and the powdery face of a bespectacled nun appeared with an angry scowl and her pale lips shaped into a perfect O.

"I need a phone."

"Your head is bloody," she said, stepping back, her face softening.

"I slept here," he said. "I need a phone."

The nun hustled him down a long hallway and into a barren office, where a phone rested silently on a scarred wooden desk. Teuch dialed, unconcerned with whether the nun heard him or not. He got his man and in Spanish directed him to drop everything and get to the shelter, to bring him a gun, clothes, money, and enough junk and needles to keep him high for a month.

"We don't allow trouble here," the nun said, her back rigid as he slouched past.

"Sometimes it just comes," he said, and he ambled back to the cot where he'd spent the night and lay down to wait.

CHAPTER
49

"SHOULD I BE JEALOUS OF MANDY CHASE?" CASEY asked José. She pulled her Mercedes up the driveway, following a long midnight-blue Bentley with glittering rims to the red carpet that welcomed patrons to Nick and Sam's.

"It wasn't like that," José said, climbing out and giving her a dirty look over the roof of the car.

"She didn't just charm you with her silicone?" Casey said, handing off her keys to a red-jacketed valet.

"Are you serious?" he said under his breath, taking her arm and walking her through the double doors of wood and beveled glass.

"An EPA agent pulled a gun on me today," Casey said, putting on a smile and waving to Paige.

Paige stood in a small group of others back by a dark wood bar lined with fat white candles in silver holders.

"That tells me anything's possible," Casey said.

They passed the hostess's stand and noise from the restaurant washed over them. Although it was early in the evening, the dining room didn't appear to have any empty tables and the dark, spacious bar area overflowed with men in tailored suits and women wearing high heels. On the back wall, facing the bar, a seventy-inch plasma screen flickered and glowed, its sound all but drowned in chatty laughter.

"Come on. This is what we wanted," José said, wearing a forced smile of his own, taking her arm, and marching toward Paige's group. "He'll crumble."

"I'm teasing you," she said, tugging him close, squeezing his hand, and brushing her lips against his ear. "We've got him. Tomorrow I unleash my depositions, my subpoenas, and I plaster him in the press. It's all so good, and I'm so happy you're with me for this."

Casey turned and embraced Paige, bussing her cheek, then Luddy's, before stepping back to receive introductions to two other couples, similarly wealthy. A small gathering, Paige had told her. The Golds and the Treemores, two *very* eligible philanthropists for her clinic.

"And this is José O'Brien," Casey said, turning to José. While his blue blazer and jeans appeared wilted next to the crisp suits and white shirts of the other men, he more than made up for it with his height, his posture, and his dangerous good looks.

José shook hands and looked hard into their eyes before he asked if anyone needed a drink. The rich men all rattled their ice and ordered Chivas Regals, thanking the ex-cop for his generosity. The ladies allowed their champagne glasses to be refilled from the bucket of Dom Perignon behind the bar. What José ordered, no one knew.

"That tequila?" Treemore asked, blinking behind his small, round glasses.

"Only when I want to go *todo loco*," José said sternly. Then his face softened. "No, it's vodka. Absolut. Straight up."

Treemore's pale cheeks went pink and he nodded.

"Well," Casey said, raising the champagne glass José offered her. "To friends, old and new."

As they raised their glasses, Paige's eyes passed over Casey's shoulder and the light in her face went out.

"Christ," she said, flicking her eyes at Casey before returning to the back wall, "you're on TV."

Paige pushed through their small group and the bigger crowd in the middle of the floor, making way for Casey and the rest to follow. As they did, the people craned their necks at Casey and the festive din subsided. Beside the newscaster's face was a blown-up publicity photo Lifetime had used of her when the movie was released.

". . . Jordan has called a press conference of her own for tomorrow," the newscaster said, looking solemnly into the camera until the picture cut to Senator Chase at a podium in front of a dark blue curtain bearing the senate seal and flanked by flags of the United States and Texas.

"The accusations fabricated by Casey Jordan are outrageous and pathetic, but those who know this woman lawyer will not be surprised," Chase said, looking up from the podium to make his point. "The same Casey Jordan, a self-made character in the recent Lifetime movie, is being sued by her own husband for defamation, has recently threatened the Dallas district attorney with a gender-biased smear campaign evolving out of her role defending a murderer who signed a confession, and, incredibly, has been shut down by the EPA for operating a workplace where she knowingly exposed employees to toxic substances. This from a woman who claims to run a charity, but uses the money to pay herself a six-figure salary, drive a Mercedes-Benz, and do work for criminals connected to organized crime. Additionally, we have learned that ten thousand dollars was recently wired from her account to an unknown location in Mexico."

Chase looked up again. "If this woman's present grab for money and notoriety weren't so hurtful and destructive, I might have to laugh at its audacity."

Chase returned to his notes. "To attempt to capitalize on the tragedy that my family and the family of Elijandro Torres have had to recently endure is sick, and it won't surprise anyone to know that Casey Jordan has in fact undergone serious psychological treatment.

"Finally," Chase said, looking up one more time and sighing dramatically, "it is important to know that Casey Jordan has aligned herself with a disgraced police officer from the Dallas PD. José O'Brien, her investigator and boyfriend, is a dirty cop. O'Brien was linked to Mexican gang activity including the smuggling of narcotics, and human trafficking for a prostitution ring. Three years ago, O'Brien was discharged from duty as an officer without pay and without his pension."

Casey felt her mouth drop open. She turned to José and saw the ripple of muscles in his jaw. He wouldn't face her, and she dropped his hand from her own.

On the screen, Chase looked up and addressed the cameras with a practiced stare. "These are the people working against me. Before it became public, I wanted the people of this great state to know exactly what is afoot and to personally deny any wrongdoing on my part."

The newscaster's face appeared on the screen and

said, "Joining Senator Chase at that impromptu news conference was Casey Jordan's former husband of ten years, Taylor Jordan, the notable Austin philanthropist."

"Christ," Casey said, her eyes glued to the enormous screen, but still conscious of the glances flashing at her from all quarters.

Taylor, handsome, conservatively dressed, and gray around the edges of his wavy hair, sniffed and looked up with red eyes. "My ex-wife, Casey Jordan, has slandered me publicly and privately. I am pursuing her in court for the shame she's brought on my good family's name, and I'm here to tell the truth about her, so that this good man, a hero to many of us for his stand on American values, will not have to suffer the humiliation that I have. It's wrong. It was wrong when she did it to me with that . . . that movie. And it's wrong now."

The newscaster appeared, silent and shaking his head in disgust before getting back to business. "In Iraq today, twenty-seven—"

Casey looked at José, aware of the uncomfortable quiet that had settled on the room.

"José," she said, speaking low, "I am so sorry I dragged you into this."

José clenched his hands and looked up, his nostrils flaring, but with eyes that glistened. He turned and headed for the door.

Casey went after him, catching him outside and grabbing hold of his arm to stop him from getting into a cab.

"What?" she asked. "I said I was sorry. José?"

José shook his head, unable to meet her eyes.

"Come on," she said. "What's wrong?"

José shook his head again, looking down.

"José? It's not true, is it?"

"Not all of it," he said, clenching his teeth and looking up at her. "But some, I guess."

"What part?" she said, her words sounding desperate, her mind racing back over the allegations: gangs, drugs, prostitution.

José wouldn't answer. He pulled away, his face tight and flushed with shame, and headed back for the cab.

Casey let him go.

CHAPTER
50

Showered, shaved, and high, with his hand on a chrome .45 automatic and a cigarette dangling from his lip, Teuch rode beside Adulio, his brother-King. Slouched down in the front seat of Adulio's pimped-out '73 Impala, they rumbled down the steaming street past the Catholic church in Wilmer. The church's doors swung open and there stood the priest. Teuch might have thought the priest meant to welcome them, except he knew the priest could not have known that Teuch would be back in Wilmer.

"Stop," Teuch told Adulio in Spanish, taking a final drag before pitching his cigarette out the open window.

"*Qué?*" Adulio asked, looking around, his bald brown head swiveling.

"Back up," Teuch said. "To the church."

They did, and the priest studied them without moving from the stoop, a watering can cradled in his arms. The priest's face suddenly relaxed and he approached the car.

"You look terrible," the priest said, in Spanish. "I didn't recognize you."

"Guess I fucked up," Teuch said in Spanish, offering up a placid grin. "Last time I saw you, Father, you offered me a blessing. I should have taken it."

Teuch pointed at the white helmet atop his head. "Cop blew half my fucking brains out, Father. Now I got some sense."

"To blow out half of his?" the priest asked, raising an eyebrow and switching to English.

"To see what you wanted me to see before, Father," Teuch said in Spanish, "to take your blessings this time. Bring me some luck."

"I hope to bring you the Lord's blessings by showing you the work I believe your brother died for," the priest said, returning to Spanish, resting his watering can on the gravel next to the small plot of flowers surrounding the stunted belfries. "I told you that days ago. Did the men who killed your brother do that to you?"

Teuch touched the dressing and smiled at the pain, now muted by heroin. "Yes. I'd like to know more."

Teuch got out of the car and followed the priest up the hard-packed dirt walk lined with small round stones. The priest swung open the dark door and they entered a musty nave with rough-cut dark wood pews that faced an altar lit by a single arched piece of stained glass and watched over by a large wooden Jesus, bleeding on his cross. Along one wall the priest went, turning in to a flickering chapel no bigger than a motel room. Teuch eyed the wooden Jesus above the main altar and sniffed before turning in to the chapel himself and seeing a hundred or more small photographs taped to the plaster wall in rows. Beneath them stood two racks of candles, their small orange flames guttering low and dribbling clear white wax.

"The people say '*Triángulo de Bermudas*' behind my back," the priest said. "These are the missing, their photographs. Some from right here, they simply disappear. Most of them have sent word that they are coming and then, nothing. Back home, in Mexico, the people say they went. Here, they wait, but no one comes."

"Coyotes," Teuch said with a nod.

"Maybe," the priest said. "But why hasn't anyone heard? Some of them are bad, these coyotes. They take advantage of the weak. But their stories are told. These people"—the priest nodded at the wall—"there is nothing. They simply vanish."

"And my brother?" Teuch said.

The priest nodded vigorously. "He didn't tell me what it was, but I found him here in this chapel, late one night, just before he died. I don't know how he got here, or what he was doing, but when I asked him, he told me these souls might not be lost. That was all he would say, but I took it to mean something."

Teuch studied the souls. A young girl. A man with a full white beard. A fat mother with two grinning children. Smiling, random faces with no connection to one another beyond their Mexican heritage and their quest for a better place. Teuch chuckled and turned away, waving his hand.

"Ghosts and demons and smoke and mirrors," he said. "The work of priests."

Teuch stopped in the middle of the nave. The priest

had followed him, but with a head hung in disappointment.

"Bless me anyway, Father," Teuch said, turning toward him and eyeing the bloody wooden savior. "For luck. I can't say it's God's work, but it is work I think He'd want done."

CHAPTER
51

CASEY WOKE TO THE SOUND OF HER CELL PHONE rising above the alarm she'd been too lazy to shut off. She cleared her throat and coughed, picked it up, and answered.

"Where are you?" Stacy asked.

Casey swatted the clock radio into silence, woefully eyeing the bottle of sleeping pills on the nightstand. She widened her eyes, worked her jaw, and wagged her head to clear the ill effect of the pills.

"I'm coming," she said, clearing her throat again.

"You sound like shit," Stacy said.

"I feel great, though," she said.

"Sorry."

"You saw that last night?" Casey asked.

"How's José?"

"I better get going here," Casey said.

"The TV trucks got here before me. I showed them where to set up."

"How do they look, the reporters?" Casey asked.

"Hungry, I guess."

"Good. They're about to get fed," Casey said, then hung up.

A cold shower cut through the fog of the sleeping pill. She dressed quickly, gulped down a glass of tomato juice, and hurried out the door with her briefcase tucked beneath her arm.

She darted in and out of the morning traffic, which was thinning now with the lateness of the hour, until she found herself in front of the courthouse with a pounding headache. TV trucks jammed the drive with more than just the local news and she pulled up her Mercedes behind one of them like just another reporter risking a ticket and a tow. She found three Advils in her purse, swallowed them dry, and checked her makeup in the rearview mirror. She got out into a sun standing well above the horizon, too bright and too hot to look at.

Stacy appeared beside her wearing a new dress and high heels that made Casey stare.

"I figured," Stacy said, looking down at herself, "TV and everything."

Casey nodded. "Thanks for coming."

Although there was no press podium for her, the media had coagulated around the usual spot on the granite steps, in the shadows of the main entrance, where lawyers, jurors, and families of the accused hurried to and fro to receive their portion of justice. Among the media, she thought she detected mic flags from CNN, E!, and *Access Hollywood*. Casey breathed deep and fiddled with her hair, tucking it in and out from behind her ears as her own mind wavered between images of a powerful, meticulous lawyer and of a sympathetic woman unjustly accused. As she stepped to the spot in front of all the lights, cameras, and microphones, she went with both, one side of her red hair pinned back behind her ear, the other falling loose across the edge of her cheek and jaw.

She set her briefcase down on the steps, extracting her five-page statement with trembling hands. After the blazing morning heat, the deep shadow of the courthouse tower sent a chill down her spine. She forced a smile at the reporters, thanked them for coming, and began to read.

Somewhere in the midst of her denials and pointed counteraccusations, she began to wish she'd postponed speaking to the press. Her consternation over José, a bad night's sleep, and a hangover from the sleeping pill left her feeling nauseated and less than sharp mentally. Not knowing how to go back, though, she plowed through to the end, thinking she could make a quick exit before she threw up.

But when she finished her statement and the questions came zipping at her like traffic on a busy highway, her legs seized up.

"Are you saying that your history of mental illness isn't connected with these wild allegations?"

Wham.

She scowled, searching for the source of the question.

"That is a lie," she said, gritting her teeth, knowing she shouldn't even address it, knowing she should just leave, but somehow unable to keep her mouth shut. "I have no mental illness."

"We've seen your date book from two years ago," said a bleached blonde in a red skirt and jacket, pointing at Casey with a microphone. "You saw a Dr. Eppilito over a dozen times. The psychotherapist. Are you saying you have no mental problems?"

Casey sighed, smiled wanly, and asked, "Who doesn't have problems? My marriage was a train wreck. A former client tried to kill me."

"And you took antipsychotic drugs for your mental illness?"

"What's wrong with you people?" Casey barked, even while the lawyer in her shouted to walk away. "A man was murdered. They cremated his body to destroy the evidence. The US government deported his wife and baby to cover it up, and you want to know about a couple Xanax I took two years ago?"

Cameras flashed and clicked and the reporters began to jostle one another, undulating like a polluted sea, their questions coming like breakers, jumbled together and smashing into her. Gangs. Drug deals. Movie contracts. Corruption. Dirty cops. Murderesses. Madness. Sex. They hit her with everything, until, finally, her stomach heaved. She snatched up her briefcase, choking back the bile, and vacated the steps.

They followed her in a pack, snapping at her with insistent and outrageous questions and accusations. Stacy locked an arm into Casey's and acted as buffer, escorting her down the steps with a stiff back, jutting out her chin and glowering. At the bottom of the steps, the young bleached blonde in the red skirt and heels darted in front of them, microphone first.

"Are you going to return the money you've taken from charity?" she said, her blue eyes bulging and spittle flying from her cherry lips.

The foam bulb on the end of the microphone bumped Casey's nose hard enough to make her eyes water.

"Are you!" the reporter yelled.

Casey grabbed the microphone and yanked it. The reporter held tight, crashing into Casey and careening off of the elbow Stacy fired into her ribs. The reporter sprawled to the pavement, her long legs akimbo. She screamed, but gripped the microphone with both hands and stabbed it at Casey.

Casey knocked the mic aside, stepped over the woman reporter, and marched on toward her car. The pack closed in and the tirade of questions, now indignant and angry, cascaded down on her and Stacy.

"Fucking animals," Stacy said with her arm across her face.

Casey jerked open the car door and looked up at the mob.

"This *shitbox* is my *Mercedes*!"

She threw herself inside, and crawled away through the swarm with her full weight on the car's horn.

CHAPTER
52

HEY, BUDDY," KEN TRENT SAID, "WHERE YOU AT?"

José squinted at the clock on his phone and wormed his swollen tongue around inside his mouth, searching for moisture. He cleared his throat and said, "In my truck. Why?"

"Where in your truck?"

José went rigid at the tone of his ex-boss's voice. He sat up, kicking a trio of empty Budweiser bottles across the floor mat. He studied the tree-lined street in front of him where Casey lived, and scoured the nearly empty parking lot of the small, shrub-trimmed shopping center. On the pavement outside, the rest of the empty beer bottles stood in their cardboard container next to a shimmering puddle of piss.

The third-floor window to Casey's back bedroom stared down at him with a half-shut pink shade, a watchful eye that somehow accused him of cowardice for sitting there and drinking all night without going inside to talk to Casey.

He said, "On my way to a job."

"In town?"

"Yeah," José said. "Why? What's up?"

The police captain took a turn at silence before he said, "I think you need to come in and see me."

"I got a wife about to come out of an aerobics class with some college kid," José said. "Husband's an insurance agent, paying top dollar, so you gotta do better than a tip on the Mavs game."

"I can't tell you, exactly, José," he said. "It's important. It's got to do with that thing you're working on down in Wilmer."

"Tell you what," José said. "I can't get down there, but I'll meet you. There's a shopping center across the street from my job, the place just off the Colinas exit on 114. You can buy me a Starbucks."

"Half an hour, okay?" Ken asked.

"Cappuccino?" José asked. "If I get there first?"

"Just the closest thing to regular black coffee," Ken said.

José always kept a spare set of clothes behind the backseat. He removed the duffel bag and crossed the street, dialing Casey's cell number but getting no answer. Casey kept a key in the flower box outside the back door. José dug it out of the dirt and let himself in to use the shower and change clothes. Clean and smelling much better, he jotted out a note telling her that he'd used the shower and explaining that if it hadn't been urgent and involving the Senator Chase case, he never would have been so bold as to use her spare key to let himself in. He added a postscript that said he hoped she'd forgive him for that, even if she couldn't forgive him for his past.

He drove over to the shopping center ten minutes before the appointed time, but instead of entering the large parking lot, he passed by and pulled into the adjoining apartment complex perched on the hill above. Parking out of sight, he walked with a pair of field glasses to the edge of the wrought-iron fence by the apartment complex's pool. He scanned the Starbucks and saw Ken Trent outside in a gray blazer and black slacks, talking to an undercover cop who nodded, looked around, and then hurriedly returned to the unmarked car, where he slumped down in the seat next to his partner.

When Ken disappeared into the coffee store, José studied the other cars in the lot and came up with a second unmarked car, where two more cops sat slumped low, one of them talking into a cell phone.

José checked the loads in his guns as he crossed the lot toward the back. He hopped the fence and shuffled down the dirt hillside into the back of the shopping center where the AC units groaned from the rooftop and the smell of garbage floated past on warm zephyrs. He jogged the length of the center and came around the opposite side, slipping into the side door of the coffee shop and sneaking up on the police captain at his table against the wall.

"Sorry I'm late," José said.

Ken jumped and spun. "Jesus."

"Thanks for getting the coffee," José said, slipping into the chair across from him and taking a drink from the other cup. "Double espresso. You remembered. That's sweet."

"Who else drinks that shit?" Ken said, taking a careful sip from his own cup.

"Look at the line, that's who," José said, nodding toward the counter crowded with businesspeople, most of them talking rapidly into cell phones or bending over their BlackBerrys.

"What's up?" José asked. "That class finishes in about ten minutes and then I'm on."

Ken's face went sour. "We've been friends for a long time. I want to help."

José nodded slowly. "Okay."

They stared at each other for a minute. José took another sip.

"You want to tell me something?" Ken asked.

"You want to tell me something?" José asked. "You're the one acting strange."

Ken winced and looked at him hard. "They found your aunt and the other woman, dead. Execution style, José. No struggle. And right there with them? That little popgun you own. The one you keep in the crack of your ass."

José felt his mind casting free, dizzy from the night before and this news, but he gripped his legs under the table and dug in with his fingertips.

"What about the others?" he asked, thinking of Isodora and the baby.

"Others?" Ken said, studying him.

"A woman and her baby girl," José said. "What about them?"

Ken shook his head. "If you're trying to distract me, don't. I'm doing my best to make this easy."

José paused, but only for an instant, and said, "I'm a serial killer all of a sudden, right? A basement full of bodies somewhere?"

"You admitting to the two?"

"Of course I'm not," José said. "You're not serious. I'd leave my own gun there?"

Ken just stared.

"You giving me a chance to run?" José asked. "That your help?"

"You know it's not," Ken said. "I told you and told you, back in the day. You can't play on the edge. Sooner or later, you lose your balance. It just happens. I just thought it could be you and me and make it easy that way, not taking you down like some banger in the street."

"Cup of coffee and a friendly surrender, huh?" José said. "You're a pal."

José flicked the coffee without warning, blinding the cop, whipping out his automatic, and clipping Trent with a backhand across the temple. José grabbed him under the arm so he didn't fall to the floor, scanning the café over his shoulder. One woman looked, her mouth agog, but when her eyes met José's, she raised her newspaper. The rest kept their phone calls going.

José propped his old friend up against the wall. A small trickle of blood seeped down along his hairline, draining into his ear. José turned again, scanned the café, stashed his gun, and slipped out the back.

CHAPTER
53

THE OTHER PATRONS AT WHO'S WHO NUDGED EACH other and stared at Casey. Paige, her big blonde mane radiating, glared around the deck until they dropped their prying eyes and the buzz of conversation recommenced. With a curt nod Paige grabbed hold of her burger with two hands and took a bite. The big diamond on her hand flashed, blinding Casey for a moment with a dash of sunlight.

After swallowing, Paige dabbed her lips and said, "Honey, I got one chit and one chit only, with Mrs. Cavanaugh. You telling me I need to use it?"

"I can't think of any way to get to her except through you," Casey said, sipping her Diet Coke. "Especially with everything going on."

"It's awful," Paige said before falling silent.

"I'm sure she's not keeping score," Casey said. "This isn't that big of a deal for her."

Paige shook her head violently. "When I stepped down at the Bovine Ball so her daughter could win that crown, she told me point-blank in the French Room Bar of the

Adolphus Hotel and I'll never forget it, she said, 'You'll get one favor from me for this. Don't you dare ask for two.'"

"This isn't much of a favor."

"She's an old German," Paige said, wrinkling her nose. "Her husband is the Cavanaugh. One is one with her."

"I'm sorry," Casey said.

Paige patted her hand across the table. "No, don't be. I just wanted to make sure you really needed it, honey. You know there's nothing I wouldn't do. Especially now, with that so-called senator and don't even get me started about Taylor Jordan. He'll be passed over on some holiday parties if I have anything to do with it. You can believe that."

"Mandy Chase needs to know this is totally private," Casey said. "Everything is confidential. I'd like to talk with her in a little more detail about some of the things she told José."

Paige frowned and clutched Casey's hand again. "And I am so sorry about that. And me the one telling you to sleep with a Mexican, my God. The men last night after you left? My God, you should have heard them carry on about it when I told them I encouraged you. Told me we both got just what we asked for, and I'm supposed to be your friend."

Casey clamped her lips tight, stared at the table between them, and said nothing.

Paige sighed and finished her burger, urging Casey to at least take a bite from her own.

"I'm not really hungry," Casey said. She'd told Paige that before she ordered the sandwich, but her friend insisted on buying it anyway.

After wiping her mouth, Paige took out a small mirror and touched up her face before putting in a call to

Mrs. Cavanaugh's personal assistant and arranging for an emergency meeting to discuss the favor.

Casey rode with Paige in her little green Aston Martin at Paige's insistence that it would look better when they arrived at the Cavanaughs' great stone mansion. A butler showed them into a sitting room with lush satin curtains and what looked like a genuine Renoir above a white marble fireplace. A maid brought them a silver tray with a pitcher of iced tea and small sandwiches, which they both simply looked at. It took another half an hour before a young woman came through the double doors in a pin-striped charcoal suit, tortoiseshell glasses, and her dark hair pulled into a tight bun.

Paige craned her neck to see into the hall. When the young woman closed the doors behind her, Paige frowned. The woman introduced herself as Shelly Frye, Mrs. Cavanaugh's personal assistant, and sat down across from them with her back to the broad windows overlooking the garden.

"You'll need to tell me exactly what it is you need from her," Shelly said, poising a Montblanc pen above her clipboard.

"I said on the phone," Paige said, thrusting out her chest so that it strained against the cream linen dress, "I'm here about the favor."

"Yes," Shelly said, blinking. "What favor? She'd like to know."

"The *one* favor she promised me in the French Room Bar at the Adolphus Hotel the afternoon before the Bovine Ball. She said not to ask for two, so this is the one. You can write that down."

"She'll still want to know what it is," Shelly said. "I'm sorry, that's my job."

"I'm sorry, she'll have to hear it from me," Paige said.

Shelly looked at Casey, but she gave away nothing.

"So," Shelly said, looking down at her pad, "the favor you want is to talk with her without telling her what the subject is."

"No," Paige said, her red nails digging into the embroidered armrest of her chair, "the favor isn't to *talk* to her. I want to talk to her about the favor."

"You'll have to make an appointment to do that," Shelly said, apologetically, but with great comfort. "She has a full schedule today."

Paige looked at the woman for a moment and Casey thought she heard a low growl from her friend's throat.

"Don't you even try to do this with me," Paige said, her voice lower and softer than before. "You go tell her I'm here to talk. You tell her that trashy little columnist from the *Star* has been after me for three years to confirm the rumor about that Bovine Ball and her daughter ending up with the Hunt fortune. You tell her I don't go back on my word, unless someone else goes back on theirs. Then you check her schedule."

Shelly peered at Paige for a moment through her dusty glasses before nodding and leaving the room. Paige exhaled and fanned her face and drank some tea.

"Wow," Casey said.

Paige set her glass down on the tray. "Damn right."

The door opened several minutes later and without looking at either of them Shelly said, "She'll see you, but you'll have to talk while she works."

Paige winked at Casey and without a word she raised her chin and followed the young woman out of the room, down a long hallway, and out into an elaborate circular rose garden. At the garden's center, a marble fountain cascaded like spring rain. Four arched trellises, thick with roses, marked the beginning of four separate paths extending from the center toward each point on the compass. The stout old Mrs. Cavanaugh wore a sun hat and heavy canvas gloves. She sat sideways on a small marble bench next to the eastern trellis while she snipped away at the buds surrounding a single yellow rose. When she saw them, she stood and opened her arms.

"Why, Paige, you darling girl," she said in a syrupy drawl. "It's so good to see you. I'm sorry Shelly kept you waiting like this, you never have to wait with me, darling. Next time you just tell her to make sure I know it's *you*."

Shelly kept her lips tight, but gave a final little bow and receded beyond the trellis they'd come through before snapping open her cell phone and going back to work.

"She tries so *hard*," the old woman said, shaking her head. "You don't mind if I keep working, do you, darling? I am so busy, you'd think I didn't have single servant, let alone two *dozen*."

Paige smiled sweetly. "You just do what you have to, Mrs. Cavanaugh. I wouldn't even bother you, but you were so kind once to offer me a favor if I ever needed one, and I do."

"Helping people is one of my great pleasures," the old woman said, intent on her work, twisting a stalk in her fingers and snipping a tiny bud. "It's nothing to do with your husband, I hope. Marriage is the work of God, you know."

"No, not that," Paige said. "This is my friend, Casey Jordan."

Mrs. Cavanaugh looked up at Casey as though she had appeared from thin air.

"Oh, hello, dear. Excuse me for not getting up. An old woman's prerogative."

"Not at all," Casey said.

"I don't know if you've heard about some of Casey's problems," Paige said. "Things in the news."

"Certainly not my business," Mrs. Cavanaugh said, returning her attention to the plant.

"I only say it because I want to ask you to arrange a meeting between Casey and the senator's wife," Paige said. "She needs to see her right away. This afternoon. I don't think anyone but you could do that."

The old woman shook her head, softly clucking her tongue. "I have very little influence over others."

"You're so highly respected, Mrs. Cavanaugh."

"Well," she said with a palsied nod that jiggled the wattle under her chin. "I'd be happy if I could do a favor for a friend. Let me see what I can do. If I am able to, would the meeting take place here?"

Paige looked at Casey and Casey shrugged, but held up two fingers, nodding before she changed to three fingers, shaking her head no.

"That would be fine," Paige said. "As long as the two of them could talk privately."

"I'm sure I won't want to be there," Mrs. Cavanaugh said, drawing herself up straight and touching her breastbone.

The old woman raised a finger so slightly and so quickly that Casey wasn't sure she'd done it at all until Shelly appeared.

"Get me Mandy Chase, dear," Mrs. Cavanaugh said, "and show our guests back to the Renoir room. I don't want them to have to stand in this heat."

CHAPTER
54

MANDY CHASE ARRIVED IN A CREAMY YELLOW SUMMER dress, carrying a white purse that matched her shoes. Casey watched her approach from one of two decorative wrought-iron chairs beside the rose garden fountain, to which Shelly had escorted Casey fifteen minutes earlier. When Mandy passed through the trellis, Casey rose and extended a hand, surprised to feel her firm grip returned.

"I don't know how much José told you about me," Casey said. "Will you sit down?"

Mandy sat at an angle with her knees and ankles pressed tight and her hands folded together on top of the purse in her lap. She offered Casey a wan smile and said, "Only about your lawsuit against my husband and your plans to cross-examine me. I didn't expect it to happen in Mrs. Cavanaugh's rose garden."

"This isn't a cross-examination," Casey said. She reached over to touch Mandy's arm. When the senator's wife went stiff, she retracted her hand. "Not even a deposition. Nothing official. I don't know if you saw the things they're saying about me."

"I watch TV," Mandy said.

"Hopefully enough to know that it's sometimes far from accurate," Casey said. "From what José said, I thought I might be able to count on your help."

Mandy narrowed her eyes. "I'm not interested in lawsuits or rebuilding your TV image."

"Do you care about Elijandro's family?" Casey asked.

Mandy considered her for a moment, then said, "I do. Them, and the other people being loaded into trucks in the middle of the night."

"And you know that's what I care about, too? Don't you?" Casey asked.

Mandy forced a sigh and said, "Ms. Jordan, I don't know anything these days."

"Would you talk to me about what you do know?" Casey asked.

"That's why you wanted to meet with me?"

"José said he thought you'd help."

"José, the dirty cop? Or was that all made up by the media, too?" she said. "If it is true, then maybe this is really more about some drug war, people coming and going. Mules."

"Women and kids?" Casey said. "I doubt that, and I bet you do, too."

"Come on, you know most mules are just that."

"José said you and Elijandro saw a truck being loaded at a stone quarry. Can you tell me about that? How you got in? A service road?"

"Why should I believe you?" Mandy asked. "Why should I trust you?"

"Use your instincts," Casey said. "Do you really believe the news reports? Your husband's press conference? Do I look crazy? Do you get the sense that I'm chasing your husband's money, or conning people? Stealing from my own charity? Do your instincts tell you that?"

Mandy studied her. "No, they don't."

"Good," Casey said. "Because I care about Isodora and her baby and the husband she lost. If I can show why your husband and Gage wanted him dead, then I can prove that he didn't shoot Elijandro by accident."

"I don't completely know why," Mandy said, shaking her head. "Only that it has to be because of those people in the trucks on their way to Mexico, but that's not enough."

"Help me find out more," Casey said. "Do you remember anything about the trucks? Any signage?"

"Do you have a piece of paper?" Mandy asked.

Casey took a legal pad from her briefcase and handed it over along with a pen. Mandy explained as she drew a map of the service entrance, the abandoned work trailer, and the place where they'd seen the truck full of people.

"You can go yourself and see. There could be a truck full of people there right now, for all I know," Mandy said, handing the map to her.

"How often do you think they do it?" Casey asked, studying it. "How many people in all do you think we're talking about?"

"No idea," Mandy said.

"Like some vigilante deportation?" Casey asked. "Is that what this is?"

Mandy started to say something, then closed her mouth before she said, "No. I honestly don't know what.

Ellie heard something, but he wouldn't say until he was sure." Mandy shifted uncomfortably. "Who would think that being married can be lonelier than having no one?"

"Me," Casey said.

"That José," Mandy said, "did you know all that stuff about him?"

"No."

"And now you're doing this alone?"

"For the moment, it seems," Casey said. "I don't know where José is exactly. Evidently some of the things your husband said on TV are true and José needs to deal with it, but this case can't wait.

"This helps," Casey continued, holding up the map. "A lot."

"Good," Mandy said, standing up. "It didn't come from me, though. Don't prove my instincts wrong."

"I understand. Thank you. One other thing."

Mandy inclined her head.

"If your husband can whisk people out of the country," Casey said, "why didn't he just do that with Isodora and her baby? Why bother with ICE?"

"My husband didn't call ICE," Mandy said. "Once she found out Isodora was in custody, he made sure they got deported, but he didn't make the initial call."

"Gage?" Casey said, wrinkling her brow.

"Me," Mandy said. "As soon as I heard about Ellie, I used a favor to get ICE to go out there right away. Unfortunately, the person who helped made it into a bigger thing than I'd have liked—social services, taking the baby—but that's protocol and I wasn't in the position to be choosy. I figured if I didn't, they'd end up on one of those trucks."

Casey nodded with understanding.

Mandy started to go, then turned to Casey. "When the kids were little, we had an Irish setter. She had a litter with the Jack Russell from the barn and my husband had a fit because it was my job and the kids' to keep her locked up when she was in heat. He wanted to breed her for some bird dogs."

Casey furrowed her brow and tilted her head.

"My husband took the kids out back and put those puppies in a burlap sack and he whipped that sack against the big oak tree out there until the puppies went quiet."

Mandy's eyes welled with tears and her mouth assumed a cruel twist. She sniffed and said, "Don't let him catch you."

CHAPTER
55

THE SUN DROPPED BEHIND THE HOUSING PROJECTS across the street from José's aunt's home, darkening the street. From an abandoned row house in the project, José watched the last police car pull away from the curb. He leaned back from the crack between the boards in what had once been the front window and let himself out the back door. To shield his face, he tugged down on the bill of the Astros baseball cap and turned up the collar of the sleeveless denim jacket he wore over his white tank top. With his tattoos and a pair of grubby jeans hanging low on his hips, José blended in easily in the barrio. He crossed the street, pausing for a broken-down Dodge Dart, its muffler scratching up sparks as it roared past.

When he came to the yellow crime-scene tape, José scanned the neighborhood. He noted a pack of punks on the corner, cigarettes slung low on their lips, sipping from drinks hidden in brown paper bags. A hooded banger sitting on a stoop slipped a vial to a hunched and sallow-eyed customer. A crooked old woman pushed a broken grocery cart full of potted plants.

José lifted the yellow tape and ducked under. He slit the police seal on the door and used his key to slip inside, pausing to survey the street before he completely shut the door. The reek of blood, urine, and excrement overcame the ubiquitous smell of mothballs coming from his aunt's coat closet. José swallowed and willed his legs to take him through the front sitting room to the kitchen, where pools of blood had congealed into a macabre pudding on the floor. Two human shapes in fetal positions had been marked in chalk where they had once lain.

He glanced around. Everything rested in its usual place. With no sign of a struggle, it made sense to José that the detectives had presumed the killer knew the women. On the floor, marked A and B, were the spots where the brass bullet casings would have lain before detectives tweezed them into plastic evidence bags. Dust from fingerprint powder coated the table and he could discern the chalk outline of the small snub-nosed .38, the same model as his own, the one that he'd given to his aunt for her protection.

He moved through the house slowly, carefully, examining details like a hunter in the woods, reading the story. As he worked, the light of day continued to fade until he needed to use the penlight from his aunt's kitchen drawer to finish his labor.

In the back laundry room he checked the door and saw the splintered wood where the killer, or killers, had entered. That alone should have excited doubt in his old boss, but Ken Trent had acted as though there were little question as to José's guilt. José continued upstairs, where the beds showed nothing more than that they were the unmade resting places of four people. Yet Trent had acted as if he hadn't known about Isodora and the baby. José ground his teeth together, sensing an obvious frame-up. He doubted his old boss would do something like this, but the reach of a US senator went far and wide and deep.

José returned to the front sitting room where he could watch the street. He flipped open his phone and dialed the police captain.

"You're only making it worse on yourself," Trent said, his voice tight. "You hit a cop? You think I can keep that quiet?"

"You're keeping other things quiet," José said. He let the silence hang for a moment before he said, "Why would I break into my aunt's house? Did anyone tell you someone broke in the back? I got a key. Why would I leave my own gun on the table?"

"How do you know the gun was on the table?"

"I still have friends," José said.

"I've got a bump on my head like an egg and you think I'm going to listen to you?" Trent said.

"Maybe it's just sloppy work your people are doing on this murder investigation and not corruption," José said. "Who's the lead? Cartwright?"

"Gibbons."

"Gibbons?" José said, shaking his head. "So maybe it's just incompetence. Have you even seen the crime scene? There are two people missing besides the ones who're dead. You can see where they slept. The people I asked you about, Isodora and her baby, the woman whose husband Senator Chase shot and their little girl. You want to find them and really know what happened at my aunt's house? Go find the person who broke in here and left you two bodies. Go talk to the senator. He'll know."

"I knew you dealt it," Trent said, "but I never thought you'd start smoking it."

"You're wrong on both counts," José said. "That what you believed all these years?"

"I was never sure until all I've seen lately."

"You think a man like Chase can't swing something like this?" José asked. "Taking out a handful of Mexicans, a crazy woman lawyer, and a cop like Gibbons? He's like a teenager playing with little kids, pulling quarters from your ears."

"You're the cop who went bad," Trent said.

"Nice try, friend," José said when he heard the metallic clicking sounds on the line. He snapped the phone shut to keep Trent from triangulating the signal.

José left through the back door, searching the dusty ground and worming his way through the spot in the faded fence where a slat board had gone missing years ago. On the other side he found several footprints around the edge of a mud puddle, some from combat boots and one from a cowboy boot. He knelt at the puddle's edge and poked at a Marlboro filter half buried in the mud. He traced the edge of the smooth flat boot print with his index finger to test its age. He stood and placed his own size twelve into the print, proving to himself that the man who had made it wore something north of a fifteen. It must have been Gage.

José headed off down the garbage-strewn alley and flipped his phone open again. He walked as he dialed, heading for his truck and listening to the steady ring, his heart knocking as he anticipated the sound of her voice.

CHAPTER
56

CASEY WATCHED THE SUN DROP BELOW THE BANK OF clouds to the west, then waited for the blue to burn down to a dark purple before she pulled out of the Quik Mart and drove the last two miles of the map, turning off the road into the gravel drive of the quarry. Off to one side the earth gave way, plummeting several hundred feet before its broken shards came to rest on a stone floor yet to be blasted into usable pieces. Scrub trees and ragged weeds bordered the rocky slope on the other side of the path. She killed her headlights and rolled slowly down the path, coming to a stop just this side of two sentinel boulders guarding the road before getting out.

Crickets trilled, celebrating the cool night air. Casey moved among the weeds, their dew soaking her pants legs and shoes. Peering out from behind one of the ten-foot rocks, Casey studied a moonscape of broken rock, chasms, and pitted slabs that stretched nearly to the purple furnace of the horizon. Off to one side, a decrepit trailer sagged in its bed of weeds like a wet cigarette. Beyond that a tractor trailer rumbled, puking diesel into the crisp air, its running lights strung up like those of a carnival freak show.

Casey's breath shortened. Her heart galloped and her fingers gripped the rock's cool face. A man in jeans walked the length of the trailer with a machine gun slung over his shoulder. The latch clanged and the tall door screeched as he swung it open and peered inside, shouting something in Spanish and pointing into the container. He shouted again and shook his gun, waving to someone inside, then fired a single shot into the sky. Casey heard the cries of distress and saw the bearded man reach into the trailer and yank a young girl out by the arm. The chilly air carried her gasping sobs across the open space, turning Casey's stomach.

The man slammed shut the door and retreated, dragging the sobbing girl into the weeds, where she grew quiet. Casey swallowed the bile back down her throat and considered a series of wild actions she could take, none of which made a bit of sense. The shadows deepened, however, and she moved forward from her hiding place, determined, if nothing else, to get close enough to see the plate numbers of the eighteen-wheeler. Crouching, she scurried across the rough ground until she could worm her way under the edge of the old construction trailer, crawl through, dampened and dirtied, and part the hem of weeds.

Casey widened her eyes, then narrowed them, trying in vain to discern the license-plate numbers. She studied the rest of the eighteen-wheeler, Tracy mud flaps, a red cab with a black rooster on the door and a circle of words around it Casey couldn't read.

She focused on the spot in the weeds where the man

and the girl had disappeared. She thought she saw some movement and heard a low groaning. She plotted a path forward to where she might get a better look at the plate and the logo on the cab. Just as she started out from under her hiding place, she heard, beyond the hammering of her own heart, the crunch of gravel and tires. Headlights glowed beyond the eighteen-wheeler, their beams thick with dust and bugs. The man popped up from his spot in the weeds, slipped the machine gun strap over his neck, and struggled with his belt buckle as he ran for the eighteen-wheeler. He knelt beside the tractor trailer, the gun raised to his shoulder until he recognized the car, a police cruiser, and stood to wave. As the man with the gun strode toward the car, Casey forgot about the license plate and calculated the distance between herself and the girl lying in the weeds. Her heart felt tight and adrenaline surged through her veins.

She crawled on her belly from beneath the trailer, staying low and out of the beam of the headlights, which now outlined the dark shape of the big eighteen-wheeler. Into the weeds she went, frantically parting their brittle stalks, afraid the rasping sound would be heard, but urged by a growing panic. A sniffle broke the silence around her and she realized she'd gone past the girl. She pushed through the growth toward the sound and nearly fell over the young girl who cowered, clutching the torn dress to her naked body.

Casey knelt and helped drape her with the tattered remnants. She froze at the sound of Gage's voice. She peeked over the tops of the scrubby vegetation, and he emerged like a giant from the police car.

The big cop fixed the tall hat on his head and swung

open the rear door of his cruiser, snarling and snatching at whoever sat in the back. When Casey saw Isodora, her spine went rigid. With her little girl crying softly at her breast, Isodora tottered alongside Gage with deadened eyes. They lifted her into the back and then turned their attention to the weeds.

"Come on," Casey said, hissing and dragging the young girl by the arm, crawling away from the eighteen-wheeler.

Behind her, she heard the voices of Gage and the man with the machine gun moving closer. Casey and the girl broke free from the brush and crouched on a flat open space of rubble between the weeds and a rising mound of slag that wrapped itself around the work area, broken only by the boulder-lined road. If they scaled the slag they'd be seen, but no other cover existed except for a pile of enormous old tires resting next to a hill of broken rock.

"This is where she was," the man's voice said from deep in the weeds.

"Come out, you little bitch!" Gage said, bellowing in the dark and moving their way.

Casey grabbed the girl's arm, hissed at her to be quiet and stay low, and half dragged her across the naked ground toward the tires. When they reached the pile, Casey poked her head up, then ducked as a beam from Gage's flashlight played over the mound of spent rubber. Motioning for the girl to follow, Casey wormed her way into the pile. The upright tires stood nearly six feet high. When they got close to the center of the pile, Casey shoved the girl into one of the tires that lay flat on the ground, signaling for silence before stuffing herself into the other half. The smell of rubber filled her nose and the dry dusty air nearly set off a sneeze. Casey pinched her nose shut.

The men's voices reached the edge of the weeds, and they, too, saw the tires. Gage redirected his light, and the shadows grew and shrank all around Casey as he drew nearer.

"Where are you?" Gage shouted. "Get out here now or we'll cut you up into little pieces!"

The other man shouted in Spanish and Casey could see the girl's wide-eyed face in the wavering light and she pressed her finger tight to her lips, shaking her head. She found the girl's hand and squeezed. The scuffing sound of boots punctuated the men's heavy breathing.

"You think in there?" the other man said in a low voice.

"Maybe," Gage said, and the pile of tires shifted as he pushed several aside.

The girl's face crumpled and tears began to spill from the corners of her eyes. She shook her head and her breathing grew louder. Casey tightened her grip. The center of the beam exposed the old tires around them, sweeping back and forth, then coming to a dead stop.

Gage filled his lungs like two big tanks. A small whistle sounded in his nose.

He kicked the tire they hid in, but Casey kept herself molded tight to the inner edge.

"Is that something?" the other man asked.

Gage said nothing for several moments before the beam disappeared.

"No," he said. "She's not in here."

The rasping sound of their boots on the stone began to recede. Casey exhaled and patted the young girl's hand in the darkness.

Then Casey's phone rang loudly, reverberating around the tire. Her hand snapped to her hip and silenced it.

Her stomach heaved and the sounds around her seemed amplified.

Boots slapped the stone, and Gage tore at the tire pile, roaring as he threw them aside one by one, stirring a storm of dust. When he reached their hiding place, he tried to raise their tire. With a wild cry, he reached inside and tore the young girl from her spot, clubbing her head with the butt of his gun and slamming her to the ground.

Then he came for Casey.

CHAPTER
57

GAGE TWISTED HIS FINGERS UP IN CASEY'S HAIR AND dragged her from inside the tire. Casey shrieked and swung her fists and kicked at Gage's groin, doubling him over in pain, but not enough to loosen his grip.

The other man chortled, and Gage sprang up, backhanding Casey as he did. Stars exploded in front of her eyes. Her ears rang, and she tasted blood. Gage punched her in the stomach so hard she felt her legs go slack, and she crumpled to the ground, gasping. Above her Gage wheezed, and placed his hands on his knees to catch his breath. His flashlight lay at a crazy angle, lighting up the tire pile and glinting on the blood that flowed down the young girl's face.

The girl groaned and began to crawl. Gage saw her and sprang, stamping on her hand, crushing the bones. She screamed as he ground his boot, then lifted her by the hair and kicked her toward the eighteen-wheeler.

"Take her," Gage said. "Close it up and get the fuck going."

"What about her?" the man said, waving his gun barrel at Casey.

"She look Mexican to you?" Gage said in a growl. "Don't be stupid. I'll take care of her."

The other man grinned and nodded and took the young girl by the scruff of the neck, disappearing into the weeds. Gage bent over again, collecting his breath. Casey heard the rear doors to the eighteen-wheeler squeak shut and the bolt was rammed home. After a minute the eighteen-wheeler's engine whined, its gears clanked, and its brakes hissed before it rumbled off into the night.

"You keep coming around me for a reason, girl," Gage said, raising his head and grinning her way. "Must be you only learn the hard way. Yeah, that happens."

Casey tried to thrash her legs, but they barely moved. She groped the rocky ground, clawing herself away. She felt Gage's thick fingers on her skin as he stuffed one hand into the waist of her pants and wound her hair around his other fist, lifting her off the ground with incredible ease. He propelled her forward, through darkness and the weeds, her feet barely touching the earth until they reached the vehicles. Gage slammed her down on the trunk of his cruiser, knocking the wind out of her, dizzying her with pain, then disappeared for an instant. Casey rolled off the trunk, lost her balance, and began to crawl.

She heard Gage coming. He lifted her from the ground and again slammed her facedown on the trunk, sending fresh waves of pain through her nose. Her face slipped on the car's painted surface in a smear of her own blood. Gage rolled her on her side, winding tape around her wrists even as she struggled. He loosely bound her ankles, then yanked a bandana from his pocket and stuffed it into her mouth before wrapping her face with a third band of tape.

"Now you'll sound good," he said, breathing heavy and rolling her onto her stomach. "Just a little whimper."

She heard him click open a knife, then felt the prick of its tip just beneath her eye and she went rigid, squeezing her eyes shut. Gage bent over her, leaning close enough so that she could feel his breath on her face as he whispered.

"What did I say to you?" he asked plaintively. "I said, 'This is not your business,' but here you are, sticking your nose in."

Casey choked and gagged, gulping down the blood that ran from the back of her nose into her throat. She felt the point of the blade pushing up underneath her eyeball and she fought against her own scream.

The only shriek came from Gage.

The pressure from the blade's point disappeared at the same instant.

Casey's eyes shot open and she saw him flopping in the dust like a tarpon on land, his legs helpless as fins, his hands groping for the haft of the blade buried in his lower spine.

On the edge of the foggy glow of light stood a ghoulish figure, his head wrapped in bloody rags, baggy clothes draped slack over bony limbs, grinning maniacally at the thrashing cop. The ghoulish man ran into the light and stomped on the knife in Gage's back, intensifying his hellish screaming before dodging back, his mouth open now in a jackal's laugh. Casey saw the gun in his hand and she wormed her way off the trunk, spilling to the ground on the far side of the car from Gage.

Casey struggled, squirming toward the darkness, but before her third step the ghoul was on her, poking her temple with the barrel of a gun.

He made a soft clucking noise as he unwound the tape around her ankles. In a heavy Mexican accent, he said, "You not going anywhere. Get up."

He grabbed the collar of Casey's shirt, dragging her up while keeping the pistol planted firmly against her head. Gage had grown quieter, sobbing now, his arms feebly flopping in an effort to dislodge the knife. The ghoul walked Casey next to the car, away from the moaning cop, and reached inside the window of the cruiser to pop open the trunk. He then led her back to the open trunk and pushed her in, slamming the lid shut.

In the pitch-blackness, Casey heard the man talking to Gage.

"You fuck with the wrong people, you piece of shit," he said. "Now tell me where they go."

"Fuck you," Gage said through his agony.

After a moment of silence Gage screamed again and again, his howl ending in renewed sobs.

Casey struggled with her bound hands to dig into the front pocket of her cut-up jeans. She got hold of her cell phone and flipped it open, illuminating the inside of the trunk. The light revealed a jagged edge of sheet metal. She stretched her wrists toward it and began to cut the tape, but stopped when she heard more talking outside.

"Big man," the zombie said with his jackal laugh. "Now I make you a little girl."

"No! God, no!"

"You don't got no God."

"I didn't do it! It was Chase. He killed your brother!"

Casey looked at the phone. With her thumb, she clicked it to video mode and began recording what she heard, the picture nothing more than the metal ribs of the trunk.

"And you, too."

"I covered it up. That's all. No, Jesus, don't."

"What about his little girl?"

Gage was bawling now. "Don't do it."

"The girl!"

"Oh, God," Gage said. "They're gone. They're all gone."

"Where?" the zombie asked, calm and quiet.

"Mexico," Gage said. "I don't know where. I *don't*. Chase knows. *He* knows. Don't! No!"

Gage screamed again, a new agony that ended with a gagging sound and a choking before everything went quiet.

Casey's heart battered her ribs. She heard footsteps coming for the car and snapped shut her phone, killing the light. Her hands trembled in the blackness, but the trunk stayed shut. She heard the man get into the car and slam the door shut. The engine started. The car lurched forward. Casey smashed into the rear of the trunk, the phone spilling from her fingers in the dark. The wheel spun rocks up into the well next to Casey's head. As they bounced along the quarry road Casey groped blindly for the phone. Then they stopped and Casey froze. She heard voices speaking Spanish. Another car started its engine and took off. The cop car did the same, going the other way, hitting the pavement of the rural highway and racing off into the night.

CHAPTER
58

JOSÉ RETURNED TO HIS TRUCK, TAKING GREAT CARE to keep to the darker shadows. After he slid behind the wheel, he scanned the street carefully before pulling away from the curb and setting off down Commerce. When his phone rang, he dug it free from his pocket and saw Casey's number. He looked at the display for a moment and placed it on the seat beside him, just driving and thinking.

The phone kept ringing.

He focused on the road, then scooped it up and flipped it open.

"Yeah," he said.

"José," Casey whispered.

"What the hell?"

"Elijandro's brother killed Gage," she said.

"Good riddance."

"I saw it."

"Call the cops."

"I have a slight problem right now," she said.

"Why are you whispering?"

"Well, I'm in a trunk for one thing. I called 911 but they thought I was nuts and I don't know where I am."

"Slow down. Whose trunk?"

"Elijandro's brother is driving Gage's car. He killed Gage at the quarry, and now I'm pretty sure he's going to kill me. So let's put our differences aside, good by you?"

"You're at the quarry?" José said, stepping hard on the gas, heading for the interstate.

"I was."

"Which way did you go?" he asked, punching Wilmer up on his GPS.

"I'm in a goddamn trunk."

"Which way did you turn? When you left the quarry?"

The line was quiet and José swallowed before hearing her say, "Left. It was left."

"How long?" he asked.

"A minute ago."

"Stay on the phone. Tell me when you turn again."

"Jesus, this trunk stinks," she said. "Smells like chewing tobacco and piss."

"You're in Gage's vehicle?" José said, pulling onto Route 45 himself and rocketing down the left-hand lane. "A cop car?"

"Yes. This guy just showed up."

José glanced at the GPS, then touched the zoom.

"You'll hit Belt Line any minute," he said. "I'm on 45 already. I'll be there."

"No problem," Casey said. "Take your time. The trunk is roomy and I have a homicidal maniac at the wheel. It's all peachy."

CHAPTER
59

Teuch sent Adulio off in the opposite direction in the Impala while he turned left out of the quarry, heading for Interstate 45. He checked himself in the rearview and poked at where the gauze sagged on his forehead. He looked like shit and turned away from his reflection, gripping the wheel tighter. He liked riding in the cruiser. It had a big macho engine, and no one would mess with a Po Po's ride. No one would find an empty cop car, either, and start looking for the cop who went with it. He didn't need that. The cop was just one down. He still had the senator to go.

The Kings had a junkyard and chop shop in Irvine, where he could lose the whole package, except for the girl. You couldn't chop down a girl. He knew some people who would do that for a price but that wasn't the way Teuch rolled.

He felt like he'd seen her before even though he had no idea where. Teuch punched up the cop radio and listened to the regular chatter about speeders and grocery snatch-

and-grabs and then turned it off, finding a good Norteño station, letting the windows down and lighting up a fat spliff he'd saved for the right time.

The pain subsided to the sounds of Los Tigres del Norte. The smoke and the sweet accordion took him back as he listened to "Directo al Corazón." He found the switch for the flashers and siren and gave them a twirl, laughing, and reaching into the glove compartment to find a sweet .38 Chief's Special fully loaded.

A bridge came into view, rising up over the Trinity River, a high point where he would be able to see traffic coming and going. The guardrails glowed in the beam of the headlights, nothing but blackness beyond. Teuch checked the mirror for traffic behind and saw the same kind of empty road that lay before him. He drove to the high point of the bridge and pulled over as far as he could and carefully studied the landscape around him to make sure they were alone.

He smoked the spliff down to a roach, seeing nothing but the lights of a distant farm and hearing nothing but the sweep of water beneath the bridge. Satisfied, he popped the trunk, hopped out, and rounded the car. On his way, he tossed the bloody knife over the guardrail, pausing to hear it splash as he rounded the back bumper.

He hoped the bitch could swim, as he tucked the newly found .38 into the waistband of his jeans.

The woman lay blinking up at him in the weak light of the trunk, a cell phone in her hand.

"Stupid," he said, reaching for the phone.

The woman clutched the phone but Teuch grabbed for it and twisted away. He shook his head and drew the gun from the back of his pants.

"Puta."

From the corner of his eye, Teuch now detected a faint glow from up ahead. He snorted at the sight of headlights, distant, but moving his way. He cursed in Spanish and slammed the trunk shut again and hustled back behind the wheel. With the cop car in gear, he eased away from the guardrail and started across the bridge.

Instead of continuing, the oncoming vehicle, a truck by its size, swerved into the middle of the bridge, blocking Teuch's path. Thirty yards away, it came to a stop. The truck's high beams kicked on and Teuch winced and jammed on his brakes. Blocking the bright lights with an arm, Teuch threw the car into reverse. He sped backward, but the truck advanced and bumped his front end, spinning him and causing him to crash into the guardrail.

Teuch punched the gas again, but the car only whined and tugged against the guardrail, which had hooked its crumpled edges into the car. The truck stopped again, high beams still blinding him. Teuch dove across the seat, flung open the passenger-side door, and rolled out onto the bridge. Still shielding his eyes, he drew the gun with his other hand, popped up the roof, and fired into the truck.

Ducking down, he scurried up to the front end and eased around the bumper, ready to fire again. Nothing moved. The truck's engine rumbled over the top of Teuch's rapid breathing. Teuch studied the shadows inside and around the truck and moistened his lips.

The red-and-blue lights on Gage's cop car flashed; the sounds of the Mexican radio station came softly from inside the car.

Finally Teuch yelled, "Come out!"

Nothing happened. No one moved. Teuch crept along

the guardrail, staying in the shadows, his eyes locked onto the truck with his gun aimed and ready. He inched closer, heart hammering fast. Out of the headlights' beams, he could see the bullet hole at the center of the frosty web that made up the damaged windshield. When he reached the door, he stood listening for several minutes before wrenching it open. Instead of a bloody body, only the soft sound of a bell and the dim glow of the dome light greeted him.

"Drop it, fucknuts," a voice behind him said.

Teuch stood still and raised his hands, turning slowly.

The voice told Teuch to drop it again, this time in Spanish and including a nasty curse on his mother.

Teuch saw an automatic pointed at his head and he dropped the .38. When it clattered to the pavement, the man covering him allowed his eyes to flicker at the sound. Teuch dropped and rolled, hitting the pavement for an instant before finding his feet and propelling himself forward into the shadows. The blast of the gun seemed to split his head open, but the bullet zipped past his ear in the same instant. He dodged twice, first one way, then the other, before reaching the guardrail and leaping into empty black space.

CHAPTER
60

CASEY HEARD JOSÉ SHOUT AND THEN A SECOND gunshot. Her fingers found a tire iron and she clutched it tight.

The trunk popped open.

"Miss me?" José said.

Casey held the tire iron, sweating and breathless.

"I should knock you in the head," she said. But she dropped the tire iron and grabbed hold of him. He pulled her out, and she gripped the front of his shirt, planting a solid kiss on him.

"I did what they said," he said, "but it wasn't like that. I had to help some people. A container of girls, children, ready to go on a ship for Singapore. There was a big drug kingpin down in Nuevo Laredo who had the information I needed. That's all. I didn't do it for money. The drugs had nothing to do with me, but I cut a deal."

"Do I look like a give a shit right now?" she said, looking up at him. She kissed him again.

"Yes, you do," he said. He put his hand on the lower

part of Casey's spine and led her to the truck. "They killed Amelia and my aunt, and someone is trying to make it look like me. Gage was one of them, but it wasn't him alone. They took Isodora and the baby."

"I know," Casey said. "I saw them."

"You know where they're taking them?"

"Gage brought them to the eighteen-wheeler at the quarry," Casey said. "I don't know how many people were in it, but it's gone. I didn't get the plate."

José scratched his chin. It looked as if he hadn't shaved in days. He looked at the windshield of his truck and shook his head.

"What did the truck look like?"

"The cab was red and it had a black rooster with a circle of words around it. Does that help?"

"You work with what you got." José wrapped his hand in his denim shirt to bang out the damaged windshield before helping her in.

"What about Teuch?" Casey asked.

"My guess is he stopped here to toss you into the river. We've got to get your car and then get out of here. When they find Gage's car, I need to be in another place."

José shut the door and circled the hood. He jumped in beside her, put the truck in gear, and took off toward the quarry. They rode in a terrible wind, unable to really talk. José asked her to point out the service entrance to the quarry and she did.

They pulled in and stopped and Casey said, "Check this out."

José cast a puzzled look at her cell phone.

"Listen," she said, then played back the video she'd recorded from inside the trunk.

"Play that part again," José said, grabbing Casey's arm.

"What part?"

"What Gage just said."

Casey reversed the recording ten seconds and hit play.

José didn't say anything. His hands gripped the wheel and he hunched his head forward as he put the truck back in gear and they bounced along the gravel road. Finally he slowed down and said, "It could be anything. Use your imagination. Those people are no one. They leave Mexico to come here. People down there don't hear from them and they have no idea what happened. The people here don't know if they went back to Mexico or got a better job somewhere else. That's what they figure. There's no record of these people. No one can check. No one can know anything. These people can just disappear because they don't exist."

"What about Nelly? Chase's maid?"

José pulled to a stop with his headlights shining on Casey's dusty blue Mercedes and shrugged. "She's an illegal, and one day she has trouble with the boss. Next thing you know, she's gone. Even if they want to complain, who do they call? No one.

"Get in your car and follow me," José said. "We can drop my truck a few exits down and head for the border."

"Why?"

"If that eighteen-wheeler is going to Mexico, we might beat it to the crossing. Even if we don't, I've got a friend there who might be able to help us pick it out based on the red cab and the rooster. He'll give us the plates, and we can track it down."

Casey hesitated and said, "I'm grateful to you, José, but are you going to tell me the whole story behind that news report?"

He stared out the empty window for a few moments, then said, "It'd be easy to say they made it *all* up, that my work brought me into close contact with the bad guys."

"That happens," Casey said quietly. "But there's more, isn't there?"

José nodded and clenched his hand, gently pounding the dashboard. "Not the prostitution. I have no idea where they got that. But I took some money. I could say it was because of my wife, but that's bullshit. These people have so much cash it's like lawn cuttings. I took some. I got caught. That's it. Am I dirty? I guess I am."

"How much?" Casey asked.

José shrugged and said, "About twenty thousand."

He held up his wrist, shaking the steel Rolex, and said, "I bought this watch with part of it."

Casey reached out and put a hand on his shoulder. "I've seen a lot worse."

José dropped his arm, sighed, and said, "Well, we've got to get your car out of here, either way. Come on. Follow me. If you want, we can dump this truck, get you some clothes and things, then hit the road. That's if we're still in this thing together."

José held out his hand.

Casey took it and nodded.

CHAPTER
61

CASEY WOKE AND BLINKED AT THE BLINDING SUN.

"You drove all night?" she asked José.

He gave her half a smile. "Like a stakeout. How 'bout we stop for some doughnuts?"

Casey's phone chirped. She opened it.

"Seventeen messages," she said, studying the numbers of the calls that had come in as she retrieved the messages. She listened to the first three before snapping it shut.

"Everyone wants an interview," she said. "You save some teenage mother and her baby from being beaten by Dad, the drug dealer; no one cares about that. But if you're a mentally ill woman lawyer going after a US senator and Susan Lucci played you in a crap movie? Do you even like Susan Lucci?"

"I see you more as Lucille Ball."

"And you as Desi?"

"She was just the first redhead I could think of. I don't know who'd play me, maybe George Clooney."

"Poor Lifetime can't afford George. I think you'll have to be happy with Lorenzo Lamas."

"Fantastic," José said.

After a minute, José looked her way and said, "I waited outside your apartment, thinking of how to tell you the truth about all this bullshit. Then I fell asleep."

She thought about what that meant, then said, "The 'shrink' I saw was a friend of a friend, during the divorce. He gave me some Xanax to help me sleep, of which I took about three."

José nodded. "Ah, the media."

"Can we get some coffee?" Casey said, yawning. "And, yes, doughnuts. Doughnuts would be good."

José pointed to a foam cup with a plastic lid in the cup holder between them.

"Still hot," he said. "You were sleeping too good. They didn't have doughnuts. I checked."

"Where are we?" she asked, peeling off the lid and sipping the coffee.

He nodded up ahead. Casey saw the lines of traffic, mostly trucks, and the booths filled with agents.

"My guy's on the midnight shift," he said, turning left and crossing the lane of oncoming traffic, pulling into the parking lot of the drab brick government building with its flagpoles for the United States and the State of Texas. "They got him on a desk right now, working on some unmanned-aircraft thing. Usually he's out on a four-wheeler."

José pulled into a space and flipped open his cell phone to let his friend know they'd arrived. A couple of minutes later, a man with bronze skin and a brush-broom mustache walked their way wearing the dark blue uniform of a border agent. José got out of the Mercedes and greeted him with a hug before the agent climbed into the backseat and reached forward to shake hands with Casey.

"Tony Chehenga," he said.

"Can I buy you breakfast?" José asked, starting the Mercedes.

"Dinner for me," Tony said. "Sure. There's a Perkins one exit up."

José pulled out of the lot and headed back up the highway.

"So what's all the mystery?" Tony asked.

"I thought they might be listening to your calls," José said.

"Not our government," Tony said, sitting back in his seat. "We respect your privacy. So, what is it you need?"

"Let's get you something to eat," José said.

"That bad, huh?"

"We've seen worse," José said.

"That's no comfort, José," Tony said.

Tony asked Casey how she got mixed up with José and she told him.

"I had a partner killed by these Mexican bangers from M-13," Tony said. "He was visiting his ex-wife and kids up in Dallas. José worked the case, that's how we met, but we've done a few favors for each other over the years."

Casey suspected there was a story behind the favors, but they pulled into the Perkins and she didn't ask.

Tony ordered steak and eggs, then handed the menu to their waitress. "Okay, I don't have to actually have the food in my stomach. What's up?"

"We need to stop a truck from going into Mexico," José said.

"No problem," Tony said, flipping his cup and accepting some coffee from a waitress with a toothy smile. "I'll call President Calderón."

"Or at least know when it went in and where it's going."

Tony looked at the flag on the shoulder of his uniform and said, "You got me confused with a *Mexican* border agent."

"Don't you know those guys?" Casey asked.

"Last time one of our guys crossed the line to ask if they wanted to put together a softball team to play us, they arrested him. We're not real close."

"Really? Arrested him?" Casey said.

Tony nodded. "Really. They had to go halfway up the ladder to get it worked out. I could get what you need, though. I just have to go through channels. We have a Mexican liaison. I know they've got cameras, same system as us, so you could run the plates and it'll come right up. It'll cost you some cash, though. Nothing happens over there without grease."

José glanced at Casey and said, "We don't have a plate number."

Tony tapped the tines of his fork against the spoon, looking from one of them to the other as if waiting for the punch line, before he sighed and said, "I could get you some DVDs, I guess. You'll have to watch them yourself, though."

"We'd be looking for them right away," José said, checking his watch. "The truck we want could've come through here any time since, I don't know, two a.m. if they were making time. Or it might come through any time now if the driver stopped, which I doubt."

"Maybe you should sit out there on the road and watch until I know I can get a copy of it," Tony said.

"I guess we'll have to," José said.

"I was kidding. What happens if you see it?"

"I ask for another favor," José said.

"And I'm going to find what in this truck?" Tony asked.

"Let's talk about that if we get to that point," José said. "How long would it take you to stop it if we see it heading into the border?"

"A phone call," Tony said. "Providing it's as urgent as you're making out."

"If we found the truck on the video, could you have them pull the destination?" Casey asked. "Would they have that?"

"For the right price, they'd give you a limousine ride there," Tony said. "*Todo es para la venta*, they say. Everything is for sale."

"Even women and children," Casey said under her breath.

CHAPTER
62

CASEY BLINKED AND RUBBED HER EYES WITH THE palms of her hands, clicking the pause button on the computer.

"I can't even keep my eyes open," she said, hiding a yawn in her elbow and swinging her legs off the motel bed. The room was a room like a million others, flowered bedspread with assorted stains and spots, cheap furniture, and a small television with a pay-per-view box for porn on top. José had dismantled the box and hooked up the laptop.

"Eight lanes of truck traffic," José said, his voice trancelike. "Too bad half of the hundred billion we export to Mexico comes from Texas."

He sat slumped down in the desk chair, his eyes half shut but unblinking as he stared at the screen. He picked up the menu of television choices from a little table by a bank of windows. "*Lord of the Cock Rings*? Must be epic."

"You're losing it," she said. "You're running what? Thirty-six hours without sleep?"

José held his Rolex out in front of his face, then moved it farther away, trying to focus. "Forty."

"We have to do this," Casey said, "but we also have to sleep. You should see what you look like. Come to bed."

"You go," José said, his eyes glued to the screen. He flipped the porn menu into the trash can.

Casey shook her head, got up, and went into the bathroom. She examined the hint of crow's feet in the corners of her eyes, then stretched the skin taut to make them disappear. She ran the water hot enough to fill the small tiled bathroom with steam before dropping her clothes and stepping into the shower. She got clean and let the water run over her hair, covering her face.

A hand on her hip made her jump and let out a shriek. "Jesus," she said.

José stepped in behind her and wrapped his arms around her middle, pulling her tight and resting his head on top of hers.

"Something about those three words," he said. "I lost my concentration."

"What three words?" she asked, turning to kiss him.

His lips grazed hers and his hands moved down the small of her back. In a whisper, he said, "Come to bed."

————

Casey woke with a start, sitting up in bed and feeling for José even as the sight of him back at the computer registered in her brain. The streetlight outside their window cast a trapezoid of pale light across the musty carpet.

"I'm guessing 'come to bed' doesn't work twice in the

same night?" Casey said, sweeping the hair from her face and looking at the clock. "It's four o'clock."

"Can you come here?" he said, still hunched over, his voice laced with excitement.

Casey broke free from the covers and crossed the small room. She put her hands on his shoulders and leaned past his neck.

"Look familiar?" he asked.

Casey sucked in a breath of air at the sight of the black rooster painted on the truck's red cab.

"That's it," she said.

"Then we've got him."

CHAPTER
63

THE SUN WENT DOWN AS THEY DROVE SOUTH. THE red cracks in the sky cast deep shadows across the east end of Nuevo Laredo, the Mexican sister to Laredo, Texas, just across the border. With the license plate of the eighteen-wheeler and some cash, Tony had been able to get them the truck's destination, but not the name of the facility. When Tony showed them exactly where it was on a map, they realized the eighteen-wheeler was headed for the same factory they'd passed on their way up from Monterrey with Isodora and her baby, the same place the *federales* had smashed Casey's camera. José and Casey had only been able to stare at each other and shake their heads.

While Casey argued to scope out the factory, José insisted that he make use of some old contacts before they made another move.

Heavy purple clouds roiled in the red light, dropping rain in sporadic sheets as they wound their way off the highway and into the city. TV antennae, water towers, and chimney pots stood out against the crimson light like sentinels atop row houses and tenements. Laundry drooped on sagging lines hung from one building to another like bunting.

"That's the place," José said, pointing down into a dark alley.

A green neon sign for a bar named Perro Rojo glimmered in the downpour. Garbage spilled from cans and an emaciated yellow dog trotted their way, ears flat, with a plastic bag in its mouth. A drunk peed on the crooked brick wall, steadying himself on the ladder of a rusted fire escape. At the far mouth of the alley, three men stood in dripping cowboy hats around an oil drum whose burning contents cast flickering light across their hardened faces. José recognized two of them, even from a distance.

"And I'm supposed to just leave you here?" Casey asked.

"I can't take you in," José said, "Machismo culture and all that. And no way in hell are you waiting around here. Just go back to the motel. I'll get a ride back with someone. You can watch one of those movies. I'll pay for it."

"Because you *know* these people," Casey said. "Right."

"From my past life."

"I think you said something about some 'drug kingpin.'"

José opened the door and got out. "This side of the line, some of them are a little more reliable than the rest. Be careful backing that thing up. You gotta use the side mirrors to dodge the drunks. I'll see you back at the motel later."

He closed the door before she could say anything and turned in the rain. By the time he reached Perro Rojo's doorway at the end of the alley, the rain had stopped. José looked up at the thick slab of purple sky with its crimson glow, the light too weak to plumb the narrow depths or to allow José to read the face of the man who sat on a wooden stool just inside the yawning doorway.

"*Doscientos pesos,*" the man said in a rough voice, holding out a large gnarled hand that glinted with thick rings until he turned it palm-up.

José dug into his pocket and handed the man an American twenty-dollar bill. The man snapped his fingers a few times and kept his hand out until José added a five. He then gave two quick double raps with his knuckles against the wood, and the door swung open. The smell of smoke and the pulse of Tejano music came from inside the building. Waves of bass and synthesizer cut through with an accordion and a twelve-string guitar. José let his eyes follow the counterclockwise spinning movements of the Tejano dancers in the room as he descended the long metal stairs along the far wall of the club.

At this early hour, he had his pick of several stools at the bar. Behind the shelves of liquor, fogged glass changed colors, fading from one to the next, completely out of sync with the music from the stage. José got himself a beer and asked the bartender if Flaco had arrived yet. The bartender, a small-breasted brunette in a spandex top, cowboy hat, and jeans, nodded toward a velvet booth in the far corner, then turned away. José took his beer with him. Eyes adjusted now to the low light, he became aware of the three men stationed on the lighting catwalks twenty feet above who carried, not the short-barreled MAC-10s or TEC-9s he'd come to expect from drug dealers, but what looked like M24 sniper rifles with laser sights.

One by one, as José closed the gap to the booth, he felt the guns swing his way.

CHAPTER
64

C ASEY MISSED A TURN AND ENDED UP IN A NEIGH-
borhood where people milled through the lightless streets
like phantoms, reaching for her car with worn hands,
knocking on windows and pleading. Casey locked the
doors and checked to make sure the windows were up all
the way. The burgundy sky burned down to the color of
charcoal ash. The few other vehicles on the street rolled
slowly forward, some tooting their horns, some rocking
with loud thumping music.

Casey looked out at the dark faces from the seat of her
Mercedes, knowing that if they stopped her and yanked
her out, there wasn't much she could do. Some of the men
wore straw hats and carried sticks. Others held machetes
alongside their legs that glinted like the bellies of fish in
the light of tiny gutter fires. Casey felt for the guns José
had left beneath the seat and kept her eyes ahead, trying
not to let the car stop moving.

When she finally found the main highway, it was for
the southbound lane. She got on it, anything to get clear

of the neighborhood. She didn't know if the idea to go to scout out the factory on her own sprang up because of the direction she traveled, or because of the anger she felt at being left behind by José and his code of machismo, or from being lost in the slums and scared. Whatever the reason, she knew that she wanted to regain her sense of control. So she kept heading south, knowing twenty minutes away was the factory where the eighteen-wheeler from the quarry was bound, the same factory they'd seen only weeks before. A place rumored to conduct experiments with human beings. A place people went into by the truckload, but apparently never came out of.

When she reached the plain south of Nuevo Laredo, she sensed the open space around her, even in the darkness. She knew from before that the hilly banks of the Rio Grande lay off to her left, and straight ahead lay the distant mountains guarding Monterrey and the land to the south. Her eyes scoured the empty roadside.

She actually passed the gated factory entrance before she noticed the guttering of a greenish chemical flame, venting from a distant smokestack off to her left. She stopped and looked hard into the darkness, seeing what she knew was the high metal fence a hundred feet or so off the road. She turned around and backtracked, slowing when she came to the wide gravel road, flattened nearly smooth from the weight of heavy truck traffic.

At the gate, two uniformed guards approached her from opposite sides, neither moving with any kind of urgency, both with submachine guns slung over their shoulders. She put her window down and let her voice take on a ditzy Texas drawl.

"I'm so glad I found someone. I'm nearly out of gas."

The man looked at her blankly.

"*Usted tiene qué marcharse*," he said.

Casey looked at him blankly, then smiled and said, "See? I told my husband, you can't just take me down to Mexico when I don't speak the language, but no. He don't care nothing. *No hablo. No hablo español.*"

The other guard rounded the hood and stood with his compatriot. They wore a dark blue uniform Casey didn't recognize, probably from a private security firm, but were armed with weapons beyond those of normal security.

The second guard chattered at her in Spanish and she gave him more of the same dummy talk. When he leaned into the window and realized she was pointing at her gas gauge, he motioned for her to get out.

"I'm not going anywhere," she said, shaking her head and smacking the wheel. "I want to speak to someone who speaks English. *Hablo ingléses.* You understand?"

The second guard said something sharp to the first one and raised a walkie-talkie to his mouth, speaking quickly and getting an immediate response. In the distance between them and the plant, Casey saw the lights of a vehicle turn onto the road and speed their way. A tall blond man with a crew cut jumped out of the jeep and strode through a small opening in the gate. His uniform was different from the guards' and he wore no gun.

"Problem?" he demanded of her, his English sounding perfect.

"Thank God," Casey said, splaying her fingertips against her chest, sighing, and pouring on her Texas accent. "I'm lost and almost out of gas and my daddy works for one of these plants in Texas. This is SmithKline Labs, right? We Americans got to stick together, especially south of the border, if you know what I mean."

Casey flicked her eyes at the two Mexican guards.

"This is a private facility," the man said coldly. "You have to leave."

"My daddy probably plays golf with your boss, so don't be a pain. Okay, sweetie pie?"

The blond man rolled his eyes. "This is not an American company, and I don't work for your daddy. Turn around and take this vehicle back onto the highway. If you run out of gas, the police will help you. I can't."

Casey glared at him and said, "How about telling me the way to Nuevo Laredo? That too much for you?"

"Make a right when you get back to the highway and keep going," the man growled, leaning toward her. "That's my advice to you."

She now saw that the patch over the breast pocket of his shirt read KROFT LABS.

Casey swallowed and averted her eyes. She nodded her head and put the car in reverse, backing out and checking on them in her rearview mirror. She checked the mirror several more times as she raced up the highway, then tried her cell phone. The phone had no service. By the time she closed in on the lights of Nuevo Laredo, she was able to ring up Sharon.

"Catch you at a bad time?" Casey asked.

"Where the hell are you?" Sharon asked in a whisper. "Hang on. I just put the kids down."

Casey heard Sharon's breathing and a long pause before a door closed and Sharon spoke in a normal voice. "Did José kill those women?"

"Of course not, one was his *aunt*," Casey said.

"They're making it sound that way," Sharon said.

"*They*," Casey said in disgust. "Listen, I need you to do some research for me."

"Now?" Sharon asked. "Wow, okay. I haven't pulled an all-nighter since college. Steven's in Miami and Matthew's got the croup, but what the hell."

"It's a company called Kroft Labs," Casey said. "Everything you can find, but specifically anything they've got going in Mexico in Nuevo León. They've got a facility here. I don't think it's American. If I had to guess, I'd say European."

Sharon paused for a moment, then said, "Their offices should open over there any minute now. I'll get on it."

"Sharon?"

"Yeah?"

"I want to know what they could be doing with a couple hundred people."

"People?"

"They disappear at that place."

CHAPTER
65

From the lounge chair on the master bedroom terrace, Mandy watched the red sun melt into the inky tips of the live oaks to the west and fanned her face. She swirled the shavings of ice in the bottom of her glass, then sucked out the remnants of diluted Grey Goose before rolling an olive around the inside of her mouth with a tongue she could barely feel. In the bowels of the master suite behind her, she heard her husband's cell phone ring and his impatient answer. Something about the tone of his voice, which seemed secretive and furtive with an edge of desperation, pricked her ears.

He had no way of knowing she sat there, drinking away the sunset. He'd expect she'd left for her scheduled dinner with three women from the SPCA, which had begun half an hour ago at a downtown restaurant. Right now she was supposed to be listening to their concerns, which she would then report back to the assistant of her husband's chief of staff. She allowed her husband's people to schedule her for one such dinner a week. She consid-

ered such things to be part of her penance, and one way
to pay homage to her mother's unforgettable words upon
learning Mandy was pregnant.

"You made your bed. Lie in it."

She tipped some more vodka into her glass, the ice no
longer necessary.

"If you're here already, then get your ass upstairs where
we can talk," her husband said, raising his voice and coming her way. "They'll wait. I'll be on the terrace."

Mandy groped for the bottle and glass and swung
her legs off the chair, finding the floor and swaying to
her feet. She made for the bronze sculpture in the corner and would have been caught but for the sound of
her husband stopping to clip the end off his cigar and
the hiss of the butane flame. She crouched down behind
the statue's base in the depth of the shadows, stuck hiding now for the duration of his stay. She listened as his
footsteps strode to the railing's edge, then peeked out
between the bronze centurion's legs at him as he gazed
out at the bloody-looking sunset.

He exhaled, wreathing himself in a rich blue smoke
she could smell from her corner. From this angle, in this
flattering light, she recognized a sliver of the man she'd
worshipped for a short time so many years ago. As if he
sensed her, his back stiffened and he turned, destroying
the image, the distended middle pushing through the gap
in his tuxedo jacket, the aquiline nose gone bulbous with
indulgence in drink and whores, and the bags of distrust
and greed weighing on the skin beneath his eyes, jowls,
and chin. He narrowed his eyes and took a step her way.
She ducked down and, except for the pattering of her
heart, she froze.

The voice of Jeff Macken, her husband's chief of staff, let her breathe. At the sound of Macken's subdued greeting her husband turned away, growling for him to spit it out.

"They're down in Mexico," Macken said. "She fucking showed up at the Kroft gates. I saw the surveillance tape."

"Where is she now? Did they let her go?"

Macken gripped the railing and leaned into the darkness. He shook his head and said, "They had no idea. She acted like some hick, said she was lost."

"She's bluffing," Chase said. "Desperate."

Macken nodded.

Chase scowled at him and removed the cigar from his mouth. "Where's Gage?"

Macken shrugged.

"That idiot," Chase said. "He's not paid to fucking sleep one off when we need him. When I call, he better come in a sprint."

Macken shook his head. "He had a shipment the night before last."

"The woman and her child?"

Macken nodded. "With the rest."

"And you spoke to Gage afterwards?"

"No, but I didn't hear anything went wrong," Macken said. "The truck made it."

Chase replaced the cigar, whipped out his cell phone, and punched a button before plastering it to his ear. He waited, then said into the phone and through his cigar, "Chief Gage, someone took a shot at my herd from the road, call me when you can."

He hung up and dialed another number.

"Dolly?" he said, working the cigar into the corner of his mouth. "Yes, it's me. I'm looking for Dean."

Chase made a fist and pounded it silently on the railing.

"No, I'm sure it's fine," he said into the phone. "You know how he gets if he's onto something, like a goddamn bloodhound . . . Okay, sure, I'd love some pecan pie. You are too sweet, darlin'."

He snapped the phone shut and twisted his lips. "Have Ells track him down and call me. I still don't believe it. Christ, did he chase O'Brien down to Mexico?"

Macken cleared his throat. "That would be his style."

"His style is dry-fucking the goat," Chase said, shaking his head. "She was *at* the Kroft facility? How?"

"No one has any idea," Macken said. "She just showed up."

"Alone," Chase said. "Which means that fucking Mexican leprechaun is up to something. When you find Gage, see if you can't get him to talk to that outfit he uses. If we can put those two out of the game down there, it can be done clean, no more PR battles over my hunting accident if they don't come back."

"Senator?"

"I said, 'Do it,' boy. Get that done."

Mandy peeked up to see her husband curling his lips, baring his teeth so he could mash the end of the cigar between his molars.

"We've all made a lot of money on this," Chase said. "Maybe it's time to pull out. Even if we're rid of them, we don't know what all they've said to anyone."

"But the *real* payday, the big big money . . ." Macken said, his voice drifting off.

"It's no good if all you can buy with it are jerk-off magazines and protecting your cornhole," Chase said.

"What do we do?"

Chase looked out over the darkened ranch, his hands white-knuckled on the wrought-iron railing, and chewed the cigar.

"Simple. Get rid of them all. Then there's nothing for anyone to prove."

"Like, ashes to ashes?"

"Yeah, something like that," Chase said, drawing hard and exhaling a fragrant plume. "When things settle down, we'll get Kroft more spics."

"It could be a while," Macken said.

"If she's got something connecting us to that place, there better be nothing left by tomorrow night but some smoke and a dirty drain."

He flicked away the inch-long ash tip of his fat cigar and plugged it back into lips. The end glowed a fiery red.

———

Mandy waited until the sound of their voices faded away through the bedroom. She poured a fresh drink, downing it in three gulps, and poured another. She rose, steadying herself on the statue, and staggered toward their empty spot at the rail with the drink in one hand and the bottle in the other. On the granite floor, her husband's cigar lay in a speckling of black soot and white ash.

"You think I can't do something about it?" she said, talking to the cigar. "You think I'm one of your whores? You can keep eating that Viagra like M&M'S but you're no man."

She nudged the cigar with her toe and saw that beneath the black ash of its tip a small orange ember still lived. She thought about his wrinkled, bony hide snuggling up to her in bed, his cold limp thing on her leg and hot bourbon breath in her ear asking her for "a poke."

"I know how to stop you," she said, resting the bottle of vodka on the table and tossing what remained of her drink over the railing. "You son of a bitch. I'll do it.

"I'll *do* it," she said again. "You fucking gargoyle."

She stamped the cigar, grinding it flat into the tiles, smearing the ember into the burned-up waste and the soggy leaves, smiling as it crunched beneath her toe like a bug, dead and unknowing, and then her heels clicked across the terrace and down the back stairs to the office where he did his work.

CHAPTER
66

Twenty feet from the table, two big fat men in black cowboy hats, jeans, and Western shirts with rhinestone pocket buttons stepped in front of him. José held up his hands, shouted his name above the music, and asked to speak with Flaco. One frisked him, examining José's cell phone, while the other held a finger to his ear and spoke into his lapel before they returned the phone and let him pass. José glanced up and saw the riflemen relax.

The gold grill in Flaco's wide smiling mouth winked at José beneath a thin black mustache. Flaco's bug eyes spun around the table from whore to whore as he finished up a story that left everyone laughing. José's eyes traveled quickly over the women with big breasts and big white teeth, but lingered to study Flaco's cronies, two young punks he didn't know.

Flaco's eyes widened even more when he saw José.

"Eh, *José mi español irlandés*," he said, poking his hat back up on his forehead with a long-nailed thumb.

"You know," José said, sitting down in a space Flaco

made for him on the edge of the booth and resting his beer, "up there, they call me a Mex. Down here, I'm a mick. I'm a man without a country."

Flaco laughed and rolled his eyes at the whores and, in Spanish, introduced José as the only good cop north of the border. A waitress set down a dozen pale green shooters that shimmered in the changing light.

"You gonna like this, *amigo*," Flaco said, raising a glass. "Is green like your Irish ass."

José obliged, slammed his glass down after he swallowed its contents, and put back another before offering up a grin and telling Flaco, in Spanish, that he needed to see Soto.

At this, Flaco grew instantly serious and at the stiffening of his body, José saw the riflemen swing their guns back his way in unison, like a small school of fish. From the corner of his eye, he caught a minute red laser dot spring to life on his hand and scuttle quickly up his arm like a roach, coming to rest, he figured, at the base of his skull. Absently, he rubbed the skin behind his ear.

José took a breath.

Flaco cast an angry look at his compatriots and flicked his head. He gripped José's arm and leaned close.

"You come in here asking for Soto?" Flaco said, his words a snaking hiss. "Are you fucking joking with me, man? Does he know? Are you fucking with me? Are you wired? Because if you are, we'll gut you like a fucking fish."

The two fat men José had passed by now reappeared. Flaco glared up at them.

"He wired? You check for that?" Flaco asked them accusingly.

One of the men lifted José roughly from the booth,

and together they swept their hands up underneath José's shirt and combed through his hair. One of them examined his ears and open mouth with a penlight while the other dropped his drawers and frisked everything in his boxers and boots.

"What?" José said. "Aren't you going to kiss me first?"

After the inspection, he buckled his pants and glared at Flaco. Around them, the thin crowd continued its dancing and drinking without pause.

"You don't say his name," Flaco said, shaking his head like a dog at the kill. "Every other motherfucking badass bitch you can think of is looking for the man. The Cougar. That's what he is called."

"Well," José said, "I thought I had a marker. Maybe I was wrong."

"You think you got a marker? I think you got a fucking marker in your brain, man," Flaco said.

"You going to call?" José asked. "Or are you saying he pusses out of a deal?"

"You crazy bitch," Flaco said, sliding out of the booth. "I'll get him word. I don't promise nothing."

José watched Flaco disappear through a back door with one of the big fatties. He took a swig of his beer, but before he could enjoy a second, Flaco burst back through the door, put a hand on José's shoulder, and leaned close.

"He said for me to tell you that you got *cojones* the size of cannonballs," Flaco said. "*Muy macho.*"

José nodded and said, "Solid steel."

"We'll see," Flaco said. "Come on."

Outside Perro Rojo, a Suburban raced up the alley and came to a rocking halt. Two thugs in black cargo pants and T-shirts jumped out, handcuffed José, and wrapped his eyes with ACE bandage, taping it tight. After spinning him around like a child in front of a piñata, they helped him into the SUV, which took off with the same yip from its tires that had announced its arrival only moments before. They turned three or four times a minute for the first ten, then the road got straight. They took that for a time before pulling an abrupt U-turn, where José felt the truck nearly roll. They rode back twice as fast, José's heart in his throat, he guessed their speed at somewhere over a hundred miles per hour, before taking a sudden right and going for nearly an hour on a bumpy road. Twice, José's head bounced off the ceiling, eliciting chuckles from the two men who sat on either side of him, gripping his elbows.

When the SUV finally stopped, José climbed out and held out his hands for the cuffs to be removed.

"*Vamos*," one of them said, telling him to come on and grabbing him by the collar.

They helped him into a helicopter, buckling him in as the blades chuffed into motion. The bird lifted, tilting forward, and eased up and away from the earth. José figured they flew for twenty minutes before descending to a soft landing. They hustled him off and lifted him by the armpits up a long set of what felt and sounded like stone steps. He heard the creak of massive metal doors that clanged shut behind him before heavy hardware rattled back into place. From the echoes of their footsteps, José knew they passed into and out of two large chambers before coming to a halt in the middle of a third, where the cool air seemed to swallow all sound.

When they removed his handcuffs and unwound the bandage on his face, José saw before him the big sad eyes and heavy drooping jowls of his old nemesis Soto.

CHAPTER
67

On Soto's pinky, a fifteen-carat diamond winked in competition with the diamond Rolex Presidential on his wrist. His hair, thin and matted flat with grease, showed the band from the cowboy hat that rested on the arm of his bulky leather chair. The only thing that had changed in the five years since José had last seen the Cougar was the plastic oxygen mask fixed to his face. He nodded at José, removing the mask and placing it atop the valve of the tank resting beside him on a little cart. An empty chair sat facing Soto. A small table with a silver pot of coffee and two dainty cups separated the chairs.

With a quick glance around, José knew the gigantic space was some kind of a cave, even though the polished granite floor, Turkish floor lamps, Oriental rug, and heavy leather chairs bespoke a palace antechamber. Soto poured from the pot a thick brown stream whose curls of steam tickled José's nose with the rich scent of coffee.

"I like to offer my finest coffee to my guests," Soto said in a wheezy but still sonorous voice. "It's from Jamaica. Blue Mountain. They ship it with the coke and weed. Those crazy black bastards know good *café*."

His lips parted just a bit and the hint of a smile tugged one corner of his mouth. "Drink the coffee slow, my friend."

José saw the three thin red beams, splinters of light in the black cave beyond the rug, directed at him from different angles. He looked down and watched them move in slow steady orbits around his breastbone, only slightly left of center.

José made a show of looking at the rug around him and said, "You get a new rug for every guest or send it out for cleaning?"

Soto finished pouring, sat back with his cup, and waved a hand.

"Don't even think about those," he said, pointing at José's breastbone. "It's only a precaution."

"I feel so much better. Thanks, Soto."

After sipping the coffee, Soto lurched as though he were going to vomit, rested the cup and saucer on the arm of his chair, and quickly grasped the oxygen mask, plastering it to his face and inhaling deeply.

"Smoking?" José asked after he had settled down, nodding at the tank.

Soto shook his head.

"Bomb," he said, returning the mask to its tank and easing back into his chair.

Wearily, he fluttered his fingers at José and said, "This is why all the red dots. My life is filled with red dots now. I like that they don't seem to affect you the way they do some people."

Soto gently patted his chest. "I lost one lung and part of another, but . . ."

He shrugged and sipped his coffee.

"Well," Soto said, "let's talk about you. To do something this stupid, you must have a very big problem."

"Nothing you can't solve," José said.

Soto looked at him, unblinking. "I like to return my favors, but only to a point. Things, as you can see, are—how would you say it—constrained."

"Nothing happens in Nuevo León without your knowledge," José said, sipping from his cup.

Soto let his lids droop and he inclined his head.

"There is a factory south of Nuevo Laredo, just off the highway," José said. "Big place. Can't miss it. People are being shipped in there like frozen dinners. I need to know who and what and why."

Soto mashed his lips together, inhaled through his nose, and let it out. He took his own cup, lifting it daintily to his mouth as he leaned forward and said, "After what you did—betraying your own government to allow me my escape—in a strange way, I consider you a friend. A *loco* brother."

Soto raised the tiny cup toward José and said, "So I'll tell you what I know."

CHAPTER
68

*E*LIJANDRO LIFTED THE POT FROM THE STOVE AND *began banging it with a spoon. He smiled at Isodora and said they needed to celebrate. Paquita danced around his legs wearing an indigo crepe dress and jangling silver bracelets on her arms, bracelets belonging to her dead grandmother. The banging grew louder and louder. Paquita spun faster and turned into an enormous black whirl. The bracelets spilled to the floor like spare change and Isodora began to shout at Elijandro to stop it.*

Isodora yelled so loud she awoke and saw a guard banging her metal food bowl against the steel door.

"Wake up," he said, speaking Spanish. "Come with me if you want to see your little girl. Now."

Isodora felt for the dirty sheet and pulled it close like a shawl. Her feet swung from the narrow bed and she staggered toward the door barely feeling her legs. Her mouth, too, felt numb, so when she asked where Paquita was it came out in a garbled mess. She followed the guard, though, without hesitation. Nothing mattered but Paquita.

Down a long hallway, past dozens of cell doors like her own, she followed the guard, her bare feet slapping the cold and dirty concrete floor. Slime oozed from the ceiling, discoloring the walls with a moldy fur. The smell of human waste fouled the air.

Outside the door, she saw the starry sky above the haze of a halogen streetlight. A single box truck sat idling, spewing diesel fumes into the wind that carried them her way. The guard rolled up the door in the back of the truck and there, in the dark, lay Paquita, swathed in a dirty sheet like her own, sleeping fitfully. A small shriek escaped Isodora's throat and she threw herself onto the bed of the truck, scrabbling to climb in.

The guard grabbed her legs, lifted, and shoved her forward. She wrapped herself around her little girl and Paquita's eyes fluttered open, glassy and unfocused. Isodora began to cry.

"What do we do with these?" a voice outside the truck asked.

"We're getting rid of them," said another.

The door rolled down, slamming shut with a shudder that Isodora felt in the floor beneath her. She could see nothing, but it didn't matter.

She held her little girl tight.

CHAPTER
69

José slumped down in the front seat of the '67 Firebird, peering just over the air scoop and watching the white panel van sitting across from their motel room. The van didn't belong. The faint glow from the tip of a cigarette burned in the darkness, confirming his suspicion. The man—or more likely the *men*—sitting in the dark van outside their motel room meant one of two things: either they already had Casey or they were waiting for him to show up and planning to take them at the same time.

"Keep going," José said, slumping farther down. "Just drive past and don't look at anything."

"I'm just supposed to drop you and go," the punk said, speaking English, but in a thick accent. "I'm no tour guide."

José dug into his pocket and peeled off a hundred-dollar bill, extending it to the kid.

"Something extra," José said, allowing the kid to snatch it. "Just keep going and look normal. You can drop me around the corner."

The kid did as he said, cruising right on through the motel parking lot with the car's pipes rumbling, then screeching when he pulled into the street, burning up his mag wheels until they came to an abrupt stop at the light.

José looked back. Nothing moved except the hair on the back of his neck. "Nice," he said sarcastically.

"You said 'look normal,' the kid said with a lazy shrug, one hand draped over the steering wheel.

"I'll give you another hundred for that shitty little .22 you got in your boot," José said to the kid, opening the door.

"No way," the kid said, peering up from beneath the brim of his cowboy hat. "I ain't going naked."

José peeled off a second bill and said, "For two hundred you can buy ten of those pieces. C'mon, I'll put in a good word with Flaco."

The kid raised his pants leg and removed the steel black .22 with a broken grip, handing it to José for the two hundreds.

"You got any extra shells?" José asked.

"Man, you ain't got to shoot more'n once if you shoot straight, old-timer."

"Right," José said, shutting the door and slipping the gun into the waist of his pants before he scooted into the dark.

He made his way through the shadows and around to the back of the motel. As he studied the terrain, he dialed up Casey's cell phone, listening for tension in her voice as she answered the phone.

"Everything okay?" he asked.

"Yes," she said. "Where are you?"

"Outside."

"The motel?"

"Did you park the car by that car wash around the block?" he asked.

"Yes. What's going on?"

"Just stay calm," he said. "Don't go to the window, but I think we have some visitors out front. There's a white van. I'm out back and I don't see anything, but hang tight. Throw your things and mine in our bags. I'll ease up to the bathroom window and knock twice if it's clear."

José hung up and crept along slowly, his eyes scanning every nook and cranny, stepping into the rotten carcass of a dead animal and nearly vomiting before wiping his boot sideways in the switchgrass beyond the broken pavement. When he reached the window to their room, he studied the shadows around him one final time before rapping his knuckles softly on the glass.

Casey swept the curtain aside and her face appeared. Quietly, she opened the window and handed their bags out before climbing through herself, José helping her to the ground. He mashed a finger to his lips and signaled for her to follow and stay close. When they reached the far corner of the building he paused in the shadows and took a pair of night-vision goggles from his bag, peering around the corner and directing them at the van.

Inside the vehicle, he could make out three men in what looked like bulletproof vests carrying assault rifles and waiting, still as mannequins.

"What do you see?" Casey asked, her hand on his shoulder and her lips whispering into his ear.

"They aren't here to kidnap us," he said.

"Then why?" she asked.

"They're here to kill us. Come on."

———

Casey had dozed off and José let her sleep while he drove them back toward home. When she woke they were at a gas station and he was outside the Mercedes, adding fuel under the halogen lights. The sky showed no sign of the coming dawn and although no rain fell, the blacktop still bore the slick puddles and stains of earlier weather. Casey stretched, yawned, and got out, putting her hands on his shoulders and her face against the muscles in his back, absorbing his heat in the predawn chill.

"Want to use the facilities?" he asked.

"Where are we?" she asked.

"About an hour south of Dallas," he said. "Almost to the Lucky Star Ranch. I'm going in for a coffee with about three shots of espresso for a booster. Want one? Can you believe they have espresso in a gas station?"

She yawned and said she'd take a coffee and hit the restroom. When she returned, he fired up the car and pulled around the side of the truck stop.

"Sharon called twice," he said, glancing her way. "And a couple numbers that didn't have a name. I wanted to let you sleep."

"Did you talk to her?" Casey asked.

"I did," José said, nodding. "I also got a call from Soto, the kingpin I went to see. The information he's getting is in line with what Sharon thinks is happening. I had Sharon send the important stuff to my e-mail. If we can get a signal, I've got Verizon Wireless and you can download it."

"Don't you want to just tell me?" she asked.

"I could. But I want to see if you see it the way I do. I don't want to poison your thinking."

"Too late for that."

José booted up his computer and opened the material from Sharon before handing it over to her. She sat hunched over the computer, scrolling down, page after page, her brow furrowing deeper and deeper as she read articles from around the globe about the incredible breakthrough drugs Kroft Labs was producing.

"So, am I straight with this?" Casey asked. "They're five or ten years ahead of the competition in coming up with drugs that work on humans when the others have perfected them in animals only."

"I think you're straight," José said, his hands gripping the wheel.

"So," Casey said, "if you could use humans instead of animals for your research, you'd be way out in front, years ahead of everyone else."

"Patent the stuff," José said.

"Wipe out all the nightmare diseases everyone worries about," Casey said, musing. "Maybe win some Nobel Prizes or something along the way."

"And make a nice chunk of change."

"Billions," Casey said, picking up her phone and dialing. "And if you can make billions, what's a couple hundred people?"

"Especially if they're Mexicans," José said bitterly.

Casey put the phone to her ear and said, "Sharon?"

"Did you get it?" Sharon asked.

"Yes, I saw it."

"Am I crazy here?" Sharon asked. "When you said people disappear and I started reading that this company is coming up with all these breakthrough drugs, I'm thinking they're using people instead of lab rats."

"I think it's possible," Casey said, "anything is."

Sharon went silent for a moment, then said, "Listen, I know you haven't been checking messages on your cell phone because of all the media calls, but Stacy had the office phones forwarded here until we get new space. Mandy Chase is trying to get ahold of you. She called three times. She—"

"What's her number?" Casey asked, cutting her off. "We're heading back to the clinic. José says all we have to do to get inside is cut through some police tape. Screw the EPA. I'll meet her there."

"He told me you were planning to go there while you were asleep," Sharon said.

"So what's her number?" Casey asked.

"You don't have to call her," Sharon said. "She's already there."

"It's like four in the morning," Casey said.

"She sounded scared."

CHAPTER
70

THE CLINIC LOOKED LIFELESS UNDER THE WEAK OR-
ange glow from the streetlight on the corner. Nothing but
shadows lay beneath the old pump station roof. Mandy's
Range Rover waited for them in the back. As soon as the
Mercedes rounded the corner of the building, the Rover's
dome light went on and Mandy hopped out. She wore
a white designer jogging suit with her bleached blonde
hair pulled into a ponytail. With no makeup, the lines of
age and the red-rimmed eyes added fifteen years to her
face. Casey hopped out of the car and smelled liquor in
the air.

"I'll do it," Mandy said, shaking her head. "I'll ruin
him. He thinks I won't, but I will. Little gargoyle."

"Come inside," Casey said gently.

José led the way to the back door, cutting through the
yellow police tape and placing his hand on the warning
sticker sealing the door that announced that tampering
with it was a federal offense that would be prosecuted to
the fullest extent of the law.

"Vandals," José said, slicing through the sticker.

Casey handed him her key. He jangled the set and opened the door, flipping on the lights. The file cabinets and shelves stood open and barren. Casey righted one of the guest chairs in front of her desk, offering it to Mandy. José ducked out to the car and returned with a tray loaded with triple cappuccinos. He offered one to Mandy. She took it and sipped.

Casey took one, too, and drank gratefully, letting the caffeine rush through her empty stomach to her brain. Mandy slapped a manila folder against her leg.

"I'm glad you made it back," Mandy said, looking from José to Casey. "You wouldn't have, if he got his way. He wanted you killed in Mexico. I heard him say it."

"Anyone else with him when he said it?" Casey asked, hopeful.

"Jeff Macken."

"Who is he?"

"My husband's chief of staff," Mandy said. "He knows everything."

Casey hesitated. "Is he a lawyer?"

"Yes."

Casey's face fell.

"What?" Mandy asked.

"Privileged information," Casey said. "And you're his wife. You couldn't testify to what you heard, and anything that evolved out of your telling the story would be contaminated and excluded. We have a lot of different pieces of the story, but nothing that we can use in a court to pin it on your husband."

"We know he worked through Gage," José said. "We know he killed Elijandro. They're sending these people down to Mexico to test pharmaceutical drugs, and we know your husband must somehow be linked to Kroft, the company doing it."

"Now we need to prove it," Casey said. "If we do, even though it won't be enough to prosecute your husband, we think it'll be enough leverage to get them to stop."

"Here's your leverage," Mandy said, pushing the folder across the desk. "I heard him talking about you showing up at Kroft, so I took a look in his private drawer and found these. Offshore bank accounts in my husband's name. Deposits from Kroft Labs, in the millions. How does that work for leverage, Miss Jordan?"

"Like a crowbar."

CHAPTER
71

CASEY DROVE TOWARD THE SENATOR'S RANCH WITH her hand on José's leg, absently stroking the thick muscles. The sky ahead glowed with the promise of dawn. They turned off the country road and drove through the gates and under the metal archway that read LUCKY STAR. When the enormous hacienda came into view, Casey pressed her lips together and nodded her head. Her ex-husband came from this kind of wealth, the same fantasy world, and had been molded into the same type of asshole. Red-tiled roofs shaded the white adobe walls. Intricate wrought-iron doors and shutters graced the arched openings. Potted cacti and flowers crowded the tiled terraces and doorways, and a carefully manicured green lawn sprawled beneath giant gnarled oak trees that reached for the perfect navy blue sky.

Nearly a dozen gardeners crouched close to the ground, already pruning, digging, clipping, and sweeping in the gloom. A handsome young man wearing a white dress shirt and black slacks hurried from the house to open Casey's door and show them in. The young man's smile revealed gleaming white teeth and beads of sweat that glistened on his brown upper lip. A bronze lantern the size of a small car hung in the enormous circular foyer and a sweeping staircase ascended either side.

The young man led them into a study just off the foyer. They were greeted by Indian rugs, teak furniture upholstered in dark brown leather and animal skins, and the cool smell of old leather books. A ceiling fan swung its paddles in a lazy circle above. José slumped down in a leather reclining chair with his hands buried in his pockets while Casey took a seat by the deep barred window, clutching her briefcase tight and studying an oil painting of buffalo on a plain. They sat for almost ten minutes before the hardware on the door rattled.

When a strange man in an olive suit came through the door, Casey stood and craned her neck, expecting Chase. The man shut the door and held out his hand.

"Jeff Macken," he said.

José stared sullenly, and Casey looked at his hand until he put it down.

"Where's Chase?" Casey asked.

Macken's eyebrows shot up. "The senator? He has an extremely busy day that's already begun. He asked me to get this worked out."

"Do you know what I have here?" Casey asked, patting her briefcase. "Here, take a look."

She withdrew copies of the records Sharon had uncovered on Kroft.

"I'll lay it out for you the way I would with a jury," she said. "This is the pharmaceutical lab Kroft runs in

Mexico, the place we know they're using human beings as guinea pigs."

Macken took the papers without expression.

"These are the transport records of the truck we have eyewitness reports of leaving the senator's quarry." Casey handed him a DVD. "You'll see the truck go through Mexican customs on this, positively IDed by our witnesses."

Casey handed him a separate folder and said, "I'd say this is our star piece of evidence, but it's not. Good enough, though. Copies of bank records showing the millions the senator has received from Kroft Labs."

Casey shut the briefcase. Macken looked up from the papers and studied her face.

"Anything else?" he asked.

"Oh," she said, fishing into her pants pocket and taking out her cell phone, "right. This is the real kicker. The jury will love this, a cop on the witness stand always works wonders. Lots of credibility."

Macken shot a sneering smile at José and said, "Ex-cops bounced for corruption? Ex-cops under investigation for murder? He doesn't quite count, does he?"

Casey glanced at José, then turned her attention to Macken and said, "Oh, not José. No. Someone near and dear to your heart. Our star witness."

She hit the play button on her phone, already cued to the right point, and Gage's voice filled the room.

"*They're gone. They're all gone . . .*" Gage said.

"*Where?*" Teuch's muffled voice asked.

"*Mexico,*" Gage said. "*I don't know where. I don't. Chase knows. He knows.*"

Casey snapped it shut before Gage's scream and let the soft paddling of the fan fill the silence.

"You think he's too busy for this?" she asked.

"What do you want?" Macken asked.

"Everything I said on the phone," she said.

Macken blinked, looked at her blankly, and then said, "I think I should speak with the senator directly."

"Good idea," Casey said. "Mind if we wait outside? This place has an odor."

CHAPTER
72

CASEY AND JOSÉ LEANED AGAINST THE HOOD OF the battered Mercedes watching gardeners disappear with the coming light. Birds showed in inky patterns on lonely mesquite branches. The hills across the river lay like sleeping giants, garbed in purple robes. Pastures and woods stretched as far as they could see.

"Good land," José said, stretching his legs out in front of him and folding his arms across his chest. "Too bad it belongs to such a turd."

"Land good enough for corporate farming," Casey said. "Lots of jobs for people like Elijandro to come up here for."

"Nice if they could work some of this land for themselves," José said.

Casey kept staring at the horizon. A fountain of burning sunlight sprang up from behind the hills.

"But it's not theirs," Casey said, without taking her eyes off the sunrise. "It's ours, right?"

"What does that mean?" José asked placidly.

"A river of mud," Casey said.

"The Rio Grande?"

"You just got to be lucky and get born on the right side," Casey said as the first of the sun's rays glinted at them.

"Nice sentiment. But have you ever been to Detroit?"

"Good point."

"And a US border town ain't no Veracruz, either," José said. He nodded and raised a hand to block the burning light. "You go there, you think you're in Europe."

The front door of the hacienda swung open and Macken walked double-time down the path until he stood beside them.

"Okay," he said, his face set and serious. "But we want that recording. We want your phone. And we'd like to speak with Chief Gage."

"Last time I saw him, his mouth was full."

Macken gave her a puzzled look. José smiled.

"We're not responsible for Gage," Casey said. "Forget the deal."

"Wait," Macken said, holding up a hand. "I said we'd like to speak with him. We can proceed without him, but I have to have the phone."

"Everything else is the way I said?" Casey asked.

"Yes."

"Isodora and the baby?" she said. "Just like I laid out?"

"As long as you're willing to go to Mexico to get them, then yes."

Casey took out the phone and held it up in front of her.

"I want José cleared, too," she said.

Macken's eyes flickered to the phone. He licked his lips, nodded, and said, "Yes. Of course."

He held out one hand for the phone, extending the other to shake and close the deal.

Casey looked at him, not wanting to touch his hand. But she shook it, then surreptitiously wiped the cold sweat she'd picked up from his palm on her pants leg.

She dropped the phone into his other hand.

He smiled.

CHAPTER
73

Six days later, Stacy walked into Casey's office, shaking her head in frustration. "There are two women outside, and I'm the one who has to tell them to go away?"

Casey looked up from her computer. Sharon slid another law book into place and turned away from the shelf to see Casey's reaction.

"Tell them tomorrow," Casey said. "We've still got to get this place back together."

Casey looked down at the budget spreadsheet in front of her and sighed. From the corner of her eye, she saw Stacy hadn't left, so she wasn't surprised to hear her speak.

"Well, they both have court appearances tomorrow, so I guess they're out of luck," Stacy said, sighing dramatically and turning from the doorway.

Casey kept her eyes on the numbers, mouthing them silently with her lips, but unable to really focus.

"All right," she said, looking up and directing her voice

after Stacy. "Tell them to come around the back, though. I don't want to start an avalanche."

To Sharon she said, "Can you and Donna take these in the conference room? I can't do anything without Tina. Just do your best. José is on his way, and I'll get him to finish the books."

Sharon smiled, opened the back door, and showed the women through to the conference room. Casey tried to concentrate.

"*Muchas gracias*," one of the women said to her.

"*Sí, muchas gracias*," the other said.

Casey looked up and nodded at their grateful eyes.

"*De nada*," she said.

"Speaking Spanish, now?" José said, striding through the door and closing it behind him.

"We're not supposed to be open until tomorrow, but they have court dates," she explained, sitting back in her chair.

"I knew you were a softie," José said, setting a folded newspaper down in front of her along with a tray of coffees from Starbucks. "We'll have to see about getting that fixed. You fixed everything else."

He pointed to a small article in the paper headlined FORMER COP CLEARED. Casey read the quotes from Ken Trent apologizing publicly for the department's sloppy murder investigation of José's aunt. Casey looked up, matching José's grin.

"Step one, anyway," she said.

"You weren't nervous, were you?" he asked.

"It's been almost a week," she said, knitting her brows.

"This stuff takes time," he said. "Big things you're putting into motion."

Stacy reappeared in the doorway.

"I know, the conference room," Casey said.

"Chase is on," Stacy said, breathless. "They're cutting in on *GMA*, live from Washington."

Stacy's eyes went to the TV on Casey's shelf.

"They didn't get mine hooked up yet," Casey said, scrambling around her desk and following Stacy into the old filling station front room.

Stacy raised a small TV from behind the counter and set it out for them to see. Sharon and Donna came in, crowding around Casey.

"Turn it up," José said.

Stacy reached for the button and shot him a look that said she knew to do that already. Chase sat between two other senators on the raised panel, with prodigious notes in front of him, and spoke into his microphone.

His hair was perfectly combed and his reading glasses were low on his nose. He had already begun when the audio switched on.

"—Have launched a full investigation, with the full cooperation of the Mexican government, into human rights abuses at the Kroft Labs facility in Nuevo León. This committee does not mean to suggest that the officers or board members of Royal Kroft Incorporated are in any way culpable for these horrible acts. Instead, we fully believe that these abuses were generated on a limited and local level. That said, Mexican federal authorities early this morning have raided the Kroft facility in Nuevo León and closed down the entire operation until it can be determined exactly who is responsible and they can be brought to justice.

"It is also the intention of this committee to diligently monitor the activity of pharmaceutical operations across the globe that wish to do business in the United States, to ensure that such abuses, wherever they exist, are brought to an immediate halt."

Chase looked up with a serious expression amid a flurry of camera flashes and an eruption of questions from the press. But before he answered, he led the men on the podium in a silent prayer.

The TV picture cut to Diane Sawyer, looking equally serious.

In her low, rich tone, the TV host said, "An American senator, leading the charge for human rights everywhere. That man has guts."

Casey puckered her lips and shook her head, turning away from the TV just as José's cell phone rang. He gave her a look and ducked back into her office.

"What's up?" Stacy asked.

Without replying, Casey followed José into her office, gently closing the door. José had one hand on the corner of her desk, as if to balance himself. He snapped his phone shut and looked up with a grim face.

"This is it," he said. "We're on."

CHAPTER
74

WHEN THEY PASSED THROUGH THE BORDER, CASEY pulled over and they got out to make their call. The man put Isodora on the phone. Casey asked her what she had for breakfast, a random question the men couldn't have prerecorded. Then they waited for the text message with the video attached, showing Isodora outside their meeting place, answering the question. They had fed her cornflakes.

As they drove, Casey checked her rearview mirror, nodding at it after a while. "Company."

José glanced over his shoulder and said, "The black Suburban, I know. Also, up there."

He twisted his head and pointed up through the windshield. Casey leaned forward and bent her head back, just catching a glimpse of the small black helicopter.

"Can't blame them for making sure," Casey said.

José studied the side mirror outside his window and nodded his head. It took only twenty minutes to reach the hill overlooking the motel. They stopped the car and the Suburban shot on past, continuing without them. José rested his elbows on the roof of the Mercedes, dialing in his binoculars, scanning the motel and the surrounding area, taking long slow breaths. Behind the motel the sun had begun to sink toward a low line of dung-colored mountains wreathed in smog.

"Look good?" Casey asked, shading her eyes but not seeing anything.

"Perfect," he said with a nod, handing the binoculars over to Casey and studying the empty sky. "Helicopter's gone, too."

Casey looked through the binoculars. The star-shaped red neon sign for the Motel de Libertad blinked on and off along with the word VACANCY, letting people know that it was open for business despite its condition. In front of the long, low concrete building sat an old filling station with a grocery store add-on. In the adjacent lot, five sagging cows stood, flicking their ears at the clouds of bluebottle flies, in a wired-off mud lot riddled with hoofprints. Beside the pen stood a shack where chickens ran beneath a line of hanging laundry.

The unfinished motel building itself looked to have run out of money three-quarters of the way through. Concrete pilings in the ground projected clusters of rusty rebar. Beyond the foundation, the giant hole of an unfinished swimming pool gaped open with mud the color of coffee. Candy wrappers, plastic soda bottles, and broken concrete blocks littered the barren and rocky landscape. Out back, on the high ground, a rickety water tower stood with its back to the setting sun.

"Where?" Casey asked, her eyes still pressed to the binoculars.

"On the end by the pool," José said, "in the doorway of that last room."

Casey zeroed in on the figure of Isodora cradling her baby. Directly behind her in the shadows stood the shape of a man. She handed back the binoculars and watched the small shape of the black Suburban that had followed them pull into the dusty parking lot. Two men got out and went into the room where Isodora waited.

Casey took a deep breath and said, "Okay. Here we go."

José cleared his throat and asked, "You think it was worth it?"

Casey handed back the binoculars and said, "You don't?"

"I'm not saying that at all."

"You're the one who said the FBI couldn't shut that factory down, or the State Department," she said.

"I know. It's a different country down here."

"'An act of Congress,' your words," she said. "How many people have that kind of power?"

She looked hard at him, and he glanced down.

"I'm sorry," she said in a soft voice. "Yes, it was worth it. That place is shut down. You're cleared. And now we're going to get Isodora and the baby. That's what Elijandro would have wanted, too, more than anything. Any lawyer worth a shit knows that sometimes the best deals aren't always fair. You work with what you got."

Casey climbed in behind the wheel. José got in next to her and she started the engine and drove off.

"I saw your face when Diane Sawyer said that nice stuff about him," José said. "And the way that motherfucker bowed his head in prayer. That's a special type of evil."

"I know," she said, following the road as it wound

down toward the motel. "I think it was the smugness, the look of knowing he was above the law."

"Money and power can buy that," José said. "Or are you new to the program?"

Casey didn't answer.

After a few minutes José said, "Sometimes there's other kinds of justice."

"I don't want to talk about karma," she said as they rounded the corner of the service station and pulled into the lot of the unfinished motel. "Karma is bullshit. If karma was real, my ex-husband would live under a bridge and suffer from an incurable venereal disease."

José said, "My mother had a saying: *Fate may be slow but it's always sweet.* It sounds much better in Spanish. Most things do."

They pulled into the cool shadow of the motel and came to a stop. Except for the black Suburban that had followed them from the border, the rest of the parking lot was empty. Casey nodded and studied the black rectangle of the open door on the end unit.

There was no sign of life.

CHAPTER
75

CASEY WAITED FOR JOSÉ TO GET OUT FIRST, THEN SHE
followed.

Casey wrinkled her nose, smelling the cows, and noticing
that the numbers on the row of unpainted metal doors had
been added as an afterthought in black Magic Marker. Quiet
filled the air except for the wretched drone of the window-
mounted air conditioner on the end unit. The air conditioner
dripped down the wall beneath the window and left a damp
moldy spot on the fresh concrete stoop.

Casey touched the back of José's elbow as they approached the open door. With no more than fifteen feet to
go, José suddenly stopped and put up his hand.

Without warning, six men wearing black bulletproof
vests piled out of the room, the last of them dragging Isodora along by the collar of her white cotton dress. She
cringed and clasped her crying child to her chest with both
arms. The men quickly circled José and Casey with handguns by their sides. Dressed in black with close-cropped

hair, not one wore an expression on his face behind his sunglasses.

One of them, a man with a red crew cut and the apparent leader, stepped forward and nodded at the men behind José and Casey. Two of them grabbed José by the arms, kicked his legs out from under him, frisked him, and removed both the Glock from under his arm and the smaller snub-nosed .38 from the back of his pants.

The men tossed the guns to the leader, who caught them smoothly and quickly emptied the Glock of its bullets before tossing it aside. He dangled the nickel-plated .38 by the trigger guard and said, "I used the other one just like this to put a bullet in that old lady's head. They said she was your aunt."

José growled and launched himself at the man, only to be yanked back to his knees by his two captors, one of them twisting his arm and snapping the bone at the elbow. José screamed and Casey watched him shudder as he struggled to breathe and control the pain.

Then one of the men stepped behind her, wrapping an arm around her throat, kicking the backs of her knees, and propelling her to the dirt as well. The man with Isodora did the same, bringing her to her knees so that the three of them looked like a small prayer group with Isodora still clutching the crying child.

The leader stepped forward. As he pointed the .38 at José's temple, he turned his face toward Casey and said, "Before we end this and bury your bodies in the desert, the senator wanted me to tell you that he knew from the start you'd get down on your knees for him, one way or another."

José tried to twist free, but couldn't.

"Too bad he'll never get the message," Casey said. "You shoot him and you won't make it out of here alive."

The leader's lips curled into a sneering smile. "I'm ready, baby, give it your best shot."

"I know you are, shithead," Casey said.

The leader clicked back the hammer on the gleaming .38. He laughed at her.

"You're dead," José said. "Look at your chest."

"Boss," the man holding Isodora said, pointing at the base of the leader's neck and then at the red dot in the center of his own nose. "Wait."

The leader dipped his chin just a touch. The two small red laser dots on his neck zigzagged, crossing each other.

The leader tore the sunglasses from his face, exposing a set of pale green eyes.

"Go ahead, baby," he said. "I die, your friend dies."

"Just walk away, shithead," Casey said. "No one has to get hurt."

"Call off your shooters," the leader said, his eyes still locked on hers.

Casey shook her head. "We're not the ones who went back on the deal. You drop first."

The leader stared, then his eyes left hers, flicking from man to man, seeing the red dots. Slowly, he raised his hands up into the air.

Casey held a hand up, signaling the snipers not to fire. The man holding her relaxed his arm and stepped away. The leader angled his head toward the truck, signaling his men to move. They backed away and slipped into the SUV, fired up its engine, and spun wheels in a clatter of stones as it shot across the parking lot, heading for the highway.

Casey took a long breath.

From beyond the chicken shack, two men emerged walking with slow careful steps, their sniper rifles raised and aimed at the retreating vehicle, their cheeks pressed tight to the guns' stocks, eyes riveted to their scopes.

They both wore black cowboy hats.

José gripped her shoulder and asked if she was all right.

"You're the one who's hurt," she said.

José glanced down at the arm he held tight to his body. "A scratch."

They turned toward Isodora, who stood crying and stroking her baby's hair. The little girl continued to scream.

Casey spotted a wiry Mexican striding out from around the corner of the motel, smiling broadly, exposing an elaborate grill of gold. Two more riflemen accompanied him. His thumbs were hooked into the belt loops of his pants on either side of a belt buckle the size of a salad plate. His black hat rested at a jaunty angle on his head.

"Flaco," José said.

"Hey, *amigo*," Flaco said, tipping his hat to Casey. "*Señorita.*"

"You won't mind if we don't stick around?" José asked.

"I left two men in the water tower in case they change their minds," Flaco said with a heavy accent. "But I wouldn't hang around if I was you, either. They got a lot more where those gringos came from."

Casey led Isodora with her baby down the length of the motel, helping them into the back of the Mercedes, the child finally growing quiet. José leaned into the backseat and spoke Spanish back and forth with Isodora before he shut the door.

"Is she okay?" Casey asked, nodding at Isodora.

"You bet," José said, smiling.

"Are you?" Casey asked, nodding at his elbow.

José looked down at his arm. "I said it's a scratch. You want me to cry?"

Casey touched his cheek, then climbed into the driver's seat.

Flaco leaned in through her open window.

"Next exit down," Flaco said, pointing out at the highway. "I got two trucks with men to make sure you get to the border."

"Thank you," Casey said, nodding and starting up the old Mercedes.

Casey backed out.

"No more markers," Flaco said, walking alongside the car and talking through the window to José. "Not even for a friend."

"We're clear," José said.

Casey looked over at José. He winked at her and she put the car into drive and stepped on the gas, leaving the desert motel behind them in a swirl of dust.

EPILOGUE

Senator Chase stepped out of the glass shower at the Westin Riverwalk in San Antonio, wrapped his waist in a fluffy white towel, and swiped some steam off the mirror. He turned sideways and sucked in his gut, poking at the doughy roll well hidden by the thick silver fur on his belly. He looked briefly at his manhood, knowing the cold water had made it retreat, nothing that a few blue pills couldn't cure.

On the sink, curled at the corners, rested his speech to the ultraconservative Council for National Pride. They'd be kicking a two-hundred-thousand-dollar check his way and their early endorsement. With the CNP coming out, other conservative groups would follow soon, and then he'd have the party's base. He leaned across the speech and poked his tongue into his cheek, examining a tiny pimple and judging whether it could be overcome with makeup or if he should try to pop it.

He closed his eyes to summon up the special prayer he'd given a few weeks ago to the Texas Safari Club. It was a blessing of wealth and success to those who believe in Him.

When he opened his eyes, he jumped at the unexpected figure appearing behind him in the mirror. Chase spun around, heart racing.

"What the fuck are you doing?" he asked, snarling. "I haven't ordered anything."

The man, a Mexican dressed in hotel livery, offered a gruesome and yellow-toothed smile. A purple scar zig-zagged its way across his forehead, highlighted in the center by a concave dot. His thick eyebrows rested in re-laxed arcs over the top of intense brown eyes. His smile contorted itself into a sneer.

"But I got something for you," the man said in a thick accent.

"Well, put it down and get the hell out," Chase said, tightening his grip on the towel and pointing toward the other end of the suite.

"Something from my brother," the man said.

Chase saw the tattoo of a hooded skull on the man's neck and he swallowed.

"My brother, Elijandro."

ABOUT THE AUTHOR

Tim Green is the author of more than a dozen best-selling novels, two nonfiction works, and a continuing series of young-adult novels. A practicing attorney and former NFL defensive end, he lives in upstate New York with his wife and five children.

Casey Jordan returns in

TIM GREEN'S

next page-turning
legal thriller!

Please turn this page
for a preview of

FALSE
CONVICTIONS

Now available in hardcover.

1

Auburn, New York
1989

BEFORE THE STORM PASSED, THE RAIN HAD WASHED clean most of the blood from Dwayne Hubbard's hand, but the streetlight revealed its red stain on the sleeve of his shirt. The duffle bag over his shoulder contained only dirty socks, underwear, and a T-shirt, so he covered and rubbed at his sleeve as he climbed the hill, searching the shadows of a street-corner tavern named Gilly's Trackside Pub, wary at the sound of country music pulsing from beneath moldy green shingles and a battered white door. A train whistled and clacked down the nearby tracks, causing him to jump and urging him on that he might not miss the 10:05 bus to New York City. Instead of crossing the puddle-soaked street to avoid the roadhouse, he doubled his pace, breathing hard now from the long hike and the violence he left in his wake.

When the small fist of men spilled out the door and

onto the sidewalk, Dwayne stopped short and they turned to stare.

"Hey, look," one of them said, staggering forward. "Don't he look just like that nigger on television. *Family Matters*? The one with the high pants? Where you headed Urkel?"

"Catching the bus," Dwayne mumbled, eyeing the way around them. Dwayne was tall and thin and wore glasses. It wasn't the first time he'd been called Urkel but the first time he'd been called a nigger at the same time.

"I said, 'Where you headed, Urkel?'" the man said, his lips quivering beneath a handlebar mustache. He wore a tank top that read BOOTY HUNTER and a pair of acid wash jeans with sneakers. "You ever hear of sundown rules?"

Dwayne averted his eyes and stepped off the sidewalk.

"Look at that, Chuck," said a fat man missing two upper teeth. "He got some blood on his shirt."

"That's a mess of blood," Chuck said, laughing drunkenly and reaching for Dwayne's sleeve. The man smelled of old onions and urine. "What's up, homeboy?"

Dwayne snatched his arm free and bolted. The fat man kicked at his shin and sent him tumbling, glasses falling from his face, and they were on him as if he'd spit in their faces, punching and kicking and him fighting to his feet until he could free the blade from the small of his back and swing wildly, cutting until a scream sent them off in flight.

Dwayne ran, too, running in a blurred haze, ditching the knife in a culvert along the way. His lungs burned and his head pounded. He pulled up short beneath a streetlamp adjacent to the bus terminal, straightened his duffle bag, and assessed himself. A compact car came from nowhere and buzzed past him, pulling into the station. He rolled up the sleeve, hiding the stain in its folds, gasping for breath and trying to calm himself. He forced his legs to walk across the street and kept his eyes on the small car that had passed him as he mounted the steps of the bus. The driver took the waterlogged ticket and examined him warily before handing it back.

Dwayne held the man's gaze and said, "Some mean storm, huh?"

The driver reached over without reply, and pulled the lever, closing the door. Dwayne found a seat in the back, refusing to make eye contact with anyone. He slumped in the corner against the window as the bus eased away from the station and swung wide onto the road. They passed the roadhouse and Dwayne breathed in relief at the empty sidewalk and street. His spirit flew as they cruised past a rectangular sign marking the city limits of Auburn and rose to new heights when they passed through the toll booth and wound their way down the ramp and onto the New York State Thruway.

Somewhere on the other side of Syracuse, he fell asleep with the rumbling belly of the bus, and woke only briefly during the stop in Albany. At quarter after four in the morning, they rolled up into the Port Authority, easing to a stop amidst the throng of buses. Groggy and rubbing his eyes, Dwayne stepped down into the crowd, struck by the smell of cleaning solution and urine, awash in a sea of human flotsam, and pushing his way toward the escalators and the streets of Hell's Kitchen.

In an instant, hands grabbed either arm and his feet flew out from beneath him. He went face-first onto the floor, smashing his nose so that blood gushed into a pool he choked on.

"Stay down!" someone shouted.

Dwayne felt a hand grip his neck and the cold muzzle of a pistol against his temple. Around him a widening circle of nameless faces gaped and shrieked and the cold edges of handcuffs—something he'd felt before—bit into his wrists.

"We got him! We got the son-of-a-bitch!"

———

Beneath the overpowering smell of Old Spice, Dwayne's nose caught the distinct sharp edge of Black Velvet. Tiny red and purple veins webbed Jeremiah Potter's cauliflower ears and nose, and a dusting of dandruff coated the shoulders and collar of his old blue suit coat. From where he sat, Dwayne could see the lint and spatters of food obscuring the lenses of his lawyer's thick round glasses. The judge repeated Potter's name and Dwayne nudged him with an elbow so that the lawyer let out a snort and jerked upright to life. While his eyes had never closed, Dwayne felt certain the public defender had grown so skillful at his craft that he could sleep through court without ever being accused of it.

Potter stood and examined his notes, flipping back through the pages of doodling while his caterpillar eyebrows convulsed. So far he'd drawn a Viking, two nude mermaids, and a lion smoking a cigarette.

He scowled and stared at the prosecution's witness for a moment with his own lips trembling before he said, "Detective Bidwell, isn't it possible that the blood on my client's knife came from someone other than the victim?"

The detective pursed his lips, then leaned forward and

said, "As I said, since B positive is pretty uncommon, it's highly unlikely, but I guess it's possible."

"Objection your honor!" Potter said.

The judge glanced at the DA, sighed and said, "Detective Bidwell, please just answer the council's question."

"I'm not going to be impeached by *him*."

The judge leaned over his bench toward the witness and said, "Work with me here, Dick. No one's impeaching you. Just answer the questions he asks. No extras."

"So, it is possible, yes?" Potter asked, tilting his head back and closing one eye to better see the witness through the cleanest spot in his lens.

The detective looked up at the judge, then the jury, then at Potter and said, "Yes."

Potter slapped his hand on the corner of the defense table.

"And just because no one has been able to find the person outside Gilly's Trackside Pub who my client *did* cut with a knife, doesn't mean that person couldn't be the one whose blood was on my client's knife, does it? Yes or no, sir. Yes or no."

"Yes or no what?" the detective asked.

Potter coiled himself up a like a spring, as if the ill-conceived brown rug on his head might pop right off, his face reddening further as he looked to the judge.

"Just rephrase the question Mr. Potter," the judge said patiently, "so the witness can give you your answer."

"I don't have time for this," Potter said, his pale blue eyes igniting as a yellowed forefinger popped up in the air. "I don't like being played."

"No one's playing you, Jeremiah, just ask him again

and cut to it, please," the judge said. "I'm even confused by what you just said."

Potter closed his eyes and mouth as if in prayer and stayed that way while he asked through pinched lips, "Is it possible the blood on my client's knife came from a man outside the bar?"

Detective Billick sighed and waited until Potter opened his eyes before he said, "Yes. Possible."

"Thank you," Potter said. "I have no further questions."

Dwayne felt hope glimmer like an unsteady match flame, but the District Attorney was as sleek and mean as a battleship in her dark gray skirt and jacket, cruising forward without concern for anything around her. She was big-boned, thick, and tall, but not unattractive at all, with short dark hair, bright red lipstick. Her voice was booming and strong, as certain as a concrete wall that steered you in its own direction.

The flame flickered out when the battleship maneuvered toward the bench and asked the judge if she could re-direct the witness.

"You did damn good," Dwayne whispered to Potter as the defense lawyer sat and slouched down low, still fuming. "What's she doing now, though?"

"Piddling," Potter said, snatching up his pen and resuming his doodles. Soon the image of the district attorney took shape but instead of the dark serious suit, she wore a bikini made out of animal skins.

Dwayne rumpled his brow but didn't ask more because the DA had begun to speak.

"How many knife fights a year in this town?" she asked.

"About three or four," Billick said.

"Any at Gilly's Trackside?"

"No."

"Never?"

"Not in the eighteen years I've been on this force. It's not that kind of place."

"Did you go down there, to Gilly's, and ask questions about a knife fight?" the DA asked.

"Of course. Yes."

"Anyone know anything?"

"No," Billick said, shaking his head and trying not to smile. "Just Chuck Willis who said he saw a black man running past who ditched something in that culvert."

"Anyone even hear about a possible knife fight? Maybe that same man running past and slashing out at someone?"

"Nope, and no one showed up at the hospital with a knife wound."

"How about any kind of fight at all that night in or outside of Gilly's?"

"No. None."

"I have no further questions."

2

Dallas, Texas
2009

CASEY JORDAN CHECKED HER WATCH BEFORE HITTING
the curb, sending a shudder through the battered Mercedes sedan. Her tires skidded on the grit as she rounded the corner of the old cinder block gas station. She could hear the knocking of the engine all the way to the back door of her law clinic, remembering the day when the car had smelled of fine leather not sour carpet and coffee.

Before she reached the rear entrance, the gray metal bathroom door swung open and a Latino woman emerged with a small child trailing a streamer of toilet paper. The woman said something in Spanish and Casey offered up a smile, but shrugged, pointed to her watch, and hurried inside her office through the back door.

Stacy, the office manager, appeared with a cup of coffee, a frown, and piercing dark eyes set in a mane of light brown hair thick as yarn. "Forget something?"

"I made some notes on the Suarez file I need for Nancy Grace," Casey said.

"You know she's half-crazy?" Stacy asked and nodded toward her desk which was really the old counter where the filling station had kept its cash register. "Speaking of that, Rosalita Suarez's mother dropped off a chocolate ice box cake to celebrate your victory."

Casey had exonerated Rosalita Suarez in a highly publicized murder trial for shooting the coyote who brought her across the border after he tried to rape her.

"And that guy called again," Stacy said. "It's in the middle of the pile."

"What guy?" Casey asked.

Stacy rolled her eyes. "You know. That billionaire-guy. How many billionaires do you know?"

"In Dallas?" Casey said. "Too many. Why don't you call him back?"

"You think I care about money?" Stacy asked, raising her eyebrows and snorting. "I work here purely for the glamour."

"I know," Casey said, "you like the excitement, too."

Stacy frowned. "I thought we help people?"

"I'm the woman to call if you shoot someone in the nuts," Casey said. "What did he say?"

"Who?"

"Mr. Billionaire."

"He wants to have dinner with you," Stacy said. "I told him you've got to do Nancy Grace's show, then you've already got dinner plans. I asked him if he'd like me to schedule something, trying to give him the hint that you're busy too, and don't just drop everything because some billionaire's got an itch."

"The Freedom Foundation isn't an 'itch'," Casey said.

"And Robert Graham isn't just some billionaire. He's a philanthropist."

"Did you know the angle behind all these rich people's *foundations* is a bunch of tax write-offs and bullshit?" Stacy asked. "They like to ease their minds with cocktail parties and fundraisers. Those Timberland boots and flannel shirts don't fool me. He keeps a gold rod up his ass."

Casey sighed and shook her head. "Call Mr. Graham back and tell him I'll change my plans and ask him where he wants to meet."

"You're meeting José at Nick and Sam's at eight," Stacy said.

José O'Brien was an ex-cop who did most of the clinic's investigative work. He had also been Casey's on and off boyfriend. Right now, he was off after falling off the wagon once again.

"Apologize to José for me, will you?" Casey said.

"He's a good guy, you know."

"I know."

"But you're still mad."

"I'm not mad," Casey said. "He needs to pull it together and I don't have time to play mama."

"That's harsh."

"Sometimes harsh is good."

"Sorry," Stacy said, pausing. "To pry."

"Listen, Robert Graham is talking about a million dollars-a-year in funding if I agree to take on a couple high-profile cases for the Freedom Foundation," Casey said. "Shouldn't I find that the least bit appealing?"

Stacy nodded abruptly at that news, picked up the phone, and said, "I'll tell Mr. Graham your schedule has opened up."